4/10

Dear Christne
   Congratul
this book in
coupon. very best wishes
              Ian Walford

LURED
by the
HOARD

an Anglo-Saxon mystery

IAN WALFORD

Lured by the Hoard

Published by The Conrad Press Ltd. in the United Kingdom 2021

Tel: +44(0)1227 472 874
www.theconradpress.com
info@theconradpress.com

ISBN 978-1-914913-19-8

Printed and bound in Great Britain by Clays Ltd, Elcograf S.p.A

Typesetting and Cover Design by The Book Typesetters,
www.thebooktypesetters.com

The Conrad Press logo was designed by Maria Priestley.

LURED
by the
HOARD
an Anglo-Saxon mystery

IAN WALFORD

Acknowledgements

This story was inspired by a visit to the excellent Staffordshire Hoard exhibition in Birmingham Museum. I want to pay tribute to the museum staff and to everyone else involved in curating the exhibition: it provides a wonderful insight into a remarkable discovery.

My thanks to Martin Wall for commenting on an early draft of the novel, and for giving me some extremely useful advice. I also found Martin's writing on the Anglo-Saxon period of British history extremely helpful as I researched the background to this story.

Thank you to Rachel for her help in so many ways throughout the development of the book, and to everyone else who agreed to read drafts or extracts of the novel at different stages – Verena, Christine, Gillian, Gordon, Isobel, and Becky – and for all the constructive feedback.

I am very grateful indeed to James Essinger and his colleagues at The Conrad Press for giving me this opportunity to publish my first book, and for their support and advice through the production process.

A massive thank you to Mum and Dad for encouraging me in creative writing and interest in history from my earliest years, and for their love throughout my life.

Above all, this book is dedicated to Verena, Gordon and Rachel who mean the world to me.

Preface

This story is set in a particular time and place: 616–638 AD, in what is now central and northern England.

Real people, real places and real events are all mentioned: kings and queens; princes and princesses; bishops and monks; wars and battles; towns and cities.

The history, though, is experienced, seen and felt through fictional characters. We journey with them as they grapple with competing loyalties to family, tribe and race. We watch the past and the future pull them in different directions. We see them caught in the interplay between faith, logic and instinct. We feel the tension as they wrestle with their reactions to powerful external forces.

It's a compelling, fundamentally human story: about the strengths and weaknesses, quirks and obsessions of ordinary people.

Above all, it's a tale about how and why different people react emotionally and intellectually in different ways to the same events: why they love and why they hate, how and why they change over time, how their behaviour affects the dynamics of the groups they inhabit, why some people are cautious while others take risks.

The story plays out against a backdrop of rapid, transformational change – all the more remarkable because communication of any sort across any significant distance was so difficult. Human beings have faced opportunities, challenges and dilemmas in every period of history: but the first half of the seventh century in the British Isles posed people with more of them, and in a more acute form, than in many other periods.

After the withdrawal of the Romans in 410 AD, society and the infrastructure on which it depended disintegrated rapidly. The transition towards new structures over the next 200 years was extremely slow.

Even by 600 AD there was no resemblance to the modern social, political and religious shape of the British Isles. Power was exercised by local warlords, British and Anglo-Saxon. Some of the warlords and their tribes had amalgamated into larger blocks, but there was little sense of common purpose and loyalty.

There was no legal system; the economy was primitive; the Roman urban and transport infrastructure had decayed and not been replaced; the incoming Anglo-Saxons were exclusively pagan while the native British practised Christianity in a variety of ways; and the total population was much smaller than under the Roman Empire.

Yet by around 650 AD, a mere fifty years later, the faint outlines of the modern British Isles were becoming visible, especially in what is now England:

- There were by now only seven kingdoms spanning England and south-eastern Scotland: Kent, Sussex, Wessex, East Anglia, Essex, Mercia and Northumbria. The boundaries between the seven kingdoms were still fluid, and the borders between what were to become Wales, Scotland

and England would not take shape for many centuries: yet the broad political shape of Great Britain was beginning to emerge;

- The seven English kingdoms were all led by Anglo-Saxon elites, spoke broadly the same language (the predecessor of English), and were all Christian. There were still tensions between the Roman and Irish/Celtic versions of Christianity, but these were largely resolved at the Synod of Whitby a few years later;

- Literacy was improving, and law codes were being laid down;

- Trade was growing, some old Roman cities and towns were recovering, and currencies were in operation in some places.

Much, though, stayed the same throughout the first half of the seventh century. There were no significant technological breakthroughs. Social and class structures changed little. Agriculture was the dominant economic activity, and it remained as hard and as labour-intensive as it had been for centuries. Peasants and slaves still bore the brunt, and as a result their lives were generally painful and relatively short. Levels of infant and child mortality remained particularly high. Brutality was as normal at all levels of society as it had ever been.

So, the story is set in a remarkable period of British history almost 1400 years ago. In some respects, though, it is a highly contemporary tale. At first glance there is virtually no similarity between the lives of people in the seventh and twenty-first centuries; but there are strong echoes of the twenty-first century in many of the experiences and attitudes of the fictional characters.

Like them, most of us have to manage on a daily basis competing loyalties – to our 'tribe', our nation, our family. We get caught in the interplay between faith, logic, instinct and prejudice. We have to cope with stagnation in some areas of life, and rapid and tumultuous change in others. We experience the tension between the pull of the past, and the urge to progress and look to the future.

We often, too, see conflict today of the type described in the story: between idealists and pragmatists; between those who dream and push the boundaries of society, and those engrossed in the basics of life; between 'somewhere' people – those rooted in and focused on their communities – and 'anywhere' people – those who are more inclined to look outwards.

The story ranges across the North and Midlands of what is now England and across North Wales. The maps on the following pages show, respectively, the boundaries between kingdoms in the British mainland in the early seventh century and, by comparison, the location of cities, towns and villages mentioned in the story (and, for context, some other major modern towns and cities) in modern Great Britain.

For convenience, the story uses both modern placenames and modern timescales (hours, days, weeks, months etc). It uses 'Anglo-Saxon' as an umbrella noun for Germanic incomers to the British Isles even though the term was probably not used until well after the seventh century. And the term 'Earl' is used to denote higher nobles even though it was probably not used until later in British history.

The precise dates of most events in the seventh century are not known, and so those referred to in the story are not meant to be definitive. A timeline of some of the key historical events, as defined for the purposes of this story, is attached at the end.

An alphabetical list of the fictional characters mentioned in the story is also included at the end.

British mainland, c 600AD

Dalriada

Strath clyde

North Rheged

Bernicia

Deira

South Rheged

Elmet

Gwynedd

Mercia

Anglia

Wessex

Essex

Kent

Sussex

Great Britain, 2021

SCOTLAND

Iona •

Glasgow •   • Edinburgh
            • Coldingham
              • Lindisfarne
              • Bamburgh

                    Hadrian's Wall
Carlisle •········•• Newcastle
        Hexham • Durham

            Catterick •

                Leeds • York
        Huddersfield •   Hull
Anglesey • Liverpool • Helme • Hatfield
  Bangor • Manchester • Doncaster
        Chester •
                Sheffield
  Oswestry •   Derby •
        Lichfield • • Tamworth
        Birmingham •

WALES   ENGLAND

    Bristol •   • London
                      • Canterbury

Chapter 1

The deed is done

I was tense. My palms were clammy despite the night-time cool of the forest.

I had thought about and planned this moment for weeks. It had arrived. Why was I hesitating, questioning?

I fingered the tiny silver figure of Woden hanging round my neck. Surely our great god of war was with me? Surely Grandfather Eadwell would have approved if he were still alive?

'Come on, Aelfred, let's get on with it, we haven't got all night!' Cadmon's voice cut through my thoughts. He pulled two trowels from his cloak and handed one to me.

'You're the slave – you dig, I watch,' I retorted. Cadmon's grimace was clear in the light of the near full moon filtering through the trees. He feigned a punch, I caught his fist, we laughed and broke apart. He knew very well my command was not serious, that we were in this together as equals.

We started scooping earth, kneeling together in the square of ground I had marked out.

The pile of displaced dirt grew steadily.

I fretted inwardly, anxiety nibbling at my consciousness.

'I can feel sacking!' Cadmon whispered, a measure of his excitement rather than fear of being overheard.

A surge of relief engulfed me: we were in the right place; it was still there.

'Easy does it,' I said. 'Let's release the sack and take a look.'

The sack was nondescript, animal skin stitched together, tied with a simple cord; but it was heavy enough, and it clinked satisfyingly.

I untied the cord, my hands shaking slightly. Cadmon watched intently.

The contents glittered in the moonlight as I pulled open the sack.

Something rustled nearby. We both whipped round, our hands reaching for our daggers. A roe deer emerged, looked at us, and trotted away.

I let out a long breath, closed my eyes, threw back my head. Every nerve was taut. I was certain we had not been followed, but was I too complacent? Perhaps my demeanour, my body language over the last few days had betrayed my intentions? Had my father guessed my plans?

'This is amazing,' Cadmon whispered as he handled a few items from the sack. Gorgeous trappings from weapons of war were packed together.

'Yes,' I said, 'it's quite a hoard, isn't it? They're battle trophies of the kings of Deira, Bernicia and Northumbria; stripped from the dead and prisoners of countless victories, worth a fortune to those willing to melt or reuse them. There's gold, silver, precious stones, intricate jewellery – Anglian, Pict, Saxon, Welsh. You name it, it's probably here.'

Questions twinkled in Cadmon's eyes, reflecting both curiosity and awe. 'Later,' I said. 'I'll explain later.'

I had told Cadmon very little so far. I trusted him implicitly, but I knew the weight of the knowledge. I had felt it would be unfair, even dangerous, to share the burden with him too soon.

Cadmon accepted my assurance with the faintest nod, his eyes still wide with wonder.

I had expected two sacks to be buried. Sure enough, the second was soon released: it was equally full, equally heavy, equally stuffed with glittering treasure.

The gentle summer breeze stirred the leaves in the trees. For a moment I felt calm, satisfied: step one had been completed successfully; but I knew there were many more to navigate.

* * * * * * *

The two men started walking, bent forward under the weight of the sacks slung on their backs. Anyone watching would have been struck by the contrast between the two men.

Aelfred, leading, was the taller by about three inches. He was slim, fair-skinned, and had long sandy-coloured hair and a full beard.

Cadmon was stockier, his legs set well apart. He had short, black hair and a dusting of dark stubble around his face.

As the two men left the trees the moon still rode high. Deer scattered in front of them.

They squelched across boggy ground, across streams coming down from the low hills that were now looming in front of them.

The men's feet sank up to their ankles on either side of the ford of a shallow river.

They zigzagged slowly up the gently rising ground, each man lost in his own thoughts, focused on the effort of hauling the heavy sacks.

'Right, here we are,' Aelfred said as they reached a welter of rocks of all shapes and sizes, a lone tree standing among them looking almost forlorn. It looked as if a giant had emptied his pockets carelessly on the hillside. 'I wouldn't rate anyone's chances of trying to track us across that terrain.'

Nestling behind one of the larger rocks were two packs and sets of bows and arrows which they had left hours earlier. Aelfred and Cadmon lowered the sacks and then flung themselves on the ground. 'That was some tough shift,' Cadmon said. 'I never thought looting would be such hard work!'

'Well, it wasn't if you were born with Anglian muscles instead of Welsh mush,' Aelfred retorted.

'Give over, I heard you puffing and panting just as much as I was, you great Saxon oaf,' Cadmon snorted.

'Well, we'll see who lasts better: we've still got a long journey ahead of us,' Aelfred laughed as he spoke, not in the least offended by the insult.

'No rest for the wicked then – nor for me,' Cadmon said, and grinned as they got up again, lifted the sacks, and walked a few yards to where they had dug a deep hole earlier.

Aelfred rummaged in one of the sacks. He pulled out a gorgeous golden sword pommel, examined it closely, and then tucked it in his pack. Cadmon looked at him, his dark eyes quizzical, but as Aelfred opened his mouth Cadmon intoned, 'I know, you'll tell me later.' Aelfred nodded.

They lowered the sacks gently into the hole and then, working quickly, piled earth on top until the sacks were invisible, smoothed the ground so it was level, and rolled rocks on top.

'No sign of them, now, eh: will you remember this spot?' Aelfred asked.

'Of course – and it's only you and me who know?' The question mark was faint, infinitesimal – but it was there. Cadmon had been raised to obey, to accept his lot and his instructions – but he was tingling with curiosity. He believed Aelfred and, despite their gulf in status, expected to be treated with respect; but he sensed that this was an even more momentous episode than it appeared already.

'Yes, just you and me,' Aelfred confirmed. 'Now, just another couple of hours and I'll reveal all, and then we can get some kip!'

They both yawned, simultaneously and widely – and then laughed. 'Aye,' Cadmon said, 'It's been a long and interesting night. Let's get it over.'

Three hours later, the sun now shining, Aelfred slept deeply in a woodland hollow, his cloak pulled up to his chin, his long hair ruffled against a pillow of leaves. Beside him, taking first watch, Cadmon sat gazing into the distance as he absorbed what Aelfred had told him. Thoughts chased each other across his mind: he knew his life would never be quite the same again; he just wished he knew how it would change.

* * * * * * *

The kingdom of Northumbria had been formed in 606 when the previously independent Anglo-Saxon kingdoms of Deira and Bernicia had been united by the Bernician King Aethelfrith.

It was now 638 AD.

Northumbria had experienced tumultuous change in the previous twenty years. Throughout that twenty-year period Aelfred and Cadmon had been as inseparable as they were on this fateful night; but their origins and ancestry were incomparably different.

Aelfred's roots in Northumbria reached back almost 300 years.

Cadmon's lay even deeper, in a quite different landscape: in Gwynedd, the ancient kingdom in North Wales.

The experiences of the two men in their lives so far, and those of their ancestors for generations before, had led them to this night; they would also shape the remarkable and dramatic events of the next few weeks.

Chapter 2

Founding a dynasty

'So, you're hanging up your boots, you old dog?' Modig said with a smile.

'Yep. I went to see the commander and told him I'd done thirty years and deserved retirement – especially as I've spent the last two years dealing with mud, rain and bandits up on the Wall,' Eadrich replied.

'Aye, it's a crap posting up on that wretched Wall, that's for sure. So, what did the Commander say?'

'He was pretty decent to be honest. I said I wanted to stay near York and settle down. He granted retirement because of my long service – he even described it as honourable. He also promised me some land!'

In the middle of the fourth century, as the Roman Empire had become stretched, they had begun to recruit barbarian mercenaries from the European mainland to help defend their province of Britannia. A squadron of Anglian mercenaries was stationed in York, a lynchpin of the imperial forces supporting communications with the crucial garrison on Hadrian's Wall.

Aelfred's ancestor, Eadrich, was one of the mercenaries. A tough, grizzled soldier in his late forties he had spent the previous thirty years serving with the legions across the Empire. Eadrich had decided very quickly that Deira – with its fertile plains, wide valleys, good lines of communication to and from York, and relatively easy access to his Anglian homeland – was where he wanted to settle.

After two years of hard service, mainly on Hadrian's Wall itself, Eadrich was sitting in a garrison with a fellow Anglian soldier, Modig. They were each nursing a jar of ale. The two men had fought together in campaigns elsewhere in the Empire; they had been reunited recently in Britannia.

'Good for you, that's very well deserved,' Modig said. 'I guess it's land the Romans have taken from local tribes over the years. They've always supported the establishment of colonies of ex-soldiers with land grants. I guess they hope veterans would help to put down any native unrest. So, what's the land like?'

'It's a pretty decent patch to be fair,' Eadrich replied. 'There's pasture and woodlands, all straddling a small tributary river. I think it'll be good for crops and livestock. I've decided to call it Woden's Ford.'

'It's a great opportunity, Eadrich – and a great name,' Modig said. 'I hope I'll get the same treatment when my time comes, although I might opt for somewhere a bit warmer! So, what's next?'

Eadrich hesitated, took a deep breath, and then replied, 'Well, first I'm going to pay a few of the locals to help me build a decent home at Woden's Ford. Then I'm going to go back to the old place in Anglia, find myself a pretty young wife, bring her back, and hopefully raise some sons.'

'That sounds like you really are planning to settle down!' Modig exclaimed. 'It sounds like quite a bit of bother, too. Why don't you do what most of our men do: take a few local women as mistresses, marry one if you must, move on some-where else when you get fed up or you want to find some fresh talent?'

Eadrich was silent for a few moments, gazing into the middle distance, and then looked at his friend. 'I know that's the norm, Modig, and what I'm doing might sound a bit daft; but I'm thinking long term – and I mean really long term, like centuries ahead.'

Modig looked surprised but interested, and so Eadrich continued, 'I want to found a new Anglian dynasty. We can both see Roman power's on the wane. And we know soldiers from the north German plains are the most effective in the Roman army. I'm sure the Romans will pull out of Britannia pretty soon – it's so far away from the core of the empire. There'll be opportunities then for those ready to take them. Passing on and protecting this tough old Anglian blood will give my descendants the best possible chance.'

Modig nodded, and still looked interested, and so Eadrich carried on, 'I also want to do everything I can to preserve our way of life and our beliefs. Christianity's spreading far too fast for my liking. We both know it's a rot, and a real threat – but the emperors seem determined to support it. I want to create a colony where we can worship Woden and the gods and practice our ancient ways. Hence the name for my place.'

'Maybe it's all a bit too idealistic – but I want to give it a try,' Eadrich concluded.

Modig was impressed. 'It's quite a plan, and so good luck to you,' he said. 'I completely agree about Christianity. It feels like a religion for the weak, definitely not for us.'

'Anyway, I'd love to be able to come back in a few hundred

years and see if your plan works!' Modig continued. 'I have to say, I'll be thinking a bit more short-term when I retire: find the prettiest woman I can as quickly as I can and have some fun!'

* * * * * * *

True to his word, once he had built a house at Woden's Ford Eadrich returned to his home village in Anglia, married a distant relative twenty years younger, and together they had five children. Over the years Eadrich and his family were joined at Woden's Ford by relatives, distant and not so distant, who were looking for better farmland than was available in northern Germany.

The colony grew as the descendants of Eadrich and the other early settlers multiplied. They were joined, too, over the decades by other ex-soldiers, and by poor Anglo-Saxons who had moved from elsewhere or had fallen on hard times and become peasants and even slaves.

After 410, when the Romans effectively withdrew from Britannia, the colonists were well-placed – as Eadrich had foreseen – to annex more land in the surrounding area and bring more of the native population under their direct control. Most of the unfree tenants and slaves in the Clan territory and even the ceorls – the peasant farmers tied to the land – were from native British stock. Their ancestors had worked the land for centuries, but they adapted gradually to the new Anglian overlords and their language and customs.

Eadrich's dream was fulfilled through a strict marriage policy. A blind eye was turned when Anglian men fathered illegitimate children by native peasant and slave women. In practice the children were often supported discreetly: it was thought a regular sprinkling of Anglian blood would strengthen the predominantly native workforce.

Marriage, however, and thus legitimate descendants, was only allowed with men and women of Anglo-Saxon, preferably Anglian, ancestry. It became progressively easier for Woden's Ford's to draw from a wider gene pool in the fifth and sixth centuries as Anglo-Saxon incomers settled right across the southern, eastern and northern reaches of the old Roman province. There was tension and fighting between groups of incomers, but alliances were formed, too. Eadrich's clan drew on the alliances to find marriage partners.

* * * * * * *

By 616 Eadrich's successors controlled a swathe of land radiating in all directions from Woden's Ford. The current chieftain, Eadwell, eighth in succession from Eadrich, was a great bear of a man. Now well into his forties, he was tall, burly, with a dome-like forehead, a mane of shaggy, greying hair, and a beard which seemed permanently tangled. His dark blue eyes shone out from a craggy, handsome face. A smile seemed to play around his mouth constantly.

I am so fortunate, Eadwell thought, as he walked in the fields near Woden's Ford on a pleasant summer evening. The gradually setting sun burnished the pastures. The grazing livestock seemed utterly calm. The river shimmered in the distance as it snaked its way into the hills.

Eadwell could survey his life with satisfaction. He was chief of one of the most powerful and wealthy clans in Deira, commanded large tributes of produce and manpower, and was an important thegn – a noble with the right to bear arms – in the united Northumbrian kingdom.

He had been shaken and saddened by the sudden and premature death of his wife ten years previously, but he had never been lonely. He had fathered seven children, six of whom had survived. His eldest son and heir, Rinc, was about to be married, and so his succession appeared secure for another two generations.

Eadwell turned his gaze towards the cluster of dwellings, a few hundred yards away down the gentle slope, where he lived with his unmarried children – four sons and a daughter. At the heart of the cluster was the original wooden, thatched home built by Eadrich well over 250 years previously. It stood alongside the great hall, a massive rectangular wooden structure, and the other dwellings of various sizes many of them linked by corridors and connecting doors.

Eadwell loved and took pride in every aspect of Woden's Ford. It was a precious physical legacy which he was determined to nurture and enhance. As he looked, he wondered, as he often did, what Eadrich had been like. He must have been a determined and resourceful individual to be able to both establish a dynasty and to lay down the roots which had sustained it for so long.

The story of the founding of Woden's Ford had been passed faithfully down the centuries. Each generation had added its own tales to the stock of clan knowledge. The diet of memories had been rich indeed by the time Eadwell was a child. It had nourished his own pride in his ancestry.

Eadwell could not recall what his grandfather had looked like in any detail, but he could just about remember sitting on his knee as the old man had told him tales of the past.

His own father had inherited the task of keeping the clan memories alive. He had undertaken it with gusto. Eadwell smiled at the memory of how his father would tell stories about the history of the clan at almost any opportunity – sometimes to the frustration of all around him, especially as he had aged, and the stories had seemed to become longer and taller!

Eadwell brushed a tear from his eye as he pictured his father – not as he had been when he had died fifteen years previously as a relatively old man, but in his prime when Eadwell had been growing up. In Eadwell's memory his father remained forever a strapping, blonde-haired warrior with a booming voice and a will of iron. Eadwell had adored him.

Eadwell reflected that he had now inherited the role as the primary bridge between the generations. He could reach back in his own memory to his grandfather. He had been as passionate as his father had been about passing on to his own children the stories of his ancestors and the founding and development of Woden's Ford. And he looked forward to spending time with as many grandchildren as his sons and daughters could produce.

Eadwell felt that the gods of his ancestors had been kind, that the fates had generally smiled on him. He was looking forward to Rinc's wedding the following week. He reflected again on the uncanny resemblance between Rinc and his own father, both in appearance and in commitment and drive. He felt that Woden's Ford would be in capable hands once he was gone.

There were, though, two clouds on Eadwell's personal horizon.

The first was his health. He had been a strong, powerful man with enormous stamina, but now he was suffering from periodic and progressively worse bouts of breathlessness and dizziness. His children and brothers had teased him initially, but they were now worried, and he was frustrated. He had been used to being in control, a warrior and leader with few peers: he was now contemplating withdrawal from active military service.

The second cloud was the accelerating spread of Christianity. Early on in his tenure as chief, fifteen years previously, rumours that Anglo-Saxon kingdoms in the south were flirting with and embracing Christianity began to swirl around Deira. These soon hardened into firm news that the kings of Kent, East Anglia and elsewhere had converted and required their populations to do likewise.

Eadwell had been and remained contemptuous. He believed, as his ancestors had done, that Christianity would undermine the martial spirit of the Anglo-Saxon tribes. He and the rest of the Northumbrian nobility had set their faces against Christianity.

Nevertheless, Eadwell was worried.

Chapter 3

616 AD

An Anglian wedding

'They make a grand pair,' Edgar said, nodding towards the bride and groom leading the dance. 'I like my women a bit plumper, and with shorter noses, but Hilda's a good acquisition. I'm sure she'll breed well.'

'Now that's no way to talk about the future mother of the clan!' Eadwell responded, feigning outrage towards his younger brother. 'I'm sure they'll both be very happy. I certainly am. We've got ourselves a pretty bride for Rinc, and we've sealed an alliance with a good family. Our stock with King Edwin must rise. I know he's king of the whole of Northumbria, but he's got Deiran blood in his veins. Surely he'll look to strong Deiran clans first and foremost for support.'

Edgar laughed. 'I'm sure you're right, big brother – we've done well!' he said.

Rinc, now twenty-two, was Eadwell's oldest son and heir apparent. Eadwell and the other clan elders had planned the match carefully. His bride, Hilda, was two years younger, the product of another powerful Anglian clan further north in Deira.

Rinc was tall, thickset and fair-haired: so like his late

grandfather all his older relatives agreed. He was a hard-working, respectful, pragmatic young man. He accepted life as it was and tended to become impatient with talk about anything which wasn't solid, practical and real – 'fanciful stuff', as he described it scornfully. Generally easy-going he was known to have a bit of a temper.

Hilda was of medium height, slim, with long dusky-blonde hair and rich, brown eyes: not a classic beauty, but 'comely' was the verdict of the female grandees in her clan. She was something of a perfectionist and was intrigued by ideas. She was generally reserved, even stoical – but also a girl who could wilt if things went wrong or she couldn't get her own way.

The wedding, held in the great hall at Woden's Ford, was a grand affair attended by numerous guests from throughout Deira. The ceremony earlier in the day had been solemn, conducted by the clan priests who had stuck faithfully to traditional rituals. The couple had committed themselves to each other. They had been wrapped in a web of pagan charms. The protection of their ancestors had been sought. Sacrifices had been offered to hasten the arrival of children.

The wedding feast was now well under way. The Anglian community enjoyed celebrating and so it was a boisterous occasion. The sun had set on the late summer day, but inside the hall torches burnt brightly, music played, dancers whirled, ale and mead flowed, and the volume of conversation rose.

Eadwell and his surviving brothers, Edgar and Aldrich, were in confident and reflective mood as they chatted. 'Aye, it's certainly a good year for Woden's Ford, and a good year for Deira,' Aldrich said, wiping ale froth from his moustache.

'Everything I hear about King Edwin makes me feel really positive. King Aethelfrith was alright for a Bernician, and I certainly wasn't against unification; but I feel much happier with one of our own on the Northumbrian throne.'

'You're absolutely right,' Eadwell said. 'This feels like a double celebration. Little did we know when we planned the wedding that Edwin and his East Anglian chums would depose Aethelfrith just a few weeks beforehand. I gather Edwin's going to move the Northumbrian capital from Bamburgh to York. That'll mean we're much closer to court and to his war band. I dare say the Bernicians won't like their capital being downgraded, but they'll just have to get over it. I'm glad Northumbria will stay united, but I agree, Aldrich, it certainly feels good to have a Deiran in command in our old capital.'

'I wonder what Aethelfrith's family will do?' Edgar pondered. 'I hear Queen Acha has fled with his sons. I don't know where to, but I'm sure Edwin will be uneasy until he finds out. It's so awkward that Acha is Edwin's sister given he's just killed her husband!'

'Anyway, I hope Edwin will make Northumbria even stronger. I'm certainly looking forward to more war and more plunder!' Edgar clenched his fist and smacked it into the palm of his other hand as he spoke.

'I'm glad, too, there's no sign of Edwin having anything to do with all the Christianity nonsense,' Edgar concluded fervently.

Edgar was only a year younger than Eadwell. They were very close, but they looked remarkably different. Edgar was slimmer, shorter and neater than the average Anglian nobleman. He was in excellent physical shape for a man in his early forties and was regarded as one of the most capable warriors and hunters in Deira.

Edgar was an intense, dogmatic, many would say stubborn individual. He was an authority on pagan lore and the traditions and sagas of the clan's ancestors; by the same token he loathed Christianity, as much if not more than Eadwell did.

As the older men talked, they were joined by Grimbald, Edgar's eldest son, who was a few months younger than Rinc. Grimbald looked much more like Eadwell than Edgar – a fact which had prompted jokes throughout his life at his father's expense. He was taller, stockier and darker than his father. He had a shock of curly, dark-brown hair, a full beard, and deep-set eyes hooded by thick eyebrows.

'I don't know whether we can trust King Edwin,' Grimbald said, to the surprise of his father and uncles. 'I've heard he mixed a fair bit with Christians while he was in exile. I hope he hasn't picked up from the Welsh or the East Anglians any notion of converting us all.'

Grimbald hesitated, and then continued, 'I didn't like being ruled by a Bernician, but there's no doubt King Aethelfrith was anti-Christian! Remember, I was at the battle of Chester. I'll never forget the way his war band cut down the monks who were praying for the Welsh armies. It was carnage.'

Grimbald paused again as a shadow appeared to pass momentarily over his eyes. His listeners knew that even for this tough, young Anglian warrior witnessing the massacre had been a harrowing experience. Grimbald himself admitted he could not get the scene out of his mind, that it haunted his dreams.

'I just wish we could become a separate Deiran kingdom again, proudly committed to all our old ways,' Grimbald finished. 'I don't see why we should be shackled to the Bernicians.'

Edgar looked at his son fondly, and said, 'You may not look much like me, my boy, but you've got the right ideas, that's for certain. We must be on our guard against Christianity. Individual responsibility, turning the other cheek, loving enemies, rejecting violence: they're all part of a plot to undermine Woden's way which we've preserved here for seven generations. Eadrich would spin in his grave if he thought we were planning to convert Woden's Ford. I know the Britons kept going with Christianity when the Romans left. But we're the future, so I don't see why we should change.'

Aldrich, quieter and more peaceful than either of his brothers, laughed as he said, 'Calm down, Ed. I know it's your pet subject and you like to rant, but this is a wedding. It's time to have fun, and there isn't a single Christian in the whole hall! By the way, Grimbald, what's that cut on your wrist?'

Grimbald looked at the angry wound ruefully as he explained, 'When I was out hunting in the hills a couple of days ago I tracked down a wolf which I think had been attacking our herds. I thought I'd killed it, but when I pulled out the arrow and turned the body it had just enough strength left to bite me. Believe me, it was sore!'

The three brothers laughed, but they were impressed. Grimbald was indeed turning out to be a chip off the old block.

* * * * * * *

Hilda was just a few feet away from the men as they talked. She had taken a break from dancing and was surrounded by Rinc's two sisters – now her sisters in law – and two of her own younger female relatives. The eldest of Rinc's sisters was eighteen and recently married; the other girls were a few years younger.

The girls, dressed in their finest, were chattering and giggling excitedly, all apparently at the same time. The main topic was the suitability and desirability of boys at the reception: the girls were well aware that events like these were prime market-places for future matches. Alice, Hilda's pretty fifteen-year-old cousin, was eyeing Grimbald with interest.

Hilda had picked up fragments of the conversation about Christianity, and she had strained to hear more. Her brow furrowed slightly as she heard Aldrich claim that there weren't any Christians in the hall.

Her own parents, although they would not admit it openly, were sympathetic to Christianity. Her father had visited Kent a few years previously and had met and been impressed by some of the monks who had followed in the footsteps of Augustine's papal mission in 597. Hilda, unusually for an Anglian woman, had talked to her father a great deal about religion.

As the celebration continued and the guests became louder, Hilda met and talked to as many of her new in laws as she could; but she made a mental note to be careful what she said about Christianity to anyone at Woden's Ford.

Chapter 4

616 AD

A Gwynedd wedding

'**M**arry me,' Abertha whispered as they sat together after an energetic dance.

Gerant looked at her, startled. 'I thought it was the man who proposed,' he said, laughing. 'But don't you think we should talk to our families first?'

'So, you don't want to marry me?' Abertha said sulkily.

'Believe me, I'd be the happiest man in Gwynedd if we were to marry; but I know many older men have designs on you.'

Gerant was right; several suitors had approached Abertha's father over the last couple of years as she had matured into a beautiful young woman. Abertha's father had begun to broach the subject of marriage with his daughter, but not very successfully. She was developing a reputation for having a strong and impulsive will and fiery temper as well as good looks. Abertha had told her father in no uncertain terms that she would know the right man when she saw him.

'No need to worry about the competition, my love,' Abertha said archly. 'I've told father I'm in charge of my future, not him.'

Gerant was impressed, but far from convinced. He was

more conventional, more cautious – but equally he was besotted with Abertha. 'Let's get married then,' he said with a smile.

'Right,' she said decisively. 'Leave the rest to me.'

* * * * * * *

It was at a harvest feast in 616 that Cadmon's mother and father, Abertha and Gerant, pledged to marry.

Both had jet black hair and relatively dark complexions, a reflection of their deep ancestry in southern Europe. Both were handsome, and Abertha, in particular, was regarded as a beauty throughout the area. Her long, silky hair and soulful brown eyes complemented a lithe figure and long legs.

The two young people – Abertha was eighteen, Gerant twenty – were from different villages, but they had met on and off over the years at events and get-togethers. There had always been a spark between them; at this feast the spark had caught fire: they had danced, chatted and kissed oblivious to anyone else.

Abertha was true to her word. Gerant did leave the rest to her, and the wedding took place within weeks. The bride and groom were resplendent and radiant in traditional attire. Their parents looked faintly bemused throughout, as if they couldn't quite work out how everything had happened so quickly.

The ceremony was ostensibly Christian but owed a great deal to much older beliefs. It was followed by the customary monologue by a local bard – a reminder of the long story which the couple had joined and which it was hoped that they would help to perpetuate through their union and off-spring.

The bard was and looked old and was deeply respected as such. He was steeped in the history and culture of Gwynedd and was listened to in silence by the guests of all ages.

'Our ancestors have lived in this place, between the mountains and the sea, for almost three thousand years. They came across the sea from the deep south, the European mainland, farmers seeking new land as they explored far and wide. They overran the sparsely scattered original inhabitants and then dispersed in small hamlets along the north coast. Their lives changed little as the centuries rolled by. There was plenty of game and fish in the hills, valleys, sea and rivers, and enough land to graze stock.'

'Gwynedd is a land defined by mountains,' he continued. 'The name itself, Gwynedd, means the land beneath the White Mountain. The mountains influence the very rhythm of the year, with its routines, celebrations and milestones. They determine when we can graze our cattle and sow seed, and they have even shaped our beliefs. Each hamlet has developed its own identity over the centuries, but they are all linked to a wider community through trade and intermarriage.'

As the attention of some guests started to wander, particularly those who had heard him and other bards at previous events, he talked about local heroes and tales of courage and romance. He explained the epic history of the royal house of Gwynedd founded by Cunedda 200 years or so previously. He lamented the oppression and cruelty of the Romans including the massacre of druid folk on the Isle of Anglesey centuries ago.

The bard painted a picture of a dramatic, romantic country which remembered, celebrated and mourned its past extravagantly.

As the bard concluded, the guests burst into the expected round of applause. The fathers of the bride and groom followed with flamboyant votes of thanks.

The guests relaxed, food and drink were served, and conversation flowed. The fathers of the bride and groom were at the centre of a gaggle of relatives and friends, all eager to congratulate them.

The talk moved on from local gossip to wider matters.

'I've heard old King Aethelfrith of Northumbria met a nasty end not so long ago: apparently Edwin of Deira defeated him and is now king.' Abertha's father was talking: his listeners expressed a mixture of surprise and satisfaction.

'Serves him right, the vicious old Saxon,' one of the men said. 'I guess we all heard about the Battle of Chester. It was bad enough he beat the armies of Powys and Rhos, but I also heard he ordered the slaughter of the monks of Bangor. They were praying nearby, defenceless. They were simply hacked to death – hundreds of them. I was told about it by a cousin who knew someone who escaped from the battlefield.'

'You just can't trust the wretched Saxons,' Gerant's father exclaimed. There were vigorous nods all round. 'They're taking over more and more land. They'll be coming our way soon, you mark my words. We need leaders who'll push them back, take back the old lands. I know there are prophecies that we'll regain the lost lands in the east: but we need action not just dreams. And we need it quickly.'

'Well said,' agreed one of Gerant's uncles. 'But I did hear a few years ago from a passing trader that this Edwin was in exile at the royal court in Gwynedd for a while. So maybe he'll be a friend, you never know.'

'Maybe, but you can't trust any of them,' his brother replied authoritatively, at the same time putting his flagon down with an air of finality. 'Now the music's about to begin, and I'm going to get a dance with my lovely daughter in law: I can't leave her all to Gerant!'

Chapter 5

618 AD

Coming together

Aelfred was born to Rinc and Hilda in June 617; Abertha gave birth to Cadmon six months later in January 618.

By May 618, their vastly different lives were about to intersect.

Rinc had just returned to Woden's Ford after a visit to King Edwin's court in York. 'Hey, Father, Hilda!' he called in breathless excitement as he leapt from his horse and handed it to a servant. 'Guess what? The king's asked me to lead a raid on Gwynedd. I've to choose thirty or so good men and set off next week. I've been told the route and given the targets for the raid.'

King Edwin, although he had only been on the Northumbrian throne for two years, wanted hegemony not just in the north-east but much further afield: he wanted to be the supreme king in the British mainland, thus continuing the policy of his vanquished predecessor, King Aethelfrith.

Edwin saw Gwynedd as an early target despite having spent part of his exile at the court of its king. He did not yet feel ready to send a major expedition: his tactics for the time being were to deploy regular small-scale raids, and thus to spread fear and weaken resilience.

Eadwell was delighted. The selection of his son to lead a significant military mission was another sign of the clan's influence. 'That's great news, Rinc! It certainly won't be easy, but it's a tremendous opportunity.'

Hilda tried to be equally enthusiastic. She recognised that this was an important moment for Rinc, but she felt as if her mind were enmeshed in a tangle of dark thoughts. Aelfred's birth, twelve months previously, had been difficult and traumatic. He was healthy, but since then Hilda had suffered two miscarriages. She was suffused by grief and depression and on edge constantly. She knew that as wife of the heir apparent her primary role was to provide a steady supply of children, preferably male – and she was well aware that she was failing.

Rinc had also been affected by the double miscarriage. He swung between the fatalism imbued deep in the Anglian mindset, and bouts of fierce, irrational rage. He accepted at one level that the gods were inscrutable, that events must be accepted; at another level he felt pain and anger at being let down, at his inability to direct and control his circumstances. His behaviour had become more and more erratic.

'It sounds fantastic, Rinc, well done,' Hilda said. 'How long d'you think you'll be away?'

Hilda couldn't keep the note of trepidation out of her voice, and Rinc noticed it. 'Not that long; and I'm sure I'll be fine – no need to worry,' he replied airily, but he didn't want to be diverted into a detailed discussion about the risks, and so he said, 'I need to start planning straight away, there's a lot to do.'

Over the next couple of days Rinc, with Eadwell and his three younger brothers – Wilfred, Alwyn and Godwyn – took great care in selecting another thirty men to accompany him. They chose a mix of relatives from across the clan with the most experience of and success in battle together with some of the toughest and most reliable peasants to support them.

Wilfred, the oldest of Rinc's three brothers (just a year younger than him), and Godwyn, the youngest at seventeen, were included in the party, but Alwyn agreed to stay at home. Eadwell didn't like the idea of all the brothers going on the same raid because of the implications for the succession if it came to grief.

The Northumbrian raiders, travelling on horses and ponies, took several days to cross the country, careful to use little-known forest and hill tracks once they were outside Northumbrian territory. They had been given detailed instructions on the route and the villages to target by agents at Edwin's court who had been spying and planning for the last few months.

Once they were within a few miles of the first village they set up camp in a secluded valley, discussed the plan for the next day, and settled down to sleep.

In the village Abertha and Gerant were comforting their six-month-old baby as he wrestled with a stomach upset. It was the end of a normal day. It was to be their last together.

The next day the sun shone from a flawless sky as the raiders approached the village. They were experienced and well-armed warriors. The villagers were unprepared, and although some of the men fought back the engagement was swift and decisive.

Very soon Gerant lay dead alongside several other men.

The Northumbrian warriors were brutal and efficient. They

didn't speak the villagers' language, but their intentions were crystal clear. They wanted to leave a shadow of terror and take as many young people as they could for the slave markets: in both ways they would make the region more vulnerable to Edwin's planned invasion.

The wailing of women and children showed that they had achieved their first goal. Abertha stood out: devastated by Gerant's death her long, dark hair flew in all directions as she mingled screams of rage with howling grief. Her hands clutched at open air, and then lashed at the Northumbrian men as they tried to catch and bind her.

It was a picture of wild, raw, elemental beauty.

Rinc was entranced.

Abertha, by now holding Cadmon, was eventually bound with the other captives and ready to be marched to the nearby port where they would be sold to slave traders in exchange for precious metals and jewellery. Goods came to the British mainland through the trading networks linking Ireland to south-western Europe, the Levant and beyond; in return there was a ready market in Europe for British and Anglo-Saxon slaves.

Rinc, however, was loath to part with the young woman. He knew that Hilda had been seeking a reliable female helper since the death of her slave housekeeper. He liked the idea of pleasing her, especially because of the trauma she had suffered through the miscarriages, and at the same time adorning his household with an extremely beautiful young woman.

'I'll take the long-haired wench back to Woden's Ford – for Hilda,' he said. No one questioned his right to do so, but a few surreptitious, knowing looks were exchanged.

Abertha realised quickly what was happening and clutched Cadmon closely. One of the warriors made to seize the child, his intention to murder the boy.

Rinc shouted at him to step back. 'The boy comes too,' he commanded.

* * * * * * *

'I really don't know why they bother. The charms sound ridiculous, the sacrifices are unpleasant, and none of it seems to make a jot of difference. The clan priests and sorcerers were let loose on me after the first miscarriage, and lo and behold I had another. They're getting going again. To be honest, they're just making me feel more depressed and vulnerable with all their mumbo jumbo. They talk about wyrd, about everything being connected, about spirits. I simply can't see how it's all supposed to work.'

Hilda was talking to Alwyn, Rinc's second oldest brother. Rinc and his other brothers had been away on the Gwynedd raid for five weeks and were expected back soon. Alwyn was twenty-two, the same age as Hilda, and was soon to marry and move out to his own home. He was a similar height to Rinc, but slimmer, and his hair was darker.

Alwyn was mature and thoughtful, and Hilda enjoyed talking to him: she felt she could be more open about religion with Alwyn than with any of her other in laws.

'Well, all the rituals, ceremonies and charms have been handed down the generations: they're tried and tested, and so there must be something to them,' Alwyn said. 'I guess at the very least they simply help you feel better or more confident or whatever just because that's what you expect. There's comfort in repeating words and actions which have been used time and again by our ancestors.'

Eadwell came into the room while Alwyn was speaking. 'That's it, Alwyn, well said! If they were good enough for Eadrich all those centuries ago, then they're good enough for us.'

'But they don't work, Father,' Hilda said, not attempting to hide her frustration. 'If there was power in the magic, surely I wouldn't have lost my children.'

'I know it's hard for you, Hilda,' Eadwell replied, 'but the priests do their thing and then it's up to the gods. Our three priests here at Woden's Ford are the latest in a long family line. Men in that family have had special powers for generations. They know better than anyone how to draw down the power of the gods. That's why they conduct all our weddings and funerals. And it's why we call on them when people and livestock get sick.'

Eadwell paused, and then shook his head slowly as he concluded, more sympathetically, 'We just don't know why sometimes things work out and other times they don't. We have to accept our fate and get on with life as best we can. There's no point in getting down about it, or in trying too hard to understand.'

Eadwell was perplexed, nevertheless, even though he wouldn't admit it. He could not understand why the gods of his ancestors, who had smiled on him so kindly, should visit the miscarriages on his family.

The conversation was cut short when a servant rushed in to

say that the raiding party was back. There was a flurry as Eadwell, Alwyn and Hilda hurried out to greet the returning men.

Hilda flung her arms round Rinc's neck and sobbed as the pent-up tension of the preceding weeks was released. Eadwell and Alwyn talked excitedly with Wilfred and Godwyn who were recounting the highlights of the successful raid.

'And who's the young lady, may I ask?' Eadwell's question and the appreciative tone made the other family members follow his gaze. They saw Abertha, very obviously tired and angry but still beautiful. She was hugging Cadmon tightly as she was led away by one of the raiding party.

'She's your new house slave, Hilda,' Rinc said, looking at his wife. 'She's a present from Gwynedd. I thought you could do with a replacement for Wenda.'

'Well, she's quite a looker, that's for sure,' Eadwell said, arching his eyebrows roguishly. 'I take it the father of the bairn isn't with her?'

'No, Father, we killed him when we took their village,' Godwyn answered eagerly. 'It was no contest. I killed a couple of their men myself.'

'Well done, son,' Eadwell said approvingly. Godwyn swelled with pride.

Amidst all of the activity and banter no one except Alwyn noticed the wary look in Hilda's eyes as she watched Abertha being led away.

* * * * * * *

44

The arrival of Abertha was like metal rubbing against jagged rock. She herself was distressed, distraught, distant. Hilda, meanwhile, normally so stoical, was struggling with her emotions: so, instead of welcoming the new house slave, she suspected Rinc's motives. She saw Abertha's arrival as a rebuke for her failure to produce more than one child. Rinc's fervent assurances to the contrary cut no ice, and so he felt hurt that his gift had been misconstrued so badly.

Eadwell, in the traditional manner of an Anglian chief, sought to assert his right to sleep with any pretty woman he chose. He was shocked by Abertha's furious rebuff. For Rinc's sake he stepped back from his instinctive reaction to expel her from Woden's Ford immediately; but he was frustrated and moody.

The only people in Woden's Ford who appeared oblivious to and unaffected by the atmosphere that summer were the two boys. Doted on by their mothers they were cocooned in love. They were a distraction for all the adults, an opportunity to focus on something wholesome and healthy.

Everything changed on a brooding early autumn morning just three months after Cadmon and Abertha had arrived.

'Will you please shut that child up!' Hilda called in to the room in which Cadmon and Abertha had been installed. Cadmon had been crying as the rest of the household had stirred and begun the day. Hilda had become more and more irritated and puzzled as the crying had continued.

As Cadmon wailed ever more loudly Hilda finally entered the room. What she saw brought her to an immediate halt. She stood completely still, oblivious now to the wailing child. She felt as if her brain, indeed her whole body, had become numb. Time itself seemed to stop.

Abertha lay motionless, her beautiful face utterly pale, her body frozen in death.

Eventually, Hilda, forcing herself, went up to the bed where Abertha lay. She bent down to make absolutely sure that the young woman was dead, but she could not bring herself to touch the body.

Cadmon was now beside himself with fury. The noise seemed to suddenly impinge on Hilda. She picked the child up and hugged him and then, still clutching Cadmon tightly, she ran from the room.

She almost bumped in to Rinc who was coming to investigate the rumpus. 'She's dead, Rinc,' Hilda gasped. 'She must have died in her sleep.'

Rinc looked at his wife. He was utterly aghast. He could not hide from her the merest hint of doubt and suspicion, too – and she noticed it. The moment passed in an instant, but it left its mark for the rest of their lives.

Feelings of shock and guilt pulsed almost visibly around Woden's Ford once news of Abertha's death emerged. So did questions and rumours.

Had she been poisoned, possibly even by Hilda whose dislike of the slave had been well known? Had she died of a broken heart? Had the strain of the forced journey, combined with grief and anger, caused unbearable strain on her heart? Had she taken her own life, perhaps swallowing some deadly herbal concoction?

Eadwell and Rinc were in no mood to carry out an investigation. The body was buried quickly. The word was put out that Abertha had had a weak constitution.

In an act of mercy, however, perhaps tacit acknowledgement of regret at the way his mother had been treated, Cadmon was effectively adopted and placed in the nursery with Aelfred. They were to grow up from then on as brothers even though Cadmon was destined to be a house slave.

Chapter 6

618–624 AD

Early years

Life at Woden's Ford on the surface moved on, and memories of the tragic Welsh slave dulled; but the long-term, subterranean impact was lasting. Rinc and Hilda never discussed the girl's death other than in the most superficial terms, but the hurt and suspicion which seeped between them in the summer of 618 gradually hardened into volcanic rock, especially as two further miscarriages and a stillbirth followed.

For all their disappointment Rinc and Hilda were determined that Aelfred should be given a secure upbringing in keeping with his status and immersed in the Anglian pagan culture which had been handed down through successive generations.

Rinc was often away from home campaigning in Edwin's armies as they marched north, west and south from Northumbria. His reputation had grown since his successful raid in Gwynedd, but it meant he saw little of his son. As a result, Aelfred spent a great deal of time with his grandfather whose health was continuing to falter and so was spared military duties.

Aelfred delighted in the vivid, dramatic stories Eadwell

told of his ancestors, of the Anglian gods, and of his own war exploits. One day, when he was nearly seven years old, Aelfred had peppered Eadwell with 'why' questions in response to every story and anecdote he had recounted.

Eadwell, laughing, eventually said to Aelfred and Cadmon, 'Right, let me explain what we're all about, and where we've come from. I hope that'll answer all your 'why' questions in one go! Now, let's sit down together.'

'That sounds exciting, Grandfather,' Aelfred said, his eyes shining as he and Cadmon sat down obediently.

'The origins of our people go back many thousands of years to Anglia, and to the great god of war, Woden,' Eadwell began. 'We owe our existence to Woden. In everything we do we must strive to satisfy and please him and the other gods. That's our first duty. Our second duty is to protect and build up our kin – all the people who share our blood, and, in particular, our clan here at Woden's Ford.'

'War and violence are duties imposed on us by Woden,' Eadwell continued. 'We must either win victories in battle and gain plunder for the clan or die gloriously and bravely in the attempt. In the past our ancestors fought other clans. Now we carry out that duty mainly by fighting for our king. We also try to please the gods and find out their wishes through magic, charms and sacrificial practices passed down from our ancestors.'

Eadwell explained the various elaborate rituals which had evolved down the years many of which required dramatic and distinctive costumes, role play, singing, and fire ceremonies.

It was an exciting environment for the boys. The adults talked constantly about battles and raids. It was a self-perpetuating cycle for the clan leaders: their followers expected plunder and land and so new enemies must be sought continually. A clan or kingdom which rested on its laurels was regarded as weak.

The Anglian community worked hard, fought hard and played hard. They never missed an opportunity to celebrate and to lubricate every event with strong drink. Reserved behaviour was not understood.

The steady stream of visitors added to the variety of life at Woden's Ford. The clan often hosted emissaries from other powerful clans in Northumbria and from allied kingdoms right across Britain. King Edwin's plans for expansion were being rolled out, and so diplomatic foundations must be laid and campaign plans developed. The Eadrich clan were fully involved and so the boys witnessed many grand gatherings and feasts.

The most memorable was a visit spread over several days by King Edwin himself as he held court and received tribute from the clan and neighbouring thegns. It was a great honour for Woden's Ford to be included in the annual royal circuit of the kingdom. The whole clan was involved for weeks in preparing a programme of entertainment and ceremony fit for the occasion. The boys were captivated and enthralled, especially when Aelfred was presented to the king.

The clan was also growing wealthier, and that provided new and additional scope to develop Woden's Ford.

* * * * * * *

'Look, Pa, I think there are real opportunities here for Woden's Ford. We're producing far more than our people need – meat, wool, leather, crops, timber. We need to look at how we can trade our surplus and get things we don't have in return. More and more goods are being bought and sold in York. Traders are coming from all over. There's lots of processing happening here now, too. The tanners, for example, are doing a lot of business. That's why the whole place smells pretty bad!'

Wilfred was talking to Eadwell as the two men walked through the bustling, exotic, often stinking streets of York on a late summer day in 624. Aelfred and Cadmon were skipping alongside. The boys were agog: they passed tanneries, abattoirs, timber merchants and live animal markets scattered amidst old Roman ruins; spent time looking at the ships in the port; and listened in fascination to the different dialects and languages.

'I'm sure you're right, son,' Eadwell said. 'Even in my younger days – and that's not too far back, whatever you all think – large parts of York seemed abandoned. I know the old Roman walls have remained intact, but in many areas it looked as if nothing much had happened since the Romans left. It looked and felt really sad. So, it's good now to see trade really picking up and to hear such a buzz in the city. I guess it's helped to have a Deiran king back here for the last few years.'

'The last few years have certainly been good for York,' Wilfred said. 'We've had a bit more stability here in Northumbria. From what I hear from travellers it's the same in other parts. Bigger kingdoms and less war mean folk can get around and buy and sell more easily.'

'I see what you mean, son,' Eadwell said. 'You've done really well to begin to develop trading links for Woden's Ford. I don't think Rinc, Alwyn or Godwyn are so interested. Let's hope trade will bring plenty more wealth our way without any fighting.'

Wilfred smiled with pleasure. He was the quietest of Eadwell's four sons. He was a fierce warrior and a good farmer, but he had found most satisfaction in exploring the new world which was opening up in York. His brothers were supportive, but like most Anglians they avoided cities if they could: they much preferred to be in the fields, woods and hills.

Once the two men had completed their business, they and the two boys rode back to Woden's Ford. They were only seven years old but both boys could ride ponies well. 'So, what did you think, boys?' Eadwell asked.

'It was so smelly, Grandfather!' Aelfred exclaimed in mock disgust. 'But I loved seeing all the ships. I want to go again with you and Uncle Wilfred.'

'Well, I'm sure that'll be possible,' Eadwell said, laughing. 'I think your uncle will be spending quite a bit of time there in future.'

They all enjoyed the ride. It was a pleasant summer afternoon. White clouds scudded across the sky in a warm southerly breeze, but otherwise the sun shone brightly on the rolling landscape. As they approached Woden's Ford workers were out in force harvesting crops. They waved cheerfully to the four riders.

'Well, that was a grand day out!' Eadwell remarked heartily as they dismounted, but he was then overcome by a fit of coughing. 'Damn this cough though. I just wish our sorcerers and priests could find a way of making me well again.'

'I'm sure they will,' Wilfred said. 'Look, why don't you come over and have dinner with me and Bertha and the little ones. I'm sure Rinc and Hilda won't miss you too much. You haven't been round for a while, and I think Bertha's beginning to feel offended!'

'Right you are, son. I'll see you soon,' Eadwell said. He lived with Rinc, Hilda and Aelfred in the main house, but his other three sons and their families all lived nearby.

* * * * * * *

Just two hours later, as Rinc, Hilda and Aelfred sat eating dinner, Wilfred burst in, out of breath and clearly distressed. He struggled to speak but the others quickly got the gist: Eadwell had collapsed while visiting Wilfred and his family.

For the next two days Eadwell drifted in and out of consciousness, unable to speak and capable of communicating only through feeble inclinations of his head and weak hand signals. Eadwell's two brothers and four sons spent most of their time in Wilfred's home or at one of the other family dwellings as normal life came to a halt. Messengers were sent to summon as quickly as possible Eadwell's sisters and two married daughters from their homes in other parts of Northumbria.

It was clear that Eadwell was unlikely to survive much longer. As the end approached his brothers and sons gathered to confirm plans for the funeral and the succession. 'So,' Rinc said, attempting to keep his voice authoritative in spite of the occasional tremor, 'we're all agreed the funeral will be exactly as Father wanted, I'll be master of ceremonies, and you, Uncle Edgar, will declare me to be the new chieftain?'

Rinc looked slowly round the faces of his relatives to check that there was no dissent. The death of a chieftain was a critical milestone. Eadwell had been the embodiment and figurehead of the clan for over twenty years. It had always been accepted that the baton of power would pass to his oldest son, as it had successively for the last eight generations, but nothing could be taken for granted.

Rinc registered the requisite five nods. Edgar broke the silence, 'We're with you, lad, never fear. I'm sure you'll make your father and all our ancestors proud. And, of course, I'll be proud, as Eadwell's oldest brother, to proclaim you as the new chieftain.'

The tough old warrior stifled a sob as he finished, and the six men locked arms and shoulders in a tight scrum of solidarity.

Two hours later Hilda entered the room shared by Aelfred and Cadmon. They looked at her in trepidation. Her face was solemn as she said gently, 'I'm so sorry, boys, but there's no easy way to say this. Your grandfather is dead.'

Aelfred had hero-worshipped Eadwell and so it was a savage shock for the seven-year-old boy. For both him and Cadmon it was as if a mountain had collapsed: to their young eyes everything they had known now looked and felt different.

Eadwell's funeral was the first event that in later life the boys could recall in graphic detail. As tradition demanded,

Rinc and the clan elders ensured that the full range of ritual and spectacle was on display. The flames leaped from the huge cremation pyre. The magnificent grave goods – Eadwell's weapons, treasured possessions, and ceremonial costumes – glittered in the fire light. The oratory was flamboyant, the display of grief dramatic, the feasting and drinking extravagant.

Aelfred felt goose bumps right across his body as he watched and listened. He remembered the great Anglian sagas Eadwell had regaled. He felt transported to a liminal dimension between present and past. He sensed the presence of the gods, his ancestors, Eadwell himself.

Aelfred then and there pledged that, whatever he did in life, his main aim was to make his grandfather proud of him.

* * * * * * *

Neither Aelfred nor anyone else present could have guessed that Eadwell's funeral was to be one of the last great pagan rituals at Woden's Ford.

Chapter 7

625–626 AD

Tension rising

'Have you heard the news? King Edwin's planning to marry a Christian princess from Kent – the sister of their king. I think her name is Aethelburg.'

Rinc was talking as he and Hilda shared a meal with his cousin, Grimbald. Grimbald, now thirty-one, was an impressive man: he was tall, muscular and handsome, with long brown hair tied back and a neatly trimmed beard. Yet his eyes betrayed a nervousness and anxiety which sat oddly with his powerful physical presence. They flickered and darted, and so he rarely made eye contact.

'I really do hope you're joking, Rinc,' Grimbald exclaimed, taking a long drink from his flagon of ale. 'That would be awful. Surely there are loads of high-born pagan women he could choose from.'

'I heard it when I was in York today on pretty good authority, so I fear it isn't a joke,' Rinc replied.

'Well, if he does marry her, I hope Edwin won't take any nonsense,' Grimbald said. 'We really don't want a Christian king in Deira. It'd be the end of the world.'

'Why would it be so bad?' Hilda asked mildly. 'Kent and East Anglia and plenty of other places seem to get along just fine as Christian kingdoms. I haven't heard the world's ended there.'

The two men looked at her with pity and suspicion. 'You're not a sympathiser are you, Hilda?' Grimbald asked. His tone was confrontational, his face puckered in consternation.

He gave her no time to reply as he went on, 'Christianity's pathetic. They want to sweep away all our old practices. They worship some man who gave himself up to die entirely voluntarily. How could you even think about it, with your father-in-law dead just a few months? Perhaps you've forgotten how strongly he felt about Christianity. But then, I've heard you've said some pretty sarcastic things about our priests and sorcerers.'

Hilda made no attempt to hide her annoyance as she frowned and said, 'Hold on, Grimbald, just calm down. I didn't say I was a sympathiser, I just asked a question. Surely we can talk about Christianity without having someone jump down our throats? And, yes, I do wonder about some of the charms and rituals we've inherited. I'm not always sure what good they do.'

'There, Rinc, you see. She's on the slippery slope. Hilda'll be joining up with the new princess. She'll have us all fawning on this Jesus god before we know it.' Grimbald's eyes flashed, his voice was getting louder. He slammed his flagon down on the table.

Rinc tried to check his cousin's growing fury by putting his hand on his arm. 'Hey, Grimbald, I'm certainly not keen on Christianity, but let's see what happens. I'm sure the king'll be sensible. It's probably just a diplomatic alliance.'

Grimbald was now in full flow and shook Rinc's hand

away. 'I blame the Bernicians. There are far too many of them around Edwin. I'm sure they've persuaded him to marry a Christian. We're even bringing Bernicians in to Woden's Ford. I cannot see why Wilfred had to marry a Bernician woman. I've got nothing against Bertha personally, but we should surely be looking within our own tribes for partners.'

Grimbald paused, and for the first time looked directly at Rinc, and then at Hilda. He went on challengingly, almost belligerently, 'I really do think the time's come for the Deiran clans to get together and go it alone. If Edwin's thinking about turning us all into Christians, then why shouldn't we find another king who'll keep the old ways and give us back our independence?'

As Grimbald finished the door opened and Alwyn entered. He sensed the tension immediately. 'I'm sorry to interrupt,' he said, looking round at his three relatives inquisitively. 'I was just passing and wanted to check with Rinc about the plans for ploughing tomorrow. But I can see you're having a really good chinwag. Don't let me stop you.'

Rinc tried to lighten the mood. 'Grimbald was just telling us how much he likes Christians and Bernicians, weren't you?' he said lightly.

'No, I f…ing wasn't!' Grimbald barked, making no effort to disguise his anger.

There was a stunned silence. It was broken after what seemed like an age by Alwyn.

Alwyn had decided to tease Grimbald. He had never got on with his cousin. They were opposites in many ways. Alwyn was thoughtful, calm, intelligent, and fluent; Grimbald was impulsive, unpredictable, often aggressive, and a rough and clumsy speaker. Alwyn liked to talk about ideas, Grimbald was a man of action, never happier than when out hunting.

Grimbald was not well-liked; he also puzzled his relatives. Most Anglian men were married by their early twenties at the latest; Grimbald was still single. Many took it as an affront: difference and unorthodoxy were not understood in a community which valued collective identity more than individual choice.

'Let's talk about something else then,' Alwyn said, smiling. 'How's your love life going, Grimbald? Surely a great, handsome fellow like you must have your eye on some lucky woman.'

Grimbald looked at Alwyn with something approaching hatred, and then rose slowly. Hilda said later she thought he was going to hit Alwyn. Instead, he simply picked up his jacket and stalked slowly out of the room without a backward glance.

Rinc, Alwyn and Hilda looked at each other. 'That was mischievous, Alwyn,' Hilda said, but she was smiling. 'You know he doesn't like to be asked about all that – although I'm actually very glad to see the back of him tonight, he was in a pretty foul mood.'

'You know,' Rinc said thoughtfully, 'I don't think Grimbald's ever been quite right since he fought in the Battle of Chester in King Aethelfrith's army all those years ago. It was his first big campaign. He talks about the excitement of it. But I think seeing the massacre of those monks affected him more than he's ever let on. Look at his eyes the next time you see him and count the number of times they actually make contact. He's an incredibly nervous man.'

* * * * * * *

'So, it's true the King's married a Christian princess. Lucky her is all I can say. I'm sure she'll have lots more slaves and servants than we do. More time to have fun, and no doubt to keep herself beautiful!'

It was a few months after the incident with Grimbald. Bertha, Wilfred's wife, was speaking to her three sisters in law. The four women tried to get together once a week with their children.

'I'm sure,' agreed Alice, Godwyn's wife. Alice was Hilda's cousin – her marriage had been arranged at Rinc's and Hilda's wedding. 'I don't think it'll make much difference to me, but the men are all getting upset about Edwin marrying a Christian. They say the new queen's brought a load of Christian courtiers with her. They seem to think Edwin will convert, and then tell us all to become Christians.'

'I know,' Bertha said, a little wearily. 'I don't know why they're so worried. Even if we do all become Christians, we'll still have to spend most of our time on clothing, food, shelter – just like now. I guess the priests would change, but so what?'

'Alwyn seems more interested than the others, but he always likes to be a bit different!' Alwyn's wife, Brigit, smiled fondly. 'We'll just have to wait and see what happens. There's nothing we can do to alter the future.'

As she listened Hilda reflected that these three women, whom she knew so well, were probably her closest friends, but they were so different from each other.

Bertha was the most extrovert. Born in Bernicia, she was a large, jolly practical woman whose fair hair seemed to be in perpetual disarray, her face constantly flushed, always ready with a joke. She and Wilfred had three children.

Brigit was quieter, slighter, prettier. She had delicate features, prominent cheekbones, fine light brown hair, and hazel eyes. Like her husband, she was reflective and thoughtful. Of the four women she had moved the least distance to marry: she was distantly related to Alwyn and had grown up just a few miles away. She and Alwyn had two children.

Alice was undoubtedly the most attractive, as the others acknowledged readily. She was of medium height, and had long, yellow-blonde hair, piercing blue eyes, and a full figure. She was well aware of her beauty, and while careful not to flirt now she was married she enjoyed male company. She was bored easily both by day-to-day tasks and any conversation that did not revolve around her immediate world. She had married Godwyn three years previously – so far, they had no children.

'So, what do you think of this new princess, Hilda?' Brigit's question drew Hilda back from her thoughts.

'Oh, I'm not sure,' she said, not entirely truthfully. 'As you say, let's see what happens. I'm sure the men will make a big noise for a while, and then things will settle down.'

Hilda had, in fact, continued to think hard about religion. She had not long returned from visiting her family in north Deira. She had taken Aelfred and been away for a few weeks. Her father, still secretly, was enthusiastic about a possible conversion to Christianity. He hoped that the arrival of Christians at the royal court would hasten the process. He had told Hilda that he hoped it might lead to a kinder, less vengeful culture.

Yet Hilda was more wary than ever about saying anything at Woden's Ford which might be interpreted as either sympathy for Christianity or criticism of pagan ways.

To deflect attention from herself Hilda raised the always interesting subject of Grimbald. 'Has anyone seen much of Grimbald recently, by the way? He's certainly been making plenty of noise about Christianity. He hasn't talked to me or Rinc since we had an argument with him a few months ago. He was really rude to Alwyn, too, now I come to think about it.'

As she spoke Hilda noticed from the corner of her eye that Alice seemed to twitch slightly and colour, but the moment passed.

Bertha laughed as she said, 'Ah, Mr Angry Loner! He does seem to be getting worked up. I'm not sure Wilfred has much to do with him, either. Grimbald seems to spend a lot of time away hunting.'

'He and Alwyn certainly don't like each other, but they don't seem to be able to stay apart!' Brigit commented. 'I heard them arguing yet again just a couple of days ago. Grimbald is all about Deira for the Deirans. Alwyn thinks Northumbria should be looking outwards, open to ideas from far and wide.'

'Yes, I know Grimbald isn't keen on Bernicians,' Bertha said, laughing. 'If I were the sensitive type I might get offended. But I think it's his problem. Anyway, it's been good to catch up, but I'd better get these three back and feed them. I can't imagine how Eadwell's wife managed with seven children in nine years, even with the help of servants. Perhaps it's no surprise she went to an early grave!'

* * * * * * *

'I shall not submit. I shall not betray Eadwell and our ancestors. I've heard Edwin himself has converted. Some folk are saying it's a matter of when not if he orders everyone else in Northumbria to follow his lead. But Woden's Ford must remain true to Woden.'

Rinc banged the table and glared around at the other five men – Eadwell's two surviving brothers and his own three brothers.

It was 626 AD. The Clan council were facing a difficult decision. Every male member of the Eadrich clan was entitled to bear arms and so theoretically had a say in its affairs; but it was acknowledged that the small group of men most closely related to the chieftain was the inner council. Although he was not yet ten years old Aelfred had been allowed to sit in by his father: Rinc wanted to introduce Aelfred gradually to his future leadership role.

'I agree entirely,' Edgar said fiercely. He had been closest to Eadwell in age and his closest confidant. 'Eadwell would never forgive us if Woden's Ford became Christian; nor would Eadrich himself. It's a religion of milksops, not even suitable for the women and children of Anglian warriors.'

'Hold on,' Alwyn exclaimed, irritation apparent in his voice. Now almost thirty Alwyn had consolidated his reputation as the cleverest of Eadwell's sons. 'The king's been really canny in the last ten years. Northumbrian influence is growing across the island and way beyond. We're well-known now in the Christian kingdom of Francia, and even in Rome. The king must believe converting to Christianity will help

Northumbria to become the most powerful British kingdom. That's bound to be good for us here at Woden's Ford: it'll definitely bring more wealth and trade.'

His younger brother, Godwyn, rolled his eyes, and said, 'Don't be naive, Al. The king just wants to keep the peace in his bedchamber. He wants invitations to the feasts of his great southern in-laws in Kent. He's star-struck. He's lost interest in Northumbria, in Deira, in his roots.'

'Yes,' Rinc said, 'we must stand up for our old ways. I don't want to be part of a Christian kingdom.'

'I don't want to become a Christian either, but how could Woden's Ford maintain a separate identity against the will of the king if the rest of Northumbria were to become Christian?' queried Aldrich, Eadwell's other brother. 'I'm not hearing other clans are prepared to stand against him.'

'We're big enough and strong enough, of course we are,' Edgar retorted sharply. 'We can come to an arrangement with the king to take a different path. Where there's a will there's a way. I'm certainly not willing to become a Christian just to satisfy the king's vanity. What's more, if we were to make a stand, perhaps other Deiran clans would join us. Perhaps we could, together, make Edwin change his mind. And if he doesn't… well, I'm sure there'd be others who'd be prepared to be king of Deira.'

Alwyn's brown eyes, which normally exuded calm, flashed as he reacted roughly, 'I'm sorry, Uncle Edgar, but it'd be madness to break up Northumbria. Bigger kingdoms are the way forward everywhere.'

Alwyn then tried to get his point across in a different, more conciliatory way, 'I know we're all anxious about letting down our ancestors; but we have to think ahead, get in to the seventh century. Christianity's becoming mainstream, not just across Britain but in Europe. We don't want to be left behind, to be regarded as crazy northern barbarians. I want to be part of a Northumbria which celebrates the past, but also a kingdom which looks forward and outwards as well.'

The light faded outside the great hall, and the candles created a pool of light in the middle of the huge space where the council table was positioned. The argument continued backwards and forwards, to the young Aelfred's fascination as well as bemusement.

It was a passionate tug of war between principle and pragmatism. Tempers frayed as the ale flowed.

The mood shifted when Wilfred suggested, 'Look, none of us wants to become Christian. This Jesus god sounds pretty pathetic. But why can't we have it both ways? Let's tell the king we're prepared to accept Christianity if that's what he wants; but in practice let's carry on doing exactly what we're doing. He's surely not going to send inspectors to check on us; and, in any case, I imagine the king'll continue to make war and carry on much as now, even if he does adopt Christianity.'

Edgar continued to resist, stridently, but the others, including Rinc and Godwyn, backed Wilfred's compromise. In the end Edgar, too, grumbled acquiescence.

A few days later a messenger arrived from Edwin's court with the formal instruction, issued to all Edwin's thegns, to adopt Christianity. There were no further details as to how the instruction should be implemented, except that an invitation to be baptised would follow.

Rinc was able to tell the messenger that Woden's Ford would comply. The messenger rode off happily to his next destination.

Chapter 8

626 AD

Alwyn Investigates

Alwyn was feeling frustrated, nervous, and intrigued – all at the same time.

He was riding along the familiar track towards York a couple of weeks after Rinc had confirmed Woden Ford's nominal conversion. He was thinking about his plans for the day ahead.

His intention was to try to meet and talk to Bishop Paulinus and those around him. The bishop had come with the queen from Kent. His teaching and advice about Christianity – or, according to others, his deceit and overblown claims – were reputed to be the principal reasons why king Edwin had converted.

Alwyn had been itching to find out more about Christianity ever since rumours had started to circulate about a possible conversion, but he had been wary because feelings were running so high throughout Woden's Ford. He knew very well how much his father had loathed Christianity. He missed Eadwell, and he had not wanted to appear to dishonour him so soon after his death.

Alwyn respected the pagan traditions handed down from his ancestors. He had observed faithfully throughout his life all the rituals and conventions at Woden's Ford. They had a great deal of value in his eyes simply because they were time-honoured: they were fundamental to the identity of his tribe; as such they had been a source of the tribe's collective strength which had, in turn, brought so much success.

Yet, although he had gone through the motions, neither his heart nor his head had been fully involved for as long as he could remember. Alwyn had found the old ways more and more stifling and even puzzling. He found it difficult to worship gods who were at best distant and anonymous, but who appeared to demand so insistently that their followers perpetuate a destructive cycle of violence which cost so much.

Alwyn had long felt intuitively that there must be a better way. He wondered whether Christianity might be 'it'. He wanted to find out as much as he could. Now that the king had authorised it as the official religion of Northumbria and Woden's Ford had converted, even if only nominally, he felt much freer to do so.

But Alwyn remained very wary. That's why he had not told anyone else at Woden's Ford why he was going to York, least of all Rinc – and he was nervous in case they found out.

The discussion at the council meeting had perfectly encapsulated the conundrum he faced and why he felt so frustrated.

Alwyn was intrigued and fascinated by new ideas and ways of thinking. He enjoyed finding out what was happening in the wider world.

His relatives, on the other hand, were deeply conservative and insular. They were prepared to trade in goods, but not ideas. Alwyn knew that Edgar and Grimbald were opposed to anything which threatened the old ways. He felt that his three brothers were less dogmatic, but that they had their heads in the sand.

Alwyn sensed that the old order was passing, and that the future would be vastly different. He wondered whether perhaps his relatives did, too, and that that was why subconsciously they were so edgy about change.

Alwyn thought that Hilda was the only other person at Woden's Ford so far who had an insight into both the potential fragility of the old pagan ways and the transformation which Christianity might bring. He had enjoyed occasional conversations with her over the years, but neither of them had felt that they could get too far below the surface. Alwyn knew that as wife of the clan chief she was in an exposed position, and also that her relationship with Rinc was far from easy. He didn't want to aggravate her situation.

Alwyn felt as if he was straddling at the same time both the past and the future and his tribe and the wider world. It was not a comfortable position. Nevertheless, he was tingling with excitement as he approached York as well as feeling a degree of trepidation.

Alwyn went first to the king's court and looked out the son of another Deiran noble who was a courtier and who he had known well since childhood. Once Alwyn had explained his purpose his friend directed him to the area of the city taken over by Paulinus and his associates. 'Tell them I've sent you,' he said. 'And good luck. They're an interesting and very persuasive bunch!'

Alwyn was met by a man perhaps slightly older than himself who said that he was one of Paulinus' priests. He was tall, stocky and sandy haired. Alwyn understood him well enough in spite of his Kentish dialect and accent.

Alwyn was surprised: he realised that instinctively he had expected a Christian priest to look and sound very different to anyone he had come across before; instead, he found himself talking to someone with a similar background to himself who looked very Anglo-Saxon.

'So, what can I do for you, my friend?' the priest asked pleasantly.

'I want to find out more about Christianity,' Alwyn said bluntly. 'I'm from a noble family in Deira. Quite frankly we've found the last year or so bewildering. We've been required to convert very suddenly from ways which our ancestors had followed for centuries – but we don't know very much about why or what it will involve.'

The priest nodded sympathetically, and then replied, 'I see what you mean. It hasn't felt quite so sudden here, believe me. There were plenty of twists and turns at court before the queen and Paulinus persuaded the king to convert. But I can see that elsewhere conversion might seem to have come out of the blue. I've a bit of time just now, so let me try to fill you in. The bishop's away at the moment, but hopefully you'll be able to meet him in future.'

The priest went on to explain the fundamentals of the Christian religion, how it had started in and around Jerusalem but spread subsequently across the Roman empire and eventually to the British Isles, and the role of the Pope in the church and the importance of Rome as his headquarters.

He described how the Anglo-Saxon incomers had pushed Christianity out of large swathes of the old Roman province of Britannia, but that many natives in the north and west had remained Christian, albeit often with no or only tenuous links to Rome.

'You probably know the Roman church has been trying to reclaim this island for the last thirty years,' the priest continued. 'A delegation sent by the Pope and led by Augustine arrived in Kent at the end of the last century; but progress has been patchy since then, to be honest. The church is still strongest in Kent, but it wasn't certain for some time that Christianity would put down roots even there because of the strength of opposition.'

'Paulinus came to Kent from Italy to join Augustine's mission,' the priest continued. 'He's been working hard across the island ever since to try to establish the faith in all the Anglo-Saxon kingdoms, partly by building Christian communities and increasing the number of priests. That's where people like me got involved. I'm the third son of a Kentish noble family who converted early on. My parents offered me to the church when I was a small boy: I was destined to be a priest from then on.'

Alwyn was fascinated. He had known some of the history and doctrine of Christianity, but he had never heard it explained so comprehensively and clearly. Some of the questions that had been in his mind had already been answered, but he had more. 'So why did Paulinus and the rest of you leave Kent to come to Northumbria if that was the base of your mission?' he asked.

'That's a good question,' the priest replied laughing, 'and it's one I ask myself regularly to be honest – for example, when I'm shivering even in the so-called Northumbrian summer, or when I'm talking to folk who really don't like the church! At times it feels far more hostile up here than in the south. It's certainly an awfully long way from home.'

'To be serious, though, the bishop is always looking for God's guidance,' he continued. 'He's passionate about extending the Roman church. He saw immediately that our princess's marriage to the Northumbrian king was an opportunity sent by God. He'd been a spiritual mentor to the princess for a long time. She was delighted at the idea of being accompanied north by a large group of people she knew well. The princess – queen as she became – is a very strong-willed character. I think she relished the challenge of trying to convert a pagan kingdom just as much as Paulinus did!'

'As I've already said, it's been an interesting few years!' he concluded with a broad smile.

'I can echo that,' Alwyn said, smiling in return. 'It's been an interesting few years for many of us, that's for sure! So, can you tell me what Bishop Paulinus is like, and what he's trying to achieve in Northumbria?'

'Certainly,' the priest said. 'Firm, fair and single-minded is how I would sum up the bishop. He's Italian, but he's worked extremely hard to understand us Anglo-Saxons – our language, of course, but also our mindset, our religion, our traditions. He's a hard taskmaster and quite aloof in many ways; but he's very committed to all of us who work with him. I enjoy being with him because you always know where you stand.'

'What's he trying to achieve?' the priest repeated Alwyn's question thoughtfully. 'There's no doubt that's a big question. In some ways the answer's quite simple: he wants everyone in

Northumbria not just to be Christian in name, but to really understand their faith. To be honest, he wants to get rid of all the evidence of the old gods.'

The priest paused, as if searching for what he wanted to say next, and then went on, 'How's he going to do that? Well, he's extremely ambitious. The king and queen have authorised plans for mass baptism ceremonies and church building right across Northumbria. Paulinus sees these as the essential platform for building a common faith. He wants uniformity of belief and practice. Ultimately, I think he wants Northumbria and all the other kingdoms on this island to be committed to a single, Europe-wide church.'

Alwyn was impressed and nodded thoughtfully. The priest sensed his interest and continued, 'The bishop's really keen to bring together influential men who share his passion and commitment. It's an important part of his plan. He's forming a study group for men who want to learn more. Would you like to join?'

Alwyn was delighted and agreed readily.

Chapter 9

626–627 AD

The new royal religion at Woden's Ford

'Look, Rinc, I know it's not easy for you, but I simply don't think this compromise will hold,' Alwyn said.

Rinc and Alwyn were in the former's home a few weeks after Alwyn's first visit to York. They'd been discussing plans to fell trees to create extra pasture for sheep.

For the most part questions about religious belief were in the background as life continued across Woden's Ford. The daily routines, the hard toil of agriculture, the ebb and flow of community life all looked and felt much as they had before the Royal messenger had arrived.

Yet the subject could not be ignored: more and more questions were being asked, not least by the clan priests.

Alwyn knew that he must tell his brother about his conversations with Paulinus' people at some point even though he was nervous about how he would react. After much fretting he had decided that now was the moment.

'I've been to York and met some of Edwin's Christian advisers,' Alwyn continued. 'The most important seems to be Paulinus. He came with the Queen from Kent. It's clear he has the king's ear, too. They've appointed him bishop of York.'

Rinc's expression was frosty, but Alwyn ploughed on, 'I'm not saying I agree with the Christians, or that I'm about to turn my back on our ancestors; but the way they talk seems so, well, fresh. I know we pride ourselves on war, plunder and glory – but it's pretty destructive when you think about it. Just look at the cost in lives and wealth. They're advocating a way which is less confrontational, allows toleration, builds harmony.'

Alwyn hesitated, and then concluded, 'I've actually joined a group of other Deiran men. We're learning together from Paulinus about Christianity. It's really opening my eyes I can tell you.'

Rinc was by now scowling. He looked frustrated. 'Why did you go and meet them?' Rinc asked brusquely. 'I'm the chief, and I'm trying to tread the fine line we agreed. It isn't easy. Why can't you just let it be and get on with life?'

'We can't hide our heads in the sand, Rinc,' Alwyn responded firmly. 'I'm sure Christianity's the future. We need to understand it. Even at the most practical level, people across Woden's Ford are confused: about how they should bury the dead and marry their children, about whether they should still use the old charms and sacrifices when they fall ill, about the role of our clan priests. They're hearing in other villages that have adopted Christianity that the old pagan rituals and ceremonies are out of favour, even being banned.'

'Folk are nervous, Rinc: we need to give a lead,' Alwyn finished.

Rinc sighed and shook his head. He wished the whole issue would go away so he could concentrate on what he loved – making the land more productive, creating wealth for his people. He didn't like being caught in the middle of what often seemed to be a theoretical argument, about things you couldn't see or touch or smell.

'I know, but others are so set against Christianity,' he said eventually. 'Look at Uncle Edgar and Grimbald. They think we've gone too far already with the compromise. They simply won't accept they're Christian in any way, shape or form. If we come down firmly on either side we're going to make a lot of folk angry. Surely it's better to just keep pretending.'

'I don't think Grimbald's quite right in the head; and I like Uncle Edgar, but he's always been stubborn. Those two are living in the past, I'm afraid,' Alwyn responded authoritatively.

'I do take your point, Alwyn, I really do. I'll keep thinking about what we should do next. Let's talk about it with the others soon, too,' Rinc said wearily, running his hand through his hair. In his own mind, though, he was determined to continue to sit on the fence as long as he could.

In most other ways Rinc was delighted with life at Woden's Ford. In the last two or three years he and his brothers had stepped back from military service. There were plenty of other male relatives, ceorls and peasants who were able to join Edwin's army when the call came for men for his campaigns. In any case the king's military focus was now to the north and north-west of Northumbria, and so the Bernician clans were supplying most of the troops.

Instead, Rinc and Alwyn were busy organising the land and working with the tenants to make it as productive as possible, while Wilfred and Godwyn were developing trade and finding markets for the produce. Godwyn had been reluctant to be involved initially, but Wilfred had persuaded him, and he was now an enthusiastic trader, too.

The four brothers and their families sat in the middle of a complex network of relationships across the clan territory. The home village where they all lived, together with the priests, and their servants and slaves, clustered around Eadrich's original dwelling and the great hall, was the clan headquarters. From there they managed and directly farmed a large area of pasture, arable and forestry.

Dozens of other more distant relatives, ceorls, tenants, peasants and slaves lived in other villages, hamlets and homesteads of various sizes scattered across the clan territory. They were all beholden in one way or another to Rinc and his immediate family: they had to pay a share of all their produce in tribute, the men had to fight when asked, and Rinc could determine how the land should be used.

Throughout 626-627 markets continued to develop apace. More and more traders were coming to York not just from the southern Anglo-Saxon kingdoms, but also from Scandinavia, Francia and the old homelands in north Germany. Wilfred and Godwyn could scarcely keep up with the demand for produce. The flow of luxuries in to Woden's Ford in return accelerated sharply. Wilfred and Godwyn were also able to acquire new slaves as their buying power increased.

Yet, despite the growing prosperity, the signs of disunity at the heart of the clan were becoming ever clearer.

Edgar had agreed reluctantly to the Council's compromise, but he was sulky. He believed that his nephews had sold out even though they weren't enforcing Christian practices. 'Woden didn't intend us to be famers and traders' was one of his stock moans, a barely disguised side-swipe at the four brothers. He believed that in stepping back from personal military involvement in the King's campaigns as far as they could they were betraying their ancestors and even Woden himself.

Grimbald was even more hostile. He remained loyal to King Edwin because he was a Deiran. He even joined some of his campaigns in the north and west. Yet he was appalled by the king's conversion, and equally shocked that the clan council had not rejected Christianity altogether.

Grimbald made no effort to hide his disdain for his cousins. He underlined his opposition by moving further away physically: he built himself a small hut in the woods right on the edge of the clan territory and lived there alone.

* * * * * * *

'I'm really not sure about all this, Rinc,' Alwyn said uneasily as he looked around at the bonfire blazing up into the night sky and at the Woden's Ford inhabitants of all ages feasting and dancing by its bright light. 'I know we decided not to enforce Christian practice, but still celebrating Woden so openly and lavishly does seem to be going a bit far in the other direction. I suspect the king will be cracking down on this kind of thing.'

It was late 627. The clan council were still at odds about the way ahead. The great celebrations of the pagan gods were popular and so most of the council members were reluctant to cancel them. The four brothers were standing together, away from their families for a few minutes.

'I know you're not sure, Alwyn, so you keep telling me,' Rinc said testily. 'I do know we're going to have to become more Christian at some point; but surely there's no harm in the meantime in keeping the old feasts going. The baptism ceremony next spring is when we'll have to come off the fence. I have told you we'll all have to go, haven't I? King's orders.'

'Yes, you have,' Godwyn said. 'I assume we'll hear when and where nearer the time. By the way, I hear Uncle Edgar has said he'll only be baptised because the king has ordered him, but they can't change his heart. Grimbald's actually refusing to go at all.'

'Well, what a surprise,' Wilfred remarked with heavy sarcasm. 'I thought they'd be first in line!'

The brothers' impromptu gathering came to an end at that point as children came running up excitedly with various requests. Hilda happened to walk over, too, and Godwyn – still childless – attracted her attention as his brothers dispersed.

'How are you, Hilda?' he asked. 'I've been hoping to have a chat with you.'

'Oh, you know, enjoying all the fun,' she said in a tone which suggested the exact opposite. 'So, what can I do for you?'

'Well, it's about your lovely cousin. Do you mind if we talk completely confidentially?'

'No, that's fine, Godwyn,' Hilda said, her tone turning to surprise. 'What's Alice done – or not done?'

'I really don't know whether there's anything to worry about,' Godwyn said tentatively, looking embarrassed, 'but Alice does always seem quite … let's say, animated around

79

Grimbald. Maybe a bit too animated, maybe a bit too cosy. In fact, look at them now.'

Hilda glanced in the direction Godwyn was motioning with his head. Alice and Grimbald were indeed standing close together in the firelight, Grimbald bending down to listen to Alice, their faces only inches apart.

'Umm, they do seem to be having a good blether,' Hilda said. 'But I'm not sure I'd be too worried, Godwyn. Alice herself admits she enjoys the company of men; and I really don't need to tell you your wife is very attractive, and so men respond positively to her. I suspect she's just humouring Grimbald, perhaps even feeling a bit sorry for him. He has, after all, turned himself into a bit of an outcast.'

'She's my cousin, but I can't claim to have much influence over her. I will, though, have a quiet word with her – obviously without telling her you asked me to,' Hilda concluded.

'Many thanks, Hilda, I really am very grateful,' Godwyn said as Aelfred ran up. Godwyn was evidently relieved to have got the conversation over and hurried away.

A few minutes later Hilda managed to manoeuvre herself alongside Alice. 'How're you doing, Alice?' she asked cheerfully.

'Good, thanks,' Alice replied. 'It's nice to keep these old feasts going. I worry a bit the Christians might make life quite dull. Grimbald was just telling me that in some places in Deira the Christian priests are banning any sort of celebration. It sounds pretty sad to me.'

'That'd be harsh if it's true,' Hilda said; 'but maybe there's some misunderstanding. I've heard Christians do quite a bit of celebrating, just differently. How's Grimbald getting on by the way – I haven't seen much of him in a while?'

'He's feeling pretty down, actually. Rightly or wrongly, he was shattered by the king's conversion to Christianity. And now he feels everyone's against him because he doesn't want to be a Christian. That's why he's gone to live in that hut. I try to cheer him up when I see him – he really can be very pleasant.'

Hilda hesitated for a few moments and looked at Alice. Her cousin frowned, 'Why are you looking at me like that, Hilda?'

'We're family,' Hilda said, 'and so I've always tried to look out for you. So please take this the right way. I do see the way Grimbald looks at you, and I do worry a bit. He's a handsome chap, and you know you're very pretty. Let's hope he doesn't misunderstand any attempts to cheer him up.'

Alice looked away and said nothing for a few moments, but then turned to face her cousin. Her expression was a mixture of frown and ironic smile. Slowly, very deliberately, she asked, 'What exactly are you suggesting, Hilda?' Hilda sensed the effort that Alice was making to control herself.

'I'm not suggesting anything, Alice,' Hilda replied evenly. 'I'm just looking out for you. Appearances count. Just be careful.'

'Of course, Hilda, I will. Thanks for the advice.' Hilda tried to detect a note of sarcasm in Alice's voice, but her cousin moved on quickly to more mundane matters. The glimpse of anger had vanished as suddenly as it had appeared.

Hilda was puzzled, but she didn't feel she could pursue the matter any further. She reflected, yet again, on how the arrival of Christianity had brought to the surface all sorts of unexpected fissures and tensions.

Chapter 10

628 AD

Commitment

'But, Father, why are we becoming Christians? What would Grandfather say?'

Aelfred was riding on his pony alongside Rinc and Cadmon as he asked the questions. It was a few months after the bonfire at Woden's Ford. The time and place of the mass baptism ceremony had been confirmed – in the river Swale at Catterick, some thirty miles north of Woden's Ford.

'King Edwin has decided, and we must do what the king says. The king's arranged baptism ceremonies right across Northumbria so all the nobles and their families can attend one. But don't worry, we won't forget Grandfather and our ancestors. We can be Christians and remember them, too,' Rinc replied.

Aelfred tried another tack. 'Grandfather used to say fighting our enemies is a noble thing to do; but Uncle Alwyn says Christians should love their enemies.'

'Let's see what the king says about that,' Rinc said. 'We're warriors as well as Christians. We must look after our kin.'

Aelfred fell silent, but his forehead was furrowed. He was a quiet, reserved child, sensitive to any hint of criticism. He felt awkward with his status as heir apparent and the attention it attracted. He got along reasonably well with other children in the clan, but he was more than happy with either his own company or that of Cadmon.

Cadmon was Aelfred's slave, but also his closest companion. Cadmon had inherited his mother's dark colouring and exuberant personality but not her quick temper. He was able to draw Aelfred out of himself better than anyone else.

Rinc was worried about his ten-year-old son. He was trying to foster leadership qualities in him, but he admitted to himself that he could not get the measure of Aelfred.

After a day-long ride and an overnight camp near the Swale, the hundreds of baptism candidates woke to a cool, cloudy, blustery spring day. 'We're surely not going right down into that water today – we'll all freeze!' Cadmon exclaimed.

As ever, Cadmon was in high spirits – this was all a bit of a joke to him; but Aelfred was intrigued and slightly nervous. 'I don't think the weather'll stop them, I just wonder what it'll be like,' he mused.

'Cold and wet!' Cadmon moaned.

'I know that,' Aelfred said impatiently. 'But surely we're supposed to feel something inside if the Christians are right.' Cadmon, though, had chased off with one of Aelfred's cousins.

Marshalled by the Christian priests, many of whom had previously been pagan priests, each clan group moved forward. Folk shivered in light clothing, a mix of puzzlement and anticipation on their faces. As they got to the riverside Bishop Paulinus, the ultimate master of ceremonies, intoned, 'I baptise you in the name of the Father, the Son and the Holy

Spirit.' Each candidate waded out to the point where they could duck their head in the water, and then looped back to the riverside to get dry.

As Aelfred put his own head in the cold, clear water he held his breath – not only to avoid swallowing any, but because he was sure there would be a memorable experience. He felt nothing other than the water.

He could remember vividly the mystical feeling he had experienced at Eadwell's funeral: by contrast this was an anti-climax.

As the clan packed up to return to Woden's Ford Alwyn enthused, 'It was amazing to see the cream of Deiran society submitting en masse and so humbly to God. What a profound statement of faith in the new life!'

'But I didn't feel a thing, Uncle Alwyn,' Aelfred complained. 'What was supposed to happen?'

'It was a symbol, Aelfred: a symbol of commitment to a new Way. The past was left in the river, and new people emerged. God will honour that commitment.'

Rinc, Hilda and Aelfred all looked at Alwyn quizzically, but there was no time then to carry on the conversation. Rinc, though, realised that Alwyn was more of a believer than he had so far let on. He also knew that the King and Queen were saying exactly the same things as Alwyn. He sensed that he would have to swallow his private doubts about Christianity.

* * * * * * *

Hilda was now thirty-one years old. She had retained her slender figure and graceful appearance. She had settled into life as a mother and as wife of the clan chieftain. She performed the roles well and with dignity in spite of her sadness at her failure to produce more than one healthy child.

She often looked melancholy, though, and there were wrinkles around her eyes. Hilda still harboured doubts about the Anglian pagan heritage, customs and practices, not least because of her stillbirths and miscarriages.

At the same time, Hilda was intrigued by the debates about Christianity and the role played by Queen Aethelburg in influencing the change of official religion in Northumbria. Women in Anglian culture were generally subservient: they were not expected to play any part in or have opinions about anything other than the purely domestic and practical; and yet this young woman from Kent was turning life in Northumbria upside down.

Hilda was reluctant to voice her questions and doubts either to Rinc or to most of her in-laws, male or female. Her relationship with Rinc was cool and distant. They could discuss practicalities and everyday matters, but he would not be comfortable talking to her about religious belief even though, as she knew well, he was wrestling with similar issues. She knew that most other members of the clan, including her sisters in law, would feel the same way.

She and Alwyn, however, had always got on well. She had heard him talk often about Christianity over the last couple of years. After the post-baptism conversation at Catterick she had decided she must try to get some time alone with him.

The opportunity came at a family gathering a few weeks

later. Brigit had taken their children home, and before he could get into another conversation Hilda approached him. 'Alwyn, I wonder whether we could chat about a couple of things,' she said.

'Sure,' Alwyn replied. He enjoyed Hilda's company and felt sorry for the way his brother treated her.

'D'you mind if we find somewhere a bit more private?' she asked. Alwyn was slightly surprised, but perfectly relaxed: the party was in full swing, no one would miss them for a little while, and there were plenty of places around Woden's Ford where they could talk quietly.

Once they were settled Hilda came straight to the point, 'Alwyn, I've been really interested to hear you talk about Christianity and all you've been learning from Bishop Paulinus and his people. I could see at Catterick you seem to get it. You know I haven't exactly been convinced by all the traditional pagan stuff for many years. Frankly, I'm fed up with the bloodlust and glorification of violence.'

Hilda paused, looked away, and then continued, 'You know, it sometimes feels to me that most of us – perhaps all of us – are living out a script that someone else has written. I certainly feel as if I'm living to earn the approval of others much of the time. I wonder how many other people quietly feel the same way?'

'I'm not sure about Christianity either, to be honest,' Hilda continued. 'I really am drawn to it; but I wonder whether we're just replacing one lot of mumbo jumbo with a new lot. On the other hand, I feel as if I'm missing something. I feel emptiness, a kind of ache, a longing for something and someone I simply can't define.'

'It's not easy to talk about this kind of thing – especially to Rinc,' she concluded after a brief pause. 'As you well know, he gets impatient with what he calls 'fanciful stuff'.'

Alwyn was still and silent for a long time after Hilda had stopped speaking – to the point where Hilda wondered whether she had offended him with her frankness.

'I know exactly what you mean, Hilda,' he said finally, looking into the distance. 'I've been thinking quite a bit myself about the way we're pulled in different directions. The way I see it, the choice is ours: we can either stay in our own small stories where we feel comfortable, living from 'ought' rather than 'want'; or we can run in search of life, live from our heart.'

Alwyn paused, and closed his eyes – almost as if he were searching inside himself – and then carried on, 'It's tricky to express, and I know it sounds odd, but I think our heart's buried deep below the different 'selves' we constantly take on and off to satisfy all the people who have a stake in us. I certainly hear what I call my heart most clearly if I'm awake in the middle of the night. It feels a bit like a nagging, insistent voice – a voice that's calling us to question, challenge, to seek truth.'

Alwyn paused again, and then looked directly at Hilda as he said, 'I do think it'll be good for Northumbria to embrace Christianity willingly and genuinely. That will align us with the European and British mainstream. But I also think Christianity is far more than just another tool for kings and queens to bind their subjects or to use in diplomacy. I'm still trying to get my head around the Christian gospel; but there's something about it I find deeply attractive.'

It was Hilda's turn to be silent. She had never before heard an Anglian, man or woman, talk in this way. She was moved.

'That's so reassuring, Alwyn,' she replied quietly. 'You've put into words a lot of what I've been thinking. I'm glad I'm not the only one with a nagging heart – I thought I was starting to go mad!'

After hesitating briefly, she went on, 'Aelfred, young as he is, is really struggling, too. He so loved Eadwell, and he can't understand why Rinc seems to be betraying his legacy. I want to help him, but I'm worried I'll only confuse him!'

'Yes, Aelfred's certainly a deep child,' Alwyn said thoughtfully. 'You should try to talk to him, and I will, too – but I can see he grates on Rinc a bit. We'll need to watch that relationship closely.'

They talked for a while longer about Christianity, about the baptism ceremony, and about conflicts of loyalty between tribe and faith. They only stopped when Wilfred's wife, Bertha, came past and said laughingly, 'You two look very conspiratorial: what are you cooking up? Is the party too dull for you?'

'Oh, we're just plotting to get rid of Rinc and Wilfred so I can marry Hilda and take over as chief: that's all!' Alwyn replied in a tone of mock seriousness.

'That's alright then, I thought it might be something important!' Bertha said with another hearty laugh as Hilda and Alwyn joined her to head back towards the celebration.

* * * * * * *

Following the baptism, it was as if a tacit truce had been called across Woden's Ford. Most people seemed to accept that they must adjust to the new religion: whatever their private views, on the surface they were trying to comply.

The clan priests became Christian priests – at least nominally. They went to induction sessions organised by Bishop Paulinus and introduced Christian practice into their ceremonies. They even tried to institute regular Christian worship sessions at Woden's Ford.

There were questions about practicalities, confusion about how ceremonies should be conducted, when and where people should worship, what was allowed and what wasn't. Yet there were few arguments.

There was even some discussion about whether 'Woden's Ford' was still an appropriate name. Alwyn and some others wondered whether an alternative name would be more suitable; but they didn't press the point in the teeth of furious opposition from Edgar and Grimbald and the lack of any general enthusiasm.

It was a time of transition, of mixed belief and practice, of establishing and testing and negotiating new boundaries and mores.

For Rinc and Hilda the big looming question was how to steer their son and heir towards manhood through this time of uneasy adjustment.

Chapter 11

628–630 AD

Growing up

'Of course I want Aelfred to learn how to be a seventh century chief and leader; but I also want him to understand and cherish his past. I want him to develop the skills our ancestors valued.'

Rinc sounded annoyed. Hilda replied equally sharply, 'Please don't talk down to me, Rinc. There's a big difference between understanding the past and being trapped in it – becoming some kind of slave to our ancestors. I worry that Edgar lives more in the past than in the present. Northumbria's changing dramatically, Rinc. Deira's changing. Look around Woden's Ford: we're wearing clothes brought from other countries, cooking in and eating off utensils from far away, and we're decorating our homes with all sorts of amazing foreign goods. Yet Edgar is bored by farming and trade; he says he just wants to fight and hunt.'

Rinc tried to lower the temperature as he said, more emolliently, 'I do get it, Hilda, of course I do. I just don't think Uncle Edgar would be quite such a narrow mentor to Aelfred as you fear. He's the authority on our clan history. He can explain all the rites and rituals that have been handed down. He's also an expert hunter and warrior. I know he's not exactly keen on Christianity; but he always has the interests of the clan uppermost in his mind. I'm sure he wouldn't try to turn Aelfred against Christianity now the king's ordered us all to be followers.'

Hilda wasn't so easily pacified. 'We both know very well that Aelfred's thirteenth birthday in a couple of years will be important,' she said firmly. 'He'll become a young man then. I want him to be mentored well. I want him to become a young man, and eventually a chief, fit for the new world we're entering, not for the one we've left behind. I simply don't think Edgar will do that job. I don't think he can.'

'And what if he brings your wretched cousin, Grimbald, in on the act?' Hilda continued, irritation now evident again in her voice. 'Grimbald really would be an awful influence on Aelfred. Why can't we ask Alwyn to mentor Aelfred instead?'

'We've been through all this, Hilda,' Rinc said, a note of impatience back in his voice, too. 'There's no way Alwyn will have the time, what with his work on the estate and his family. Edgar, on the other hand, has taken a back seat. He's fifty-six now; he's picking and choosing his military commitments; and, as you say, he's not that interested in farming and trade. He'll have plenty of time. But I will absolutely stress to Edgar that we want him to mentor Aelfred, not to brainwash him.'

Hilda was reluctant to give up, but she accepted that Rinc would get his way. She felt she had extracted enough concessions. They agreed eventually that Edgar would work closely with Rinc and his brothers in making sure that Aelfred was educated about every aspect of the role of chief; and that Edgar would concentrate on teaching him about clan history and the skills of hunting, woodcraft and warfare.

Edgar was thrilled. 'I'd be delighted, Rinc, thank you so much for asking. My own glory days are long gone, although I think I have at least one more big military campaign left in me. I'd love to pass on my knowledge so it can be used by our future chief in battles to come.'

Edgar looked wistful. Rinc felt that in his mind's eye he was thirty years back in the past, seeing again some of those glory days. He couldn't help admiring his uncle. His hair was greying slightly but still essentially blonde, and there was not an ounce of spare flesh on his lean, wiry body.

'I'm sure you'll do a great job, Uncle – but remember that job will be to mentor Aelfred, not turn him into a copy of you! We want him to hear from Alwyn, Wilfred and Godwyn, too. We want Aelfred to understand what they do, and to hear their views on life today.'

'Of course, of course,' Edgar said, smiling. 'That's all understood, Rinc. I know Hilda doesn't want her son to live in the past!'

* * * * * * *

The next two years were the happiest of Aelfred's life.

He enjoyed learning about farming and land management with Rinc and Alwyn and visits to York with Godwyn and Wilfred.

Most of all he enjoyed the time he spent with Edgar, not least because Cadmon was allowed to join him. It took him away frequently from the tension that permeated his parental home and gave him time with his grandfather's closest confidant.

Edgar proved to be an excellent mentor, teacher and companion to the boys. He took them away on trips in the woods and hills, taught them the skills of hunting and survival, swordsmanship and archery, battle tactics and leadership. It was great fun for all three of them as well as hard work.

The boys learned quickly and were soon highly competent. They revelled in Edgar's tales, particularly when he talked about campaigns against the Picts, against the tribes of Rheged and Strathclyde in the north-west, and against the Welshmen of Gwynedd. Edgar lived again his experiences in the wild lands – encounters with wolves, bears and lynx, arduous marches through the mountains, dramatic, savage battles with strangely dressed and painted tribesmen.

The boys were entranced.

Edgar avoided scrupulously any overt criticism of the Christian faith. Instead, he took time to explain the purpose and meaning of the Anglian rituals, the intricacies of the clan family tree, and the place of Woden's Ford in the wider Deiran landscape. He instilled in Aelfred immense pride in his ancestry and in the achievements of the Deiran, Bernician and Northumbrian kingdoms over the previous few decades.

One day, as they hunted in the hills and he tried to explain the geography of Northumbria and Deira, Edgar told the boys about a trip he and Eadwell had made as young men. He said it had done more than anything else to give them an understanding of their land. 'Your grandfather and I took off for weeks on a trip right around the boundaries of Deira. We went on foot, lived wild, and learned so much. We got to know the mountain passes, the river crossings, the points of weakness, and the ways we could surprise enemy kingdoms.

That trip helped us to become great warriors even though I do say it myself!'

'That sounds fantastic, Uncle. Do you think it's something Cadmon and I could do when we're older?' Aelfred asked enthusiastically.

'Why not? Ask your father at some point,' Edgar replied.

Edgar was silent for a few minutes, and then continued, quietly and with a distant look in his eyes, 'I think that trip also gave us an idea about something I call 'rootedness'. Our ancestors have been here and helped to build our way of life in Deira for centuries. They've breathed the air and been intimately acquainted with the land. I've shown you where all the previous chieftains and their families were buried. Their bones have mingled with the soil. We're part of the land.'

He paused, and then went on, 'I really don't know if this is true, but I sometimes wonder whether the land is in our blood. After a people have lived and become rooted in the same place for a long time can they pass on through the womb a sense of place, a memory of the land? These are probably just the fancies of a rambling old man – but perhaps not!'

The boys were awestruck and puzzled at the same time; they didn't know what to say.

'As I say, boys, there's probably nothing to it – but maybe there is! Anyway, time now to get home.'

* * * * * * *

Edgar's mentoring role culminated in a week-long trip shortly before Aelfred's thirteenth birthday, in June 630.

Edgar rode with the boys for the best part of two days across northern Deira. Their destination was a settlement on the edge of wild hill country where there was a distant connection with Woden's Ford through marriage.

They all stayed with their relatives for the first night; Edgar then gave Aelfred and Cadmon detailed instructions and sent them into the hills on their own for the next two days and nights.

'I'll see you back here in two days,' Edgar said cheerily as he waved them off. 'I'm sure you'll be fine. Now remember all I've told you. Don't forget the route and do remember to look out for wolves!'

'Will do, Uncle – and thank you!' Aelfred replied with equal enthusiasm. It had rained hard the previous night, but the sun was out. Early mist lay low in the valley, the hills jutted out above it. A gentle breeze rustled the trees.

The boys were confident and happy as they walked into the hills twisting through narrow gorges, past deep lakes and dense woods. By late evening on the first day, they had caught a rabbit and fish, cooked them, eaten well, and were settled beside their tent.

As the late sunlight cast shadows the boys heard howling in the distance echoing across the purple hills. They looked at each other and laughed nervously. 'What did your uncle say if a wolf comes for you?' Cadmon asked.

'He said they keep away from humans, they're more scared of us than we are of them,' Aelfred replied firmly, trying to sound more confident than he felt. 'He also said we should have a spear handy so we can keep them at a distance if they do try to attack.'

'I'm sure that was a bit closer,' Cadmon said, cocking his head to one side.

'No way,' Aelfred exclaimed. 'It's heading away. Just calm down will you – you're putting me on edge.'

The boys bickered for a while, pointlessly, about whether the wolf was coming closer or moving away, and whether there was more than one. In the end they agreed to take it in turns all night to sit at the entrance of the tent to keep watch, a spear gripped in their right hand.

The next day was hard work for both boys as they followed the route Edgar had prescribed, their limbs stiff and weary through insufficient sleep. They didn't hear any wolves from their second campsite, but they agreed to do the same again that night.

The boys trailed back to their starting point on the third day, exhausted but unscathed and deeply satisfied. Edgar welcomed them delightedly. 'So, you made it – well done! How was it?'

'It was great, Uncle Edgar. We never got lost once and we slept so well,' Aelfred exclaimed.

'Yes,' Cadmon said, the words tumbling out, 'we're so well-rested; and we didn't see a single wolf!'

Edgar looked from one to the other curiously, noticed the bags under their eyes and their drooping shoulders, and smiled to himself. 'Well, that's all excellent,' he said. 'It was a tough challenge. You can be proud of yourselves. You're fully entitled now to call yourselves young men! Now come in, and let's hear all about it. We'll start heading home tomorrow, but tonight you can enjoy a good sleep indoors.'

The two-day ride back to Woden's Ford was leisurely. The

boys basked in the glow of their achievement. Edgar was more relaxed now that the boys had completed the expedition safely, and he gave a running commentary on everything they passed.

They were just a few miles from Woden's Ford when they came across Grimbald heading back along the track through the forest with a dead deer slung across his shoulders. 'So, how are the adventurers? You survived obviously. Can we call them young men now, Father?' he asked Edgar heartily.

'They did well – they're most definitely young men! I'm proud of them,' Edgar replied.

'Why don't you come back to my place before you go home,' Grimbald offered. 'I've been brewing some ale: it'd be just the thing to celebrate a successful expedition.'

Edgar accepted enthusiastically, 'Right you are, son, that'd be grand! Come on, boys.'

Aelfred and Cadmon had never been in Grimbald's solitary hut and were intrigued. It was small but surprisingly comfortable. On his own territory Grimbald was much more expansive than they had seen him in company. He was genuinely interested in the boys' experiences, and they enjoyed chatting to him.

'Well, you know where I am now, lads,' Grimbald said as they left. 'Feel free to come and visit whenever you like.'

'We will, thank you,' Aelfred replied eagerly, reflecting on the way Grimbald was regarded very negatively by many of his relatives.

As they rode on towards Woden's Ford Edgar and the boys were surprised to see Alice. She was carrying in a sling her first child, who was just a few months old, as she walked in the woods.

The boys were shy, even awkward. They knew Alice well as Aelfred's aunt, but as they had grown older they had also become very aware of her beauty. She was sixteen years older than Aelfred but still only twenty-nine: she had made the transition in their eyes from Aunt Alice to a glamorous and attractive young woman.

'Nice day for a walk,' Edgar said as they drew level. 'Are you trying to get Wulfhere to sleep?'

'Something like that!' Alice replied, laughing. 'I thought it'd be a nice change of scene for him.'

They chatted for a few minutes about how the trip had gone and then left Alice as they headed towards Woden's Ford. Edgar glanced back over his shoulder: he looked puzzled.

* * * * * * *

Aelfred's thirteenth birthday was celebrated a few days later – lavishly, as befitted the entry of the heir apparent into manhood. He was happy and excited. He hadn't forgotten the pledge he had made at his grandfather's funeral to make Eadwell proud and was still confused about why the clan had adopted Christianity; but he had enjoyed the busyness of the last two years, and for the time being wrestling with the differences between the pagan beliefs of his ancestors and the King's faith was not a high priority.

'He's coming on,' Rinc said as he chatted with Edgar.

'Thanks for all you've done for Aelfred, Uncle Edgar. He's still a bit shy and thoughtful, but he's got a presence now and doesn't seem so worried. He's a good looking, athletic lad. I'm sure he'll make a grand warrior.'

'It's been a pleasure,' Edgar said. 'I've enjoyed spending time with him – and with Cadmon. He's growing and learning well; but he's a deep one, Rinc. I suspect he plays to whichever gallery he's facing. I'm not sure we yet know the real Aelfred.'

Chapter 12

autumn 631

A surprise for Woden's Ford

'So, what do you all think the King wants us to do?' Rinc asked as he smiled at his relatives around the council table in the Great Hall. It was autumn 631 – a little over a year after Aelfred's thirteenth birthday. Aelfred was by now a regular attendee.

'Get baptised a second time, but in even colder water?' Edgar asked in mock despair.

'Yes, but only you Uncle Edgar: once was obviously not enough,' Rinc retorted, laughing. 'No, I really think this is good news for us.'

'Well, don't keep us in suspense,' Godwyn said.

'Right, I'll put you out of your misery.' Rinc grinned as he spoke. 'I was summoned to court a few days ago. I honestly didn't know what to expect – the message had been cryptic, to say the least. I was even more nervous when I was met by four of Edwin's most powerful courtiers. But I shouldn't have worried. We still seem to be in favour, thankfully.'

Rinc paused for dramatic effect, smiled even more broadly as he looked slowly around the table, and then continued, 'The King's decided to distribute the royal treasure throughout the kingdom for safe keeping. He's asked us to store a portion in a secure and secret location! It'll be arriving with an armed convoy in the next few days. We have to think of a hiding place, and not tell anyone else.'

There was a surprised silence. This was a highly unusual step as well as a great honour for Woden's Ford. 'But why?' Aldrich asked, expressing what was in all their minds. 'I thought kings usually turn over any treasure they acquire pretty quickly: in rewards, to buy influence, or in exchange for other goods they want.'

'We can come to the why later,' Rinc said. 'Let's first agree we're willing to take this on, and then decide where we'll store the treasure.'

There was some discussion about the possible risks, questions about whether it was a test of loyalty, even a trap – but the Council decided quickly to accede to the request, and then agreed on a location deep in woods a few miles from Woden's Ford.

'Let's all be absolutely clear: not another soul is to know. Aelfred, I'll show you the exact location when you're eighteen, but until then please don't tell anyone else about the secret, even Cadmon.'

They all nodded solemnly.

'So, *why* do you think Edwin is distributing the royal treasure?' Rinc asked.

'Come on, chief, spare us the inquisition,' Alwyn said, feigning weariness.

'I honestly don't know,' Rinc replied. 'I can guess, but it's important we pool ideas and information: we might be facing some really challenging times.'

'It's all about Mercia,' Aldrich said succinctly.

'Go on,' Edgar encouraged his brother with a slight nod.

Aldrich continued, 'I've had a strong sense over the last two or three years that the Mercians are fed up with Edwin's pretensions to be the most important king on the island. Their power's been growing, and so has their ambition. Penda's emerged as the leading man in Mercia. He wants to bring Edwin down a few pegs. He wants to reduce the threat to him from the north and become top dog. Every visitor I've met from the south recently has talked about Mercia's expansion plans. And last time I was in York a couple of Edwin's spies told me they had picked up lots of evidence of Penda building alliances with the British kingdoms.'

'I gather that Cadwallon, the king of Gwynedd, is particularly angry with Edwin,' Aldrich went on. 'It's not surprising really since Edwin has conquered the island of Anglesey. I think that's where most of Gwynedd's wheat is grown, so its loss is a real blow. It all points to a plan to invade Northumbria. Our king's taking precautions: if the worst comes to the worst, he doesn't want all of Northumbria's royal treasure to be left lying around in one place for Penda and the British to scoop up.'

'Well said, Aldrich!' Edgar exclaimed. 'I don't always agree with you, but I think you're spot on. Mercia's become a real threat. I wouldn't have imagined it thirty or so years ago. Mercia — the name even means border country — was seen then as a bit of a sideshow, marginal, almost a joke. The kingdom still looked and felt what it was — a very loose collection of small Anglian tribes who'd pushed west but didn't have any collective muscle. They were small fry compared with the bigger kingdoms. You have to give them a lot of credit for building a powerful kingdom. Given their location right in the middle of the island we simply cannot afford to underestimate Mercia any longer.'

'I've heard, too, Penda's the coming man,' Edgar continued. 'Apparently he has an older brother – Eowa, I think he's called; but Penda seems more likely to become the next king of Mercia. I imagine Cadwallon of Gwynedd has made the same assumption. That must be why he's keen to bring him into the alliance.'

'What's more, from what I've heard Penda is remaining true to his roots and not following the Christian fashion. I can't help admiring him for that, even though he may soon be our enemy,' Edgar added as he finished.

The four younger men listened intently to their uncles. Rinc nodded, and said, 'I'm fairly sure that's exactly the reason. Edwin's been trying to build a powerful kingdom for the long-term. He's trying to accumulate wealth rather than just push it out as soon as it comes his way. He's preparing for a major war with Mercia and the British kingdoms; scattering the treasure to try to protect his long-term investment is just one of the steps he's taking. I think we'll also be asked to provide a great many men in the near future for a major campaign.'

* * * * * * *

Several days later a group of armed members of Edwin's war band arrived at Woden's Ford leading two packhorses each of which carried an enormous and very heavy sack. They contained the royal treasure.

Rinc took delivery of the sacks, and then quickly called together the other members of the clan council. Once they were sure they were alone they opened the sacks and rummaged through the contents. The men were silent, awestruck at the obvious value. The sacks contained an astonishing collection of the most gorgeous trappings stripped from weapons of war.

'This must be Northumbrian war loot,' Edgar said in a hushed tone. 'I guess it's been gathered from the fields of victorious battles, not just in Edwin's time but even in King Aethelfrith's. It's remarkable. I suspect I was at quite a few of the battles myself.'

'Right,' Rinc said, 'let's put everything back in the sacks. We've decided on a hiding place, so as soon as it's dark let's take a torch and go down there as quietly as we can.'

Two hours later, as the autumnal night settled, the six men stole into thick woodland a few miles away from the main village. Alwyn and Wilfred laboured under the weight of the sacks; the others kept watch to make sure that they weren't observed.

Once they were in the woods, they followed a path for a little while and then struck into the deeper trees. They zigzagged through the woods, using their daggers to mark every other tree carefully with a distinctive mark: a circle with a stripe through it.

'So, here we are,' Rinc said, as they stopped under an ancient oak tree. 'Are you all happy with the way we've marked the route? Could any of us get back here on our own if necessary? And none of us will tell another soul?'

The other men nodded solemnly several times. 'Great, let's

dig.' Edgar and Godwyn had brought spades and started to dig a deep hole. The sacks were lowered in gently and earth piled back over them. The men smoothed the ground and scattered leaves, twigs and stones over the spot to make it look as natural as possible.

'Well, that's it: job done,' Edgar said. The men stood for a few minutes in the flickering light of the torch, staring at the ground which covered the treasure. They were silent, transfixed. Eventually they turned and headed back towards Woden's Ford, still saying little. All the men were struck by the strangeness of what they had just done. They wondered when they would see the treasure again.

Chapter 13

632–633

Aelfred contemplates a gathering storm

My fourteen-year-old mind was full of conflicting feelings and questions for weeks after that dramatic autumn council meeting. I sensed dimly that a storm was gathering. I wondered how it would affect us all.

I was excited and intrigued by the discussion about the royal treasure hoard. I was disappointed that I would have to wait to find out exactly where it was hidden. I thought occasionally about having a look for it because I knew roughly where it was; but I was sure Father would be angry if he found out I had done so. I contented myself with feeling important that I had been entrusted with even part of such a huge secret.

I was enthralled by the prospect of war with the Mercians and the Welsh, but also confused. Grandfather and Uncle Edgar had taught me well enough that as Anglians we should relish opportunities to fight – and even seek them out: that clans and kingdoms which sat back would become weak.

Yet I simply could not understand why Anglian kingdoms were gearing up to fight each other, and why a pagan warlord might be allying with native, Christian kingdoms against fellow Anglians.

I put these questions to Father and Uncle Alwyn as I worked with them one day.

'They're very sensible questions, Aelfred,' Father said. 'There are many, many reasons why kingdoms fight each other: but ultimately it boils down to self-protection and power. Northumbria hasn't actually been involved in a war of survival for many years. We've become the most powerful kingdom. That's why we've been doing the attacking, mainly against British kingdoms. And that's why in your lifetime, for all the talk about war, you've not known many men from Woden's Ford who've died in battle.'

Father continued, 'As you heard from your great uncles at the Council meeting, other kingdoms are getting fed up with King Edwin's domination. They don't want him to have so much power. So, they might try to cut him down to size, and even threaten our very existence. I'm afraid religion and kinship don't matter too much when daggers are drawn!'

'I do sort of get all that, Father,' I replied. 'Do you think we *will* get attacked – and, if so, how can we prepare?'

It was Uncle Alwyn who answered my question, at least partially. 'I agree with your father, Aelfred. Christians teach about peace, but at the end of the day we can't let others trample over us. Rumours about some sort of alliance against Northumbria are getting stronger. I heard them again in York just the other day. I'm sure king Edwin has his spies around the whole island. He'll let us know when we need to march. In the meantime, we have to get on with normal life. We can't just stop and wait and worry. We have to keep producing food for ourselves. And, of course, there's more and more folk who want to buy our surplus: Uncle Godwyn and Uncle

Wilfred are doing a great job in trading all our stuff in York.'

'War could well disrupt all sorts of things,' Uncle Alwyn concluded. 'We should make the most of the opportunities we have while there's still peace. I, for one, hope the Welsh and the Mercians will back off so we can keep living in peace for a long time to come.'

It all sounded very tentative to my young ears. I wanted more certainty, and so asked, 'Surely we'll win if there is a war, won't we? As you say, we're the most powerful kingdom.'

Father and Uncle Alwyn looked at each other, and Father then said, 'You can never tell, Aelfred. Our king's made himself quite unpopular from what I hear. I imagine we'd defeat any of the other kingdoms on their own, but I'm less sure what would happen if they all got together.'

Adults, I thought, it's so difficult to get a straight answer from them! I dropped the subject, but the conversation did nothing to help me sort out my competing questions and feelings.

I continued to feel both keyed up and nervous; and I knew I wasn't alone. As the year 632 progressed, life seemed to go on as normal for the most part, but I could sense from stray conversations and unexpected actions that tension, foreboding, excitement and fear were not far below the surface.

This became even clearer one day as I walked home and saw a few men gathered on a track. I could see that there was some sort of argument going on, and that Grimbald was right at the heart of it. I went to see what was happening.

A man I didn't recognise was talking, and he sounded angry and, I thought, a little scared. 'I am absolutely not a Mercian spy. I'm as Deiran as all of you. I live further south,

I'm a metal worker, and I'm on my way to York to see if I can pick up some jobs. There's plenty of wealth there, and I want some of it. I've never been anywhere near Mercia. Now just let me go on my way.'

'How do we know that's not a cover story?' Grimbald asked menacingly. 'Why wouldn't Mercia or the Welsh pay someone like you to find out as much as they can about what's going on in Northumbria?'

I could see that the man was now actually looking baffled as well as annoyed and worried. 'What could I find out by wandering around the countryside that would really help Penda and the others?' he asked.

'Who knows?' Grimbald replied darkly. 'But we can't be too careful when we see strangers about. These are dangerous times. Anyway, you can go on your way now, but keep your eyes open as you travel – there could be spies anywhere.'

The man walked off, grumbling about the unfairness of life, and Grimbald and the rest of the group dispersed. News of the incident circulated around Woden's Ford over the next few days, but I heard various versions of it. Folk were suspicious, and so more inclined to believe lurid gossip than dull truth.

There were further sightings of alleged 'spies' over the months, and although they all turned out to be false alarms each incident ratcheted up the tension a little more.

The months dragged by. The year 632 gave way to 633. I continued to work with my father and uncles, learning as much as I could, and occasionally went hunting with great uncle Edgar. Everyone was very active, but there was an unspoken sense, too, that we were waiting – that something was about to happen. It was an odd, indefinable, indescribable atmosphere.

So, it almost came as a relief when the rumours and speculation crystallised into something more solid one day in the spring. Father gathered together all the members of the clan council – of which I was an honorary member. He told us he'd received word that one of the king's courtiers would be visiting the next day with some important news. Father said that the man was visiting every thegn in Deira. He wanted all of the council members to meet him together.

I was expecting Edwin's emissary to look grander, fiercer, more worthy somehow of the stir which anticipation of his arrival had created. Instead, I found myself looking at a slender man who looked weary, untidy and somewhat careworn. I felt strangely let down, but quickly forgot my disappointment as he began to address the council.

The man's voice was quite flat – matching his appearance and demeanour – but we all hung on his every word. 'I know you'll have heard rumours about war with the Welsh and the Mercians over the last year or so. Clearly nothing's happened yet. That's highly likely to change at some point over this coming fighting season. The king's heard firm news from his various agents and spies that an alliance led by King Cadwallon of Gwynedd is planning to attack Northumbria during the summer or early autumn.'

'They don't appear to have decided yet on a definite time, but we need to be prepared from now on,' he continued. 'Their aim is to take over the whole of Northumbria: we would become subject to a British king if they were to win. King Edwin wants to wait until we know exactly when and where they're going to make their move, and then choose the best place to join battle. All the king's thegns in Deira and Bernicia are being told to get ready – we'll need every man who's available when the time comes. There's no question we'll be fighting for our lives.'

There was silence when the courtier finished. I knew that each man was reacting slightly differently, trying to understand the implications for himself and for the wider community. We'd all been expecting news like this, but it was still a shock to hear the expectation confirmed in such stark terms.

Uncle Edgar was the first to speak. I could see that he was in his element. Despite his dismay at King Edwin's conversion I knew he was loyal to the leader of his tribe: Northumbria was in danger and he would strain every sinew to protect his kin.

'I knew I had another big military campaign left in me,' Uncle Edgar said, almost gleefully. 'This is great news! We need to be tested by war. It's them or us, and may the best men win. That's why I'm absolutely determined that the men of Woden's Ford will be the best-prepared in Edwin's army. Rinc, with your permission I'd like to begin training our men immediately.'

Father was looking sombre, but he couldn't help smiling at his uncle's enthusiasm as he responded, 'Of course, Uncle, that would be great. I'm sure you'll do a grand job.'

'Thank you, Rinc, I'll certainly do my best,' Edgar replied. Then, after a brief pause, he said, 'I also think we should ask our clan priests to offer sacrifices to Woden and the other ancient gods. I know that won't go down well with all of you.

I'm not for a moment suggesting we should abandon Christianity because that would be to disobey the king; but I don't see what harm it would do to try to earn the favour of the old gods. If they don't exist it will be simply wasted effort; if they do exist it'll help us to win the war.'

I held my breath, expecting an explosion, from Uncle Alwyn at least. Father, too, glanced around at the others: none of them said anything; Alwyn merely shrugged his shoulders.

'That's agreed, Uncle – but on the understanding that reversion to pagan practices is exceptional, and only until the battle is over,' Father said. 'We're Christians now, and that's not up for dispute.'

'Of course, Rinc, of course,' Uncle Edgar said firmly, nodding his head and smiling broadly. 'I'll let the priests know.'

After another spell of silence the courtier spoke again, 'I've also been asked to check that the king's treasure that was given to you for safe keeping is still secure and in a secret place.'

Alwyn replied quickly, 'Yes, absolutely no need to worry about that. You can assure the king it's safe and sound. We check it regularly, and we'll keep doing so.'

After a little more discussion the courtier thanked us for our time and said he would get on his way to his next destination. The council meeting broke up after it was agreed that the news should be passed on to everyone across Woden's Ford as quickly as possible. It was important, Father said, that everyone should begin to prepare, and that all able-bodied men should join Uncle Edgar's training sessions.

The next few months felt peculiar – as if we were poised between peace and war but couldn't give our full attention to either.

Uncle Edgar's training regime was demanding, and so kept all the men busy. Grimbald was Edgar's chief lieutenant. I sensed that Grimbald's loyalty to his tribe, like his father's, was stronger than his personal opposition to Christianity and his passion for Deiran independence. He threw himself in to the preparations for war with gusto and, I assume, suppressed his doubts about the king's priorities.

In fact, the training regime was so tough that I heard men mutter that they couldn't wait for the battle so that they wouldn't have to do any more training!

The clan priests were delighted to revert, even though only partially and temporarily, to their old pagan ways. They offered regular sacrifices to try to secure the gods' favour for Edwin and the men of Woden's Ford. They predicted a Northumbrian victory with great confidence.

Others, I knew, were less sanguine. An old woman in one of the hamlets, reputed to be able to tell the future, claimed to foresee a great defeat for Northumbria. The news of her prophecy spread quickly as did alarm; but many argued that the woman had very rarely predicted anything accurately and dismissed her words as nonsense.

I was surprised by the reaction of my mother and aunts after the courtier had delivered his message. I knew that previously they had been quite dismissive of rumours of war. 'Men will be men' seemed to be a summary of their views. I guess they were used to the seemingly endless discussion about possible war and battles, about tactics, and about previous military action. I had often heard Aunt Bertha say, 'no amount of talk about war will clothe and feed the children.'

I noticed the change as I listened to Mother and Aunt Brigit talking one day. 'I'll admit, Hilda, I'm becoming nervous,' Aunt Brigit said. 'I know the men like to talk about fighting a lot. But, let's face it, we haven't been involved in a major war for many years. A few ceorls and peasants have been killed in battles with British armies, but we don't really know what it's like to be fighting for our survival. From what Alwyn tells me, that's what could lie ahead. There is, I suppose, a very real possibility that many of our men will die. At the worst, Woden's Ford itself could be ransacked.'

'I know,' Mother said. 'Rinc doesn't like us to be pessimistic about Northumbria's chances. And you can see Edgar is really up for the fight and getting all the men ready. But I'm not sure they're quite as confident as they like to make out. There's going to be quite a big army coming against us.'

I knew, of course, that a major war could have seriously bad consequences: but having not had any experience of one my young mind could not make the connection between the theory and the potential practical reality. I simply did not want to contemplate the possible death of many of my older relatives, the end of the Northumbrian kingdom, Woden's Ford being overrun.

Yet, as I heard my mother and aunt discussing so soberly and realistically the possibility of defeat, I felt for the first time a knot of anxiety in the pit of my stomach. I tried to ignore it, to dismiss their pessimism as 'women's talk', but there was no question that the knot of anxiety was there –

and I was to feel it regularly over the next few weeks.

On my sixteenth birthday, in June 633, I asked Mother and Father if I could join the Woden's Ford fighting contingent. Father was prepared to consider the possibility, but Mother put her foot down and Father did not press the point. It was only later that Father told me that he had seen sense in holding me back so that I could take over as chief if he did not survive the battle.

I will admit I had mixed feelings: on the one hand I expressed disappointment to Cadmon and my cousins that I would not be allowed to go to war; on the other hand, I felt a degree of private relief.

* * * * * * *

'That's it, men: at last, after all the false starts and speculation it looks like we'll be on the move soon.'

Father had gathered together his uncles, brothers and other close male family members, including Grimbald. It was August 633. I could sense the tension in the air.

'I've had orders from the king to move out and join the other Deiran contingents about thirty miles to the south, near Doncaster; that's where we'll meet the Bernicians. It looks as if the king's spies have solid information about the plans of the Welsh and the Mercians. They're expected to meet up in the north of Mercia, and then march up the old Roman road.'

'Good!' Uncle Edgar exclaimed. 'I was beginning to wonder whether it was a great big hoax. I'm sure our men'll be glad to get moving. They certainly can't say they're not prepared.'

'You're right there, Uncle Edgar: you've done a grand job,' Uncle Godwyn commented with only the slightest hint of irony. 'I still wonder why we've had to wait so long. Surely it would've made sense to invade Mercia months ago and surprise them.'

'Possibly,' Uncle Alwyn said. 'I imagine Edwin wanted to wait in case the coalition didn't materialise. And there might have been a risk of finding the Welsh closing in behind if we'd attacked Mercia.'

I felt at the same time both butterflies of excitement and the now all too familiar tightening knot of anxiety in my stomach. I looked round at my relatives. They were all looking brave and excited; but I wondered what they felt inside.

Chapter 14

633 AD

The storm breaks

'Be careful with the dog, Wulfhere, and stop teasing him,' Alice called, half laughing, half irritated. 'You don't want him to bite you.'

Her three-year-old son either didn't hear or didn't care. He continued to chase the big hunting dog round in circles, reaching for his tail, and laughing and squealing with delight as he kept just missing – until the dog stopped suddenly, the small boy crashed into him, and the pair rolled on the grass in a maelstrom of legs, arms, fur, hair, barking and laughter. It wasn't clear whether the dog or the child was having more fun.

Alice and Bertha smiled indulgently as they sat chatting on a balmy mid-September afternoon in fields near Woden's Ford. They were keeping an eye on Wulfhere, and on Bertha's three children and Brigit's two who were playing together a little further away. It was three weeks since the men had left to fight.

'Isn't that Grimbald's favourite hunting dog?' The questioner was Mildred, Edgar's wife and Grimbald's mother, who had just walked over to join the younger women.

'It was,' Alice replied, 'but he decided it had become a bit too old and slow for hunting. He gave it to me and Godwyn as a pet for Wulfhere. He's surprisingly good with children. As you can see, Wulfhere loves him'.

'I wish men were like that,' Mildred said, a little wearily.

'What do you mean, Mildred?' Bertha asked, looking puzzled.

'Well, look at Edgar,' Mildred said. 'He's pushing sixty, so you'd have thought he'd be slowing down and becoming a bit more 'pet-like'; but he's as obsessed as ever with war, ancestors, power and wealth. They should all learn a lesson from that dog and spend more time playing with little children.'

Alice and Bertha laughed. They saw relatively little of Mildred but enjoyed her quick wit and dry humour when she did venture into company. Both of Grimbald's brothers had died – one in childhood, the other as a young man had drowned in a flooded river. The second death, a few years previously, had triggered a period of deep depression; as a result, Mildred had kept a very low profile in recent years.

'I know what you mean, Mildred,' Bertha said. 'I often struggle to understand men and their preoccupations. They can seem so pointless, even counter-productive. Look at us now: most of the men are away to war right in the middle of harvest time. Well done to Brigit for organising most people who are left to gather it in, but it's not easy. I wonder how we'd get on if none of the men were to return from this wretched war? Perhaps we could turn Woden's Ford into a beacon of common sense!'

'Don't say that, Bertha!' Alice exclaimed. 'We don't want to tempt fate! Anyway, if our men didn't return, I'm sure others would come along and order us about.'

'I want them all to come back, of course I do,' Bertha said, laughing. 'I just sometimes wish life made more sense.'

Brigit, Hilda and Aelfred had approached the group as Bertha was talking. 'I like the sound of that,' Brigit said enthusiastically. 'We could all do with more sense. Have you heard some news about our men? I heard you talking about them.'

'No, still nothing,' Bertha replied, sighing deeply. 'We were just speculating how we might get on without men. How'd you fancy organising the harvest every year, for example?'

'I don't even want to think about them not returning,' Brigit said as she threw herself on the ground. 'I'm shattered. Aelfred's been an enormous help – he's obviously learned a great deal from Rinc and Alwyn; and we couldn't have managed if the four of us hadn't pooled resources over the last few weeks. But, believe me, one year of doing the harvest is more than enough for me! Anyway, I'm sure the men'll be back soon. They all seemed very confident they'd give the Mercians and Gwynedd a good thrashing.'

'I have to say I'm not quite so sure,' Hilda said pensively. 'I would love them all to return safe and triumphant, but I've a bad feeling about the whole thing.'

'Oh, Mother, don't be such a wet blanket,' Aelfred groaned. 'Of course Northumbria will win. How could you be so pessimistic?!'

'I hope you're right, Aelfred,' Mildred said, 'but they have been away for quite a while. But perhaps our boys have won and gone on to conquer Mercia, you never know. That would certainly delay them.'

'Well, maybe,' Aelfred replied as he headed off to join his

younger cousins. 'I just wish we could get some news: time seems to have stood still.'

The women were silent for a few moments: they were all as impatient as Aelfred for news, but each of them was handling the situation in their own way.

* * * * * * *

The balmy late September weather gave way to October and early autumn.

Leaves began to fall from the trees.

Still there was no news.

Aelfred tried to force himself to be optimistic.

Uncertainty was a great social leveller. The only question on the lips of women and children right across Woden's Ford, irrespective of their status, seemed to be, 'I wonder when they'll be back.'

Few dared to ask the other question which hung in the air, 'What if they lose?'

It was to be answered before the end of October.

* * * * * * *

'I'm so sorry I can't give you better news. I'm afraid our forces were simply overpowered at the Battle of Hatfield. King Edwin died, and I know many, many Northumbrians died with him. Early on the king told everyone to try to escape if he were killed. I know that's unusual. Normally a king's men are supposed to fight on even after he's died. But I think Edwin could sense the battle wasn't going to end well. I imagine he wanted as many of us as possible to be able to fight another day rather than perish. I managed to get away. I'm pretty certain others from Woden's Ford did, too; but it was impossible to stay together.'

At this point Aldrich paused, struggling to contain the emotions that were threatening to overwhelm him, but then went on, 'I'm afraid Wilfred definitely didn't make it. I saw him fighting at one point and go down. I know he didn't survive. I've already told Bertha and the children.'

Aldrich looked in despair. There were muffled sobs among those gathered around him. He continued eventually, trying to sound more positive, 'I really am pretty sure others of our folk got away and will turn up soon. It was just impossible to keep together.'

Aldrich had arrived back at Woden's Ford an hour or so previously with a small contingent of men. After going to see Bertha immediately he had asked Mildred, Alice and Brigit to join Hilda and Aelfred so that he could pass on the news to them altogether.

There was stunned silence when Aldrich finished. Aelfred felt as if a giant fist had struck him in the guts: his stomach seemed to have turned to liquid.

Aelfred could see at a glance his mother and his aunts – people he knew so well. Each of them was processing in their own way the terrible news and struggling with the uncertainty which Aldrich had spelt out. Hilda and Alice were strangely impassive, Brigit was weeping quietly, Mildred had closed her eyes and was mouthing an incantation.

Aelfred realised suddenly that if his father didn't return he would be chief. For a split second he felt as if the ceiling were spinning: he simply could not absorb the thought.

Aldrich noticed Aelfred staring vacantly into space. He put his arm around his shoulder as he said, 'Aelfred, I know how tough this is. It's horrible not knowing whether your father will make it back. I hope he will, but if he doesn't you can count on me to help.'

Aldrich had lived on his own for a number of years: both his wife and his fourteen-year-old son had died in quick succession, and his two daughters had gone away to get married. He was generally undemonstrative, and although Aelfred had never been as close to him as he had been to Eadwell and Edgar he had always appreciated Aldrich's solid dependability and common sense.

'Thank you, Uncle, that means a lot,' Aelfred said quietly. 'Can you tell me anymore about the battle? You must have had a terrible time.'

'You can say that again, son, it's been a tough few weeks,' Aldrich responded with feeling. 'After we left Woden's Ford we waited for quite a while at the muster point near Doncaster, training with the other Deirans and getting ready. The Bernicians turned up later, but I don't think as many as the king was expecting. Eventually scouts reported that King Cadwallon of Gwynedd and his allies, including Penda of Mercia, were approaching en masse. So, we all marched to the place where Edwin wanted to fight, at Hatfield. Right from the start I could see we were outnumbered. We fought hard, but it was a disaster. I did see your father fighting and doing well, but then I lost sight of him.'

At that point Hilda, Alice and Brigit came to thank and comfort Aldrich. Aelfred moved away. He wanted to be alone, to try to make sense of what he felt, to avoid talking. He simply could not comprehend the possibility that his father and uncles were all dead.

* * * * * * *

Few people across Woden's Ford slept well that night. Aelfred himself tossed and turned, all sorts of scenarios playing out in his mind.

In the morning Aelfred still did not feel like communicating. Both Hilda and Cadmon tried to talk to him, but he rebuffed them gruffly and went for a walk. It was a still, clear October morning. The trees were aflame with autumn colour. Aelfred registered nothing except pain and gnawing anxiety.

As he returned, he saw a large group of people in the distance.

He began to hear the hubbub of animated conversation as he got closer.

Aelfred started to run. He could tell that among the crowd were men returning from Hatfield. He hardly dared to hope, but as he approached hope turned into substance: his father and uncle Alwyn were at the heart of the group.

Aelfred reflected later that it was probably not the most manly way for a sixteen- year-old to welcome his father and uncle back from the presumption of death, but he ran instinctively in to their arms: both men returned the hug fiercely.

123

Aelfred dared not say much until he and Rinc were back in their own home in case he burst into tears – something he definitely didn't want to do in the presence of the dozen other returning fighters and the women and children who were gathering to welcome back their sons, brothers and fathers.

'It's really good to be back, but I'm afraid I'm not bringing much good news. We're all going to have to adjust to a new normal for a long time to come.' Rinc was slumped in his favourite chair, nursing a flagon of ale. He looked bereft as he spoke to Hilda, Aelfred and Cadmon. His voice was flat, dull, lifeless.

'I gather Uncle Aldrich has made it back already and given you some news,' Rinc continued. 'So, you've heard about Wilfred?' Three silent nods gave him the answer.

'I'm afraid there's much worse. I saw Edgar and Godwyn die. Alwyn and I managed to get away by the skin of our teeth. I'm almost certain Grimbald did, too, but we became separated from him.'

Hilda, Aelfred and Cadmon gasped, their shock visible and audible.

Aelfred closed his eyes and hid his face in his hands. 'Please tell me that's not true, Father. Please,' he almost begged, his voice breaking.

No one could say anything for a few minutes. There was nothing to say.

Eventually Hilda asked gently, 'What about the bodies, Rinc? Where are they?'

'That's the awful thing.' There was now a note of anger in Rinc's voice. 'There was nothing we could do. We had to leave them for the Welsh and the animals and birds to do as they please. They won't rest with their ancestors, and that's so awful.' He shook his head, pain etched on his face.

'So, what happens now, with the king dead?' Aelfred had just about composed himself; the future seemed unimaginable.

'It's really not clear, Aelfred,' Rinc replied gloomily. 'We did pick up bits and pieces of news from others as we headed back. It seems Penda and the Mercians have headed back south, but King Cadwallon may lead his army north towards Bernicia. He may want to install himself in Bamburgh. On the other hand, winter is approaching, so they may hunker down, do some raiding, and then perhaps bring in reinforcements in the spring for a big push to conquer the whole of Northumbria. I don't know what'll happen in Deira. We'll need to wait and see whether anyone tries to become the king of Deira – or Northumbria, for that matter – before Cadwallon makes a move.'

There was another despondent silence. It was broken by Aelfred. He had moved from incomprehension the previous evening to grief which was now combining with indignation and the beginning of a quest for scapegoats. 'Why? Why? Why?' he exclaimed vehemently. 'How could it all go so wrong?'

He didn't expect an answer, and no one gave him one. Each of them was lost in their own grief and devastation.

Aelfred knew, though, that he must try to find answers.

* * * * * * *

Grimbald returned, alone, three days later. In the evening he came to talk to Rinc. At first, they shared their grief together, their differences buried for the time being.

'So, I came back via York,' Grimbald said. 'I wanted to get some idea of what the future might hold. It looks as if the Queen and her folk, including Bishop Paulinus, are preparing to head back to Kent by ship. Good riddance, I say!'

'I think we can forget about Christianity,' Grimbald continued. 'There's some talk that Osric, Edwin's cousin, might claim the throne of Deira. I don't think he's that keen on Christianity, or on the Bernicians. So, there's a chance Osric might lead an independent, pagan Deira in a revenge attack against the Welsh. It's early days, but if that were to succeed it'd be an amazing silver lining in a very dark cloud!'

Aelfred, who was sitting with the two men, was surprised at the almost triumphant tone in Grimbald's voice. Rinc raised his eyebrows, and said, 'That would be quite a change, Grimbald. Let's see how it plays out. Everything must be pretty chaotic. I think our main job right now must be to support families across Woden's Ford. By my reckoning about twenty men are missing and so may have died at Hatfield. I guess some may still turn up, but that's a huge amount of grief. I'm also hearing many folk are afraid the Welsh will come and ransack Woden's Ford.'

Grimbald nodded, but his mind was clearly on the opportunities that Hatfield had created. 'Father wouldn't have wanted to die, but he died a warrior's death – right in the heart of the battle. I know he'd like some good to come out of it: a pagan, independent, Deiran kingdom would certainly count as good in his eyes.'

Grimbald paused, looking reflective, and then continued, 'You know, I cannot forgive the Bernicians. Not enough of them showed up at Hatfield, and that's why we lost. I don't think they ever really liked Edwin. It really is time to go it alone.'

Aelfred could tell that his father did not want to talk to Grimbald about the potential political and religious fallout from Hatfield. Rinc, very deliberately, turned the conversation to Grimbald's mother, Mildred, now Edgar's widow: he asked how she was, and what could be done to support her.

Grimbald replied briefly, but then got up to leave. 'I'll be away then. I guess you'll be inviting me on to the clan council now Father's gone. I'm sure he'd expect me to be there, to represent him as his sole survivor,' Grimbald said.

'Of course, Grimbald: I'll let you know when we next get together. Go well.' Rinc shut the door behind his cousin; Aelfred couldn't help noticing that his father rolled his eyes after he had done so.

* * * * * * *

'You've heard that Bertha and the children are heading back to her family in Bernicia? Rinc's providing an armed escort for them. It'll be a shame to see them go, but probably the right thing for just now.'

Hilda was talking to Alice who nodded, and then said, 'Yes, I know. It'll be so sad to say goodbye to them, but Bertha really is in pieces.'

'And how are you, Alice? You seem so calm. I can only

imagine what it must be like to lose your husband in such an awful way. And little Wulfhere must be missing Godwyn terribly.'

Alice looked at her cousin, clearly weighing up carefully what to say next. Hilda could not read anything in her clear blue eyes. Nothing was left in doubt though when she did speak.

'I'm going to move in with Grimbald,' Alice said in a business-like tone, as if she were telling Hilda the time of day.

Hilda blinked, and then blinked again. 'What?!' she exclaimed.

It was a rhetorical question, but Alice repeated, 'I'm going to move in with Grimbald.'

Hilda shook her head in bewilderment, as if to check that she had not misheard. 'Why?' was all she could say.

'Let me tell you the whole story; but I'm not telling another soul. I'm sure neither Godwyn if he had lived, nor Grimbald for that matter, would want it to go any further. I'm trusting you, as my cousin as well as my sister-in-law.'

Hilda nodded, and Alice continued, 'When I married Godwyn I was pleased. I'll be honest, I'd have preferred Grimbald; but the idea of marrying the brother of a clan chief was extremely attractive. Godwyn was good-looking and dashing, I was twenty-one. The future seemed bright. I knew men found me attractive. So, imagine my surprise when Godwyn refused to sleep with me! I couldn't quite believe it. I asked him why. He just said he couldn't be bothered. I asked him whether it wouldn't look bad if I didn't have children. He said we would just have to say we couldn't.'

'To say I was shocked was an understatement; but I

couldn't really talk about it to anybody,' Alice continued. 'Godwyn obviously didn't want others to know. So we kept up an appearance. I put up with it for a while, but eventually I decided I'd had enough. I still liked Grimbald, sensed that he liked me, and although he hadn't married I didn't think it was because he was scared of sleeping with women! I started to flirt with him, and I knew Godwyn was suspicious.'

Alice paused, and looked her cousin in the eye as she then said, 'I well remember our conversation at the bonfire, Hilda. I imagine Godwyn put you up to it. In the end, I told Godwyn I was going to have an affair with Grimbald, and so he'd better accept it. I'd keep his secret, but he'd have to keep mine in return. Bizarrely, I think he was actually quite relieved. I suspect he felt guilty he couldn't give me what I expected as a wife. I spent time with Grimbald in his hut whenever I could. Wulfhere is, of course, Grimbald's son, although we agreed Godwyn would claim him. Grimbald wasn't happy about that, but he got to see plenty of him because Godwyn wasn't particularly interested.'

'So, Godwyn's death wasn't such a tragedy for me,' Alice concluded. 'I know there'll be a bit of scandal when I move up to the hut. But I don't really care. There are bigger things to worry about just now than a widow moving in with a bachelor.'

Hilda was staggered. She had been reasonably sure that Alice had had an affair with Grimbald, but she had never suspected the underlying situation.

'Thank you so much for sharing all that with me, Alice. I'm so sorry you had to put up with such odd circumstances. Your secret's safe with me.'

Hilda hesitated, and then continued tentatively, 'I know this is an awkward question, Alice, but can I ask what exactly you like about Grimbald? I know he's handsome, but ...' Hilda didn't know quite how to finish the sentence.

Alice smiled a little wearily and said, 'I know most folk don't like him, and I sort of get that. He's an uncomfortable character. But there's something I find very attractive in his wildness and rawness. There's no pretence. What you see is what you get. And there's no question he likes me – and that definitely helps!'

Hilda was not usually very tactile, but she embraced Alice as she said, 'Well, I'm glad something's worked out for you, Alice. You deserve it after what you've been through.'

Chapter 15

633 AD

Aftermath

'How're you feeling, Alwyn? Have you got your head round what's happened yet?' Rinc asked.

It was a week after the brothers had returned from Hatfield. They had just finished clearing out and closing down Wilfred's and Godwyn's homes. It had been a task they had been dreading, but now that Alice and Wulfhere had moved to Grimbald's hut and Bertha and the children had left for Bernicia they had accepted they could not leave it any longer.

Alwyn stopped what he was doing, straightened up, and looked at his brother. 'I honestly don't know,' he said. 'I've been asking myself that question for a few days, and so has Brigit. On the one hand, there's the busy me: there's a great deal to be done and thought about, and I'm getting on with it. But it's as if I'm doing it automatically. I'm not really thinking about what's happened and why we're in this situation.'

'Then there's the distraught me,' Alwyn continued. 'I feel empty, hollow, drained of life somehow. I can't get the images of Hatfield out of my mind. I feel utterly bereft at the loss of our brothers, Uncle Edgar, and so many others. I'm so sad to have seen Bertha and the kids leave. I'm baffled at Alice moving in with Grimbald. I'm shocked at how suddenly the Northumbrian kingdom has collapsed. I worry desperately about the future.'

After a brief pause, Alwyn added, 'Perhaps there's also a third me. It's the one in denial. I can't quite accept that so many dreadful things have happened in such a short time. I'm expecting everything to revert to normal. Does all of that make any sort of sense?'

'I think so – sort of,' Rinc replied wearily. 'But you've always been better with words. I'm not so good at describing what's going on. All I can say is I feel ghastly: as if I've been kicked in the head about twenty times.'

Alwyn listened to his brother with sympathy and concern. He thought Rinc had aged markedly in the last week. He was sure that there were new flecks of grey in his hair and beard, and his shoulders seemed to have sagged. His eyes were cloudy. Alwyn knew that as chief Rinc carried extra weight on his shoulders: the toll now seemed very obvious.

'Rinc, man, I want you to know we're in this together,' Alwyn said firmly. 'You're the chief, of course. But you're not on your own. Wilfred and Godwyn have gone, but you're stuck with me.'

'I actually received a message yesterday from Bishop Paulinus' folk,' Alwyn continued. 'They're on the run, heading south back to Kent with the Queen. The bishop invited me and the family to join him – to make a new life down there. He'd like me to be part of their mission. I've already declined. I'm sure it'll be easier to be a Christian in Kent than in the mess we've got in Deira now. But I've told him my moral conscience would never forgive me if I were to abandon my kin in their darkest hour. It's the kind of language he'll understand!'

Rinc smiled wanly, and Alwyn went on, 'I'm telling you to reassure you, Rinc: I'm a committed Christian; but I'm equally committed to you and to Woden's Ford. Believe me, I'll do everything I can to help us all recover.'

Rinc looked at his brother for a few moments: then, in the same instant, they reached for each other and embraced.

Over the last few years Rinc's own instincts had been at war with his intellect and loyalty to his king. He had struggled with the Christian teaching which seemed so at odds with the values which had been instilled in him from birth. He had had plenty of arguments with Alwyn as his brother had embraced Christianity ever more enthusiastically.

None of that seemed to matter now. As Alwyn had said, this was a crisis, but they were in it together. They both felt as if the eyes of their ancestors who had built and sustained Woden's Ford over so many centuries were on them, and that future generations were depending on the decisions they took in the next few weeks.

'Right,' Rinc said, with more energy and purpose in his voice immediately. 'Let's decide what we're going to do. First, tell me what you've heard about what's going on in York and Bamburgh. Grimbald told me King Edwin's cousin might be making a move for the Deiran throne, and that he's not very keen on Christianity.'

'Yes, it seems Grimbald was right,' Alwyn replied. 'Osric's become the Deiran king, but I'm not sure that amounts to very much right now. I suspect Cadwallon of Gwynedd is biding his time. He wants the whole of Northumbria for himself.'

'I'm fairly certain Grimbald is right about Osric's attitudes as well,' Alwyn continued. 'I've met Osric a couple of times over the years. He's definitely interested in himself, but not much else I have to say. I don't think he's much of a thinker, either, let's just leave it at that. When Edwin converted I suspect Osric continued to oppose Christianity – but only because he wanted to attract dissenters. I imagine Osric's always been on the lookout for an opportunity to claim a crown – any crown actually.'

'That's very interesting,' Rinc replied. 'I've heard there's a similar situation in Bernicia. King Eanfrith's on the throne – sort of, anyway. He's supposed to have done a deal with Cadwallon, but I suspect his position's just as shaky. I doubt Cadwallon's in the business of sticking to deals. So, Northumbria has split back apart. All the gains we made as a united kingdom are at risk.'

Rinc paused, looked around, and then continued more quietly, as if there might be a secret listener even though they were completely alone, 'But there is a glimmer of light. Perhaps more than a glimmer. I've heard rumours Prince Oswald, the son of King Aethelfrith and Queen Acha, might mount a campaign against Cadwallon. He's been in exile in Dalriada in the far north-west ever since Edwin killed his father and took the Northumbrian throne in 616 – just before I got married, if you remember.'

'He was just a young lad when he went to Dalriada, but I gather Oswald now has strong support from the Dalriadan king,' Rinc went on. 'I really do believe we should support any move by Oswald – and buy time for him if we can. Of course, Aethelfrith was Bernician, but Oswald has also inherited royal Deiran blood from his mother, Queen Acha. And he's Edwin's nephew. He's ideally placed to bring us back together.'

'I agree completely, Rinc,' Alwyn said. 'A united Northumbria was good for all of us; ongoing occupation and division will be bad. I certainly don't want to be subject to a Welsh king. So, how can we buy time and support Oswald? I assume not much is going to happen over the winter.'

'This is what I think,' Rinc said. 'First of all, we need to avoid Woden's Ford being ransacked by the Welsh invaders over the next few months. I'm going to see what I can manage on that front. But don't ask too many questions – we might need to be a bit underhand.'

'Second, we're going to have to deal with our beloved cousin,' Rinc went on, with a sigh. 'Let's just say, I don't think Grimbald will be as dismissive of King Osric as we are. He's got it in his head Osric's going to hammer the Welsh invaders and re-establish a glorious, independent, pagan kingdom of Deira. It's all nonsense, of course, but I suspect it'll be difficult to get him to agree to support Oswald instead.'

'I agree, it certainly won't be easy,' Alwyn mused as he stroked his chin thoughtfully. But his eyes then lit up, and he went on, 'So, how about this as an idea? You told me Grimbald's demanding a seat on the clan council in place of poor Uncle Edgar. If we do agree, there'll only be four of us: Uncle Aldrich, the two of us, and Grimbald. I know it's tempting not to admit him. But if we were to exclude him, he'd make a massive fuss. So why don't we allow him on, and then use the next Council meeting to get agreement to the way ahead that we want? He'll be in a minority of one; but if the

Council has made a decision he is more likely to obey – and if he steps out of line we can call him to order.'

'That's neat, I agree, Alwyn,' Rinc replied, smiling and nodding his head, after he had considered his brother's suggestion thoughtfully. 'But I can't say I'll look forward to the meeting where we override him. I'll be in the hot seat, and I suspect it'll be a very rough ride!'

Rinc then added, 'I can see the sense in bringing him on to the Council; but I don't think we should tell Grimbald about the royal treasure buried in the woods. I simply don't trust him not to offer it to Osric and his pals.'

Alwyn nodded vigorously.

* * * * * * *

'I still can't believe what's happened,' Aelfred said for the umpteenth time. 'Who could have predicted it? It still feels completely unreal. Why, how could it happen?'

It was a month after Hatfield. Aelfred and Cadmon lay sprawled on a hillside, taking a break from hunting. It was a familiar spot: they had been there many times with Edgar. The landscape lay below them looking as it had done all their lives, and for centuries before. The trees had shed their leaves and winter was taking hold.

The boys were as gloomy as the November weather, saying little, staring into the distance. The landscape was the same as ever, but everything felt different.

Cadmon nodded. He felt keenly the loss of men he had known so well. Yet, deep within, there was an almost unacknowledged ambivalence. Cadmon knew that he had been born in Gwynedd. Over the years he had been told some of the story of his arrival at Woden's Ford; he had guessed other aspects. He had no complaints about how he had been treated by the clan: he knew his place as a slave, but he had grown up effectively as an Anglian and for the most part was treated as Aelfred's brother. Yet now, with Northumbria defeated and occupied, at least partially, by an army from Gwynedd, he couldn't help feeling just slightly conflicted.

Aelfred continued, his tone a mixture of flatness and frustration, 'Life seems so completely meaningless now. What's the point in preparing to be a chief, in marrying, in doing anything if it can all be wiped out in an instant? We might as well just sit around waiting to die. I certainly can't be bothered chasing any more deer today, that's for sure. The Council are meeting later to talk about the future and Father expects me to be there. Let's go back.'

'Fine,' Cadmon agreed without enthusiasm, and the boys began to trudge back towards Woden's Ford.

* * * * * * *

As Rinc, Alwyn, Aldrich and Grimbald sat down later Aelfred sensed around the table the sadness and heaviness which had blanketed Woden's Ford ever since Hatfield. There was none of the banter and laughter which had been such a rich accompaniment to council meetings in the past, even when serious matters were discussed.

None of the men acknowledged the loss openly, but

Aelfred suspected that each of them was thinking about the men who had been present the last time they had met but who were now dead.

Aelfred also sensed his father's determination to try to move on. 'We've talked between us about quite a few ideas and 'what ifs' over the last few weeks,' Rinc said purposefully. 'It's time now as a council to make some decisions.'

'Let's talk first about Cadwallon and his Welsh army,' Rinc continued. 'It seems they'll be overwintering in Deira, but some way west of here. I know they've started to occupy some land and turn folk out. I'm well aware many of our people are afraid they'll occupy and sack Woden's Ford, too.'

Rinc paused, and then said, 'I really don't think Cadwallon's army could take over the whole of Deira for the time being. But they'll need food and fuel over the winter, and so they'll go looking for it. They'll take stuff by force if necessary. I believe we could buy time, and perhaps stave off an attack on Woden's Ford, by offering them some supplies over the winter. What do you think?'

'Pay a bribe to the enemy to buy protection? Give some of our produce to the people who killed my father?' Grimbald asked scornfully. 'Is that really what you're planning?'

'I'm not sure I'd put it quite like that, Grimbald,' Rinc replied evenly. 'Let's be realistic: we couldn't defend ourselves if the Gwynedd men tried to ransack Woden's Ford; but I'm not sure they'll stay in Northumbria long-term – we'll come on shortly to what might happen next year. I certainly don't want to do anything that'd prolong the occupation unnecessarily; but I do want to do everything I can to keep Woden's Ford intact. Perhaps we could agree that if Cadwallon's men do come anywhere near us, we'd try to negotiate with them without in any way consenting to their occupation?'

Rinc had focused on Grimbald as he spoke hitherto, but now glanced at Alwyn and then Aldrich. Both men nodded.

Grimbald looked unhappy, but before he could say anything more Rinc continued, 'Look, we need a longer-term plan, too. I've absolutely no confidence King Osric will survive for long on the Deiran throne. And I hear King Eanfrith in Bernicia looks just as shaky even though he's supposed to have done a deal with Cadwallon. I can't imagine Cadwallon will want puppet kings in Northumbria: he wants both thrones for himself. I'm also now fairly sure Prince Oswald will mount a campaign against Cadwallon. I believe we should support any move by Oswald to become king of a reunited Northumbria.'

Grimbald fired up immediately, 'I know Oswald's mother was Deiran, but Oswald is essentially a Bernician. I've also heard Oswald's a Christian. Haven't we had enough of Christianity? It didn't do Edwin or us any good at Hatfield. And remember it was the Bernicians who let us down there. We need to put our faith in our ancestors, not in another Christian king who hasn't even lived in Northumbria for years.'

Alwyn was equally robust as he responded, 'Look, Grimbald, there's no point in blaming Hatfield on Christianity. Edwin overreached himself, annoyed some powerful enemies, and we weren't strong enough to withstand them all when they got together. The Christian God doesn't promise protection in battle any more than Woden can. Christianity's about a personal faith in a living God, a new way of living. It's a way that deep in our hearts we all know is right.'

'I'm a Christian, but I'm also a Deiran and a Northumbrian,' Alwyn continued. 'I believe having Oswald in either Bamburgh or York as king of a reunited Northumbria would be in our interests. I've said it before, and I'll say it again: I believe absolutely Christianity is the future. If Northumbria rejects Christianity, we'll be out of line with the rest of Europe. We'll look really old-fashioned and closed-minded.'

Aelfred could see Grimbald's rage mounting as Alwyn spoke. His throat went red, a muscle twitched in his temple, and his eyes narrowed. Grimbald was tempted to interrupt, but he let his cousin finish. Then the anger exploded – not in a violent outburst, but in a controlled, almost sinister voice.

'That's the most despicable rubbish I've heard in a very long time – even from you, Alwyn, and that's saying something. How could you even say all that with my father's and your brothers' bodies scarcely cold? What would your own father say if he could hear you from his grave?'

'We must be for Woden, Deira, and our ancestors,' Grimbald continued passionately. 'That's where our future lies. Not with Christians and Bernicians, still less in doing shabby deals with Gwynedd. They all want to destroy our heritage, sap us of our identity. I'm certain embracing Christianity caused the disaster of Hatfield. The gods have punished us for turning away from them. We can't repeat that mistake – either by trying to bribe the Welsh, or by supporting another Christian king.'

Grimbald's voice rose as he finished, 'I'm for King Osric. He *is* committed to our heritage. He *is* committed to taking back control for Deira.'

Grimbald sat back and looked fiercely at his three adult

relatives. He then looked at Aelfred, and said, 'And let's think about Aelfred and his generation. I don't want them to accuse me in future of selling them out.'

Rinc was well aware how much Alwyn and Grimbald disliked each other, but even so he was taken aback by the gulf between them.

Rinc looked at Aldrich questioningly. 'I'm sorry, Rinc,' the older man said despairingly. 'Don't look to me for a solution. I'm spent. You younger ones have to sort this out between you.'

Rinc knew that his uncle had been hit harder by Hatfield than any of the other survivors. He had seemed resilient immediately after the battle, but he now appeared to be deteriorating almost daily. Aldrich had told Rinc that he felt old and lonely, almost guilty for surviving, that life had become pointless. As if to illustrate his feelings Aldrich put his head in his hands and shook it silently.

Alwyn and Rinc looked at their uncle sympathetically; Grimbald stared in front of him, expressionless.

Rinc knew that the impasse must be broken, but he also knew that there would be a cost. 'Right,' he said with as much authority as he could muster. 'To state the obvious, we're not united. I'll need to make a decision, and then we must all stick to it.'

'Here goes,' he continued. 'First, I hope we won't have any contact with them, but if the Welsh occupiers do come looking for supplies this winter, and so long as any request is reasonable, we'll do our best to comply. Second, Alwyn will, on all our behalf, make secret approaches to other clans in Deira and Bernicia about how best to support Prince

Oswald's bid to become king of a united Northumbria. Third, we will not do anything to support Osric as king of Deira.'

Aldrich and Alwyn nodded assent; Grimbald looked furious. After a long pause, and in the same controlled, venomous tone of voice in which he had spoken earlier, he said, 'I hear what you say, Rinc. You'll not expect me to agree with you. I recognise your right as chief to make a binding decision. I will submit to it. But I promise it'll come back to haunt you.'

Rinc and Grimbald locked eyes for a few seconds: the ferocity on both sides was excruciating. Aelfred happened to be sitting next to Grimbald. He could almost feel Grimbald's body quivering with suppressed rage.

Rinc looked away first. Grimbald pushed back his chair, stood up, glanced at Alwyn and Aldrich, shook his head, and stalked out into the night muttering oaths.

* * * * * * *

Aelfred was still not allowed to speak in council gatherings, but his father couldn't stop him reflecting on what he saw and heard. He knew that the tribe, the clan, his kin were overriding considerations; but his late grandfather and great uncle Edgar had both instilled in him a deep suspicion of Christianity and a reverence for his ancestors.

Aelfred summed up his dilemma to Cadmon later, 'I want to be a loyal Deiran, Cad, but I can't help feeling that Grandfather and Uncle Edgar would be more in favour of Penda than a Christian King Oswald. I don't like the way Grimbald treats Father and Uncle Alwyn, but I do have a bit of sympathy for him. Maybe he has a point about the defeat at Hatfield being the result of King Edwin's conversion. But he's going to find it hard to stick to Father's decision. I don't think I've ever seen anyone quite so angry. It was actually pretty scary!'

Chapter 16

634 AD

Fallout

'**We**'ve got to confront him, Rinc. He's flouted your authority and broken the agreement we made at the Council in November. It's not good enough, especially when I'm doing my best to secretly support a coalition in Deira to back Prince Oswald – and, believe me, that's not easy.'

Alwyn was speaking to Rinc in February 634. It was a perishing day. Flurries of snow blew from time to time in a sharp north-easterly wind. Even with a fire blazing in the hearth and torches lit, it was gloomy and cold inside.

Rinc's brow was furrowed in exasperation. 'Tell me again what you've heard, Alwyn.'

'Right,' Alwyn said. 'I was in York yesterday meeting some of the men who'd been in contact with Oswald. I gather, by the way, that King Eanfrith's reign in Bernicia is already over. We knew he'd tried to do a deal with Cadwallon, but it looks as if he's been murdered for his pains.'

'Oswald's apparently planning to head towards Bamburgh with the support of Dalriadan forces,' Alwyn added. 'It's thought he'll avoid the Welsh for the time being. I guess they'll prepare for a fight later in the year. That's when Deiran contingents could try to join up with Oswald.'

'Anyway, that's all by the by,' Alwyn went on. 'There's lots of talk in York that King Osric is going to try to take on Cadwallon's army while they're still over-wintering in Deira. One of the chaps said he'd heard Woden's Ford had pledged to support King Osric. He wondered why we were supporting both causes. I said that wasn't the case, and so there must be a misunderstanding.'

'The chap then described seeing Grimbald coming away from a meeting with Osric's courtiers the day before yesterday,' Alwyn continued. 'He said he'd asked the courtiers what was going on. They said Grimbald had pledged to support Osric.'

'That's appalling,' Rinc exclaimed, shaking his head. 'It certainly sounds like he's betrayed us. We'll have to go up to his hut and have it out with him. It'll be messy, and I guess both Alice and little Wulfhere will be there. We can't duck it though. We might as well go now before a blizzard sets in.'

The two men put on thick cloaks, hats and boots and set off towards Grimbald's hut. Alice opened the door when Rinc knocked, four-year-old Wulfhere peeping from behind her. 'Well, welcome,' she said cheerfully. 'What a surprise! No one ever visits, so what brings you here on such a wild afternoon?'

'It's nice to see you, Alice, I hope you're doing well,' Rinc said as courteously as he could manage. 'We've come to have a chat with Grimbald actually.'

'I thought that might be the case,' Alice said. 'He's just round the back getting some more wood. D'you want to come in and wait?'

'No, thanks,' Rinc replied hurriedly, 'we'll go and find him. See you later, Alice.'

The brothers walked round the hut and saw Grimbald about two hundred yards away coming towards them carrying an armful of firewood.

'Hello, Grimbald,' Rinc called as he came within earshot. 'We'd like to talk to you. It's really quite important.' Rinc reflected later that this was something of an understatement given that they were about to accuse their cousin of treachery.

Grimbald didn't say anything and kept on walking towards them, his breath steaming in the cold air. He stopped a few feet away but didn't put down the bundle of wood. He was clearly not in the mood for small talk.

Rinc came straight to the point, 'Where were you the day before yesterday, Grimbald?'

Grimbald looked at him appraisingly for a few seconds, and then said, 'What business is it of yours, chief?' He lingered over the last word provocatively.

Rinc kept his patience. 'I am the chief, and so it's my business to ensure the decisions the clan council make are followed through. I will ask again: where were you the day before yesterday? And who did you talk to?'

'This is ridiculous, Rinc,' Grimbald said roughly, his dark eyes blazing. 'I was in York. Now let me go so I can keep my fire burning.'

Grimbald made to walk on towards his hut, but Rinc gripped his right arm.

'Not so fast, cousin,' Rinc said fiercely. 'Alwyn has pretty solid evidence you've pledged support to King Osric. That's something we decided we would definitely not do. If it's true, you've betrayed us.'

Alwyn had been silent, but now spoke up, 'Yes, Grimbald,

there's no question it was you. The man I spoke to in York wondered why we were backing both sides. I was doing what we agreed and making contact with Oswald's supporters.'

Grimbald looked at Alwyn for a few seconds. There was pure hatred in his eyes. He then pulled his arm out of Rinc's grasp and flung the wood to the ground.

'Right, I knew it must come to this,' he said furiously. 'You've the cheek to call me a traitor! I tried to go along with what we decided at the Council. But, you know, in the end I felt I was betraying everything I believed in: Woden, Deira, my father, all my ancestors. I simply couldn't do it anymore. We've got a chance to rebuild an independent, pagan Deira; you two want to sell out our heritage for more trade, a weak god, and some very unreliable allies. I'm proud to support King Osric. I will not do anything to support Oswald.'

With that he spat on the ground, a deliberate act of contempt for his cousins.

Alwyn said later that he'd been determined to keep to the moral high ground, but something inside him snapped when Grimbald spat. 'You're completely crazy, Grimbald!' he shouted. 'You haven't been right in the head since the battle of Chester all those years ago. How can you possibly want to drag us back to some barbarian darkness when we can build a fresh future? You'll pay for betraying us.'

Grimbald didn't hesitate. He was taller and stronger than his cousin. In one stride he was beside him, his right fist swung into Alwyn's left cheek, his left fist caught Alwyn on the nose as he reeled backwards.

Alwyn fell to the ground. Grimbald turned and strode back the way he had come – towards the woods.

Rinc was torn for an instant between chasing after Grimbald, and helping Alwyn, but recognised that the latter was the higher immediate priority. He crouched beside his unconscious brother. Within a minute Alwyn came round, opened his eyes carefully, and moaned. 'What happened?' he asked, dazed and confused.

'Let's worry about that later, we need to get you home now,' Rinc said.

At that moment Alice hurried across. 'What's going on? Where's Grimbald? I heard some noise and wondered what it was about.'

Rinc was not inclined to show any sympathy to his sister-in-law. 'Grimbald knocked Alwyn unconscious and then disappeared into the woods,' he replied bluntly.

'Oh, no!' she exclaimed in anguish, raising her hand to cover her mouth. 'Can I do anything to help?'

'I suggest you calm your man down when he returns, Alice,' Rinc said. 'We're not going to hang around for him; but we'll be back soon. There will, I'm afraid, be consequences.'

Alice shook her head but said nothing.

'You can shake your head all you like, Alice,' Rinc said angrily, 'but Grimbald cannot be allowed to get away with this. I can't help it that you've thrown your lot in with him.'

Alice was angry now, too, and said, 'I wasn't shaking my head because I disagreed with you, Rinc. There absolutely must be a reckoning. I was shaking my head because I cannot believe you men can get so worked up about such useless things. Why fight and argue about gods and spirits? Who cares about kings and ancestors so long as we have food on the table and we can get on with living our lives? It just seems so ridiculous.'

'Well, good luck when you have that chat with Grimbald,' Rinc replied, laughing mirthlessly. 'Now I suggest you get back into the warmth and look after Wulfhere.'

Alice seemed about to say something else, but instead she turned and walked back towards the hut without a backward glance at her brothers in law.

Alwyn had now recovered sufficiently for the two men to begin to walk back towards their homes, albeit at a gentle pace.

* * * * * * *

'I'm prepared to forgive Grimbald, I really am. I lost patience and provoked him. He shouldn't have thumped me, but I did bring it on myself a bit. I'm a Christian, and Christians should forgive. I'm not saying he shouldn't pay a price for his treachery, I'm absolutely not. I just think I should be prepared to forgive him for hitting me.'

Alwyn was talking to Rinc, Brigit, and Hilda. It was the morning of the next day but one after the incident with Grimbald.

'Well, maybe, Alwyn – that's up to you,' Rinc replied. 'As far as I'm concerned, Grimbald's put himself beyond any sort of leniency. His treachery and the way he dealt with us are unforgiveable. He's let down his kin in the most despicable way. The punishment must be either death or to be outlawed.'

There was a solemn silence. No one dissented.

Brigit spoke eventually, 'What about Alice? And Wulfhere? They aren't to blame for what Grimbald's done. Can we show mercy to them?'

'That's up to Alice to some extent,' Alwyn replied. 'She's our sister-in-law and Hilda's cousin – and, of course, Wulfhere is Godwyn's son. We should be prepared to give her a home if that's what she wants.'

Hilda stared at the floor at the mention of Wulfhere, but then looked up as Alwyn finished, nodded, and said, 'I agree. I can't understand why Alice wanted to move in with Grimbald, but we should at least offer her sanctuary.'

'Right, let's do that,' Rinc said. 'Now, we'll need to think about how we confront Grimbald. I can't imagine he'll come and look for us. We'll need to get a group of men together and go up to the hut.'

They were all silent again, each thinking about possible consequences. Eventually Hilda, shaking her head, said, 'Poor Alice. I really do hope she and Wulfhere come through all this.'

Then, trying to lighten the atmosphere, Hilda turned again to Alwyn and said, more brightly, 'Anyway, Alwyn, how're you feeling today? Your face is certainly very colourful – and I suspect it's just the start!'

'I'm quite a bit better after a day's rest, that's for sure – but my face feels about twice its normal size!' Alwyn said, smiling ruefully, and then exclaiming as his facial muscles crinkled his bruised skin painfully.

The others laughed sympathetically, and then looked up as there was a knock on the front door.

Hilda opened it: to her astonishment Alice stood outside, Wulfhere holding her hand tightly. Alice looked cold, windswept and flustered – and somehow diminished, a stark contrast to her normal self-possessed beauty.

Alice started when she saw the other three sitting at the table, but it was too late to retreat. Her words came tumbling out.

'Look, folks, I'm really sorry for what Grimbald did. The thing is, I haven't seen him since. And I'm getting scared. He does go away overnight sometimes – you all know how much he loves hunting; but this time was so sudden, and it's been two nights, and I don't have any idea where he is or what he's doing. And it's really lonely up in that hut.'

Hilda instinctively put her arm round her cousin's shoulders and hugged her. Alice burst into tears, and Wulfhere looked as if he was about to do the same.

The other three looked at each other, and then Alwyn said, 'Right, Alice, we'll get some men together and go into the woods to look for him. You and Wulfhere should have something to eat and try to get warm.'

'Yes, Alice, you can come with us, or stay here with Hilda,' Brigit said. 'By the way, Alwyn, you're not going anywhere near any woods today; you're still meant to be resting!'

'That's right, Alwyn, you do as you're told!' Rinc said firmly. 'I'll go and collect some men. Now, Alice, can you give us any idea where Grimbald goes in the woods and hills when he's away hunting?'

Alice had calmed down enough to be able to give some pointers to Rinc who then hurried off to collect a search party.

* * * * * * *

Rinc was soon striding up the hill with fifteen others including Aelfred and Cadmon. They were all armed with spears and daggers and were accompanied by several hunting dogs. They split into groups of two to cover as much ground as possible in the wooded hills beyond Grimbald's hut as quickly as possible, but they maintained calling distance between the pairs.

Aelfred and Cadmon formed one of the pairs. They heard from time to time, and answered, the calls of the pairs to their right and left.

The minutes passed. There was no news yet.

Suddenly their dog, a few yards ahead of them, began to bark insistently. The boys ran towards the sound. Aelfred said later that it was almost impossible to describe what they found. Lying almost side by side in a rocky hollow were the blood-spattered bodies of Grimbald and a large grey wolf. A hunting knife lay between them. The bodies had evidently been there for some time because other animals and birds had already started to gnaw at them.

The boys retched and looked at each other in utter horror. Cadmon then shouted the agreed signal. The boys heard the neighbouring pairs repeat it excitedly, and the sound was then transmitted more faintly down the line of searchers. Aelfred and Cadmon continued to stand and stare.

The sound of running, stumbling feet followed almost immediately. The pairs of men to their right and left arrived almost simultaneously. They stopped, gasped, and swore.

Their reaction was repeated almost exactly as the rest of the searchers arrived at the scene. Not a single man approached the bodies for some time, and none of them spoke: it was as if they were all petrified by a combination of instinct and superstition.

Eventually Rinc stepped forward. He looked down at the body of his cousin for a few minutes. Aelfred did not have any idea what his father was thinking.

'Here lies a brave man and a great warrior,' Rinc proclaimed, his eyes sweeping the semi-circle of searchers. The men all muttered assent, many bowed their heads.

Aelfred knew how bad his father's relationship with Grimbald had been by the end, and so how much it must have cost Rinc to offer even such a brief eulogy.

The spell was broken, and the searchers started to talk to each other. 'Look,' Rinc said to Aelfred and Cadmon whom he had summoned forward to examine the grisly scene. 'I'm pretty sure the wolf attacked Grimbald from behind and caught him in the neck. Grimbald must have had just enough strength left to reach for his knife and stab and kill the wolf, but he must have then bled to death.'

'It's strange,' he continued thoughtfully, almost to himself. 'Grimbald had a thing about wolves from very early on. He was fascinated by them. Maybe there was something of the wolf about him. He certainly lived a bit like a lone wolf for many years. So, it's ironic he died like this.'

'Right, men,' he said, turning away towards the rest of the party, 'let's get some branches and make a stretcher to carry the body back down.'

A few minutes later a dreadful procession began to snake its way back through the woods, four of the men bearing the makeshift stretcher which bore Grimbald's ravaged remains.

* * * * * * *

Rinc could not recall hearing anything like it, certainly not at close quarters. It was heart-rending, gut-wrenching, ear-splitting.

There were no words at first: Alice's scream was a feral, inhuman, visceral outburst of rage and grief. Then the words came, shouted, each one pulsating with violence, spittle spraying from her mouth, 'You've murdered him. You've always hated him. You were out to get him. Grimbald would never be overcome by a wolf. He was a brave, strong man. It took fifteen cowards to kill him.'

Rinc extended his hands, palms outwards, as if to try to stem the torrent of invective, and said, 'That's simply not true, Alice. Come and see his body. We can show you the wolf, too, if you like. Grimbald killed it, but it had already slashed his throat and he bled to death. I'm so sorry.'

Rinc then reached out, trying to take Alice's hand to comfort her. Alice slapped Rinc's hand away, and shouted, 'Don't touch me, murderer! I will never believe you. I will never see Grimbald dead. I want to remember him alive and vital. He was worth more than you and all your miserable brothers put together.'

To Rinc's horror Alice then ripped her bodice and flung herself face down, sobbing uncontrollably, her fists pummelling the floor.

There was no one else in the house. Hilda, Aelfred and

Cadmon were at Alwyn's house with Wulfhere. Alice had been left alone to rest while the men had gone in search of Grimbald.

Rinc ran the few hundred yards to his brother's home, explained the situation quickly, and then hurried back with Hilda and Brigit. Alice was still lying face down, sobbing and screaming, her voice now hoarse, her fists still beating the floor.

Her sisters in law knelt beside Alice and did their best to calm her. Alice appeared not to register their presence at all. After a while she finally lay motionless and quiet, utterly exhausted, still with her face to the floor. She had not looked even once at her sisters in law.

Hilda and Brigit stared at each other, then at Rinc who had stood behind them transfixed, his back to the door. Only then did the two women see Wulfhere standing in the entrance, his eyes wide with terror. 'What's mother doing?' he asked in a small, tremulous voice.

* * * * * * *

Aelfred had thought that the sense of loss across Woden's Ford after Hatfield could not be surpassed; but Grimbald's death seemed to tip many into even greater grief and confusion.

Grimbald had not been a popular character, but the nature of his death was shattering. Coming only four months after Hatfield it stirred up awful memories for many just as wounds were beginning to heal.

Once Grimbald's funeral was over Rinc, Alwyn, Hilda and Brigit knew that they had to make decisions – and do so quickly.

They could not work out precisely what had happened to Grimbald. They concluded that he had probably gone into the woods to calm down with every intention of returning, and that it was pure coincidence that he had been attacked by the wolf. They felt there was no need to tell anyone else about Grimbald's treachery and the retribution they had been planning since fate seemed to have intervened. Thus, it was generally understood around Woden's Ford only that Grimbald had had an unfortunate accident while out hunting.

Alice was beyond consolation. Hilda and Brigit went to extreme lengths to try to comfort her, but after a few days they concluded that she was experiencing not just grief but disintegration. Her face had slumped, her body had shrunk, her eyes were dull. She could not speak coherently and her memory had ceased to function. All they could do was sedate her with powerful herbal mixtures so that she slept for most of the time and hope she would recover eventually.

Alwyn and Brigit had taken Alice and Wulfhere into their home. Little Wulfhere was completely at a loss. He had effectively lost two fathers and now his mother within four months. He barely spoke. Alwyn's children took it upon themselves to try to distract and cheer up the little boy, but he was clearly suffering profound shock.

Meanwhile Aldrich and Mildred had been affected deeply by the events at Hatfield and since. They were in despair and felt virtually incapable of living alone, at least for the time being, and so Rinc and Hilda invited them into their own home.

* * * * * * *

'It really does feel like we've been cursed over the last few months: Wilfred, Godwyn and Edgar all dead at Hatfield; Aunt Bertha and my cousins back in Bernicia; and, just when things start to feel better, Grimbald is killed, Aunt Alice goes mad, and Great Uncle Aldrich and Great Aunt Mildred lose the will to live.'

Aelfred was speaking to Cadmon a couple of weeks after Grimbald's funeral. He continued after a brief pause, 'You know, I never felt entirely comfortable with Grimbald, but I really think he was right about why everything's been going wrong. He said the gods were punishing us for abandoning them and converting to Christianity. It sort of makes sense.'

'In fact,' Aelfred continued reflectively, 'I've been thinking that now Grimbald's gone there isn't a single adult left at Woden's Ford who really values the old ways. It's as if the song which was handed down from Woden through all our ancestors to Grandfather and Uncle Edgar is in danger of fading out. I know he was a bit tuneless, but Grimbald was the last singer. I don't think Father and Uncle Alwyn are that interested. They prefer the new song – Christian, Northumbrian, forward-looking. They expect Prince Oswald to defeat the Gwynedd occupiers and take Northumbria forward to a bright future.'

Aelfred glanced at Cadmon, nodded, and then, looking away and almost speaking to himself, said slowly and deliberately, 'I'm sure my purpose in life is to keep that old song going, to do everything to push back against Christianity.

That way I'll make Grandfather proud – which is what I promised at his funeral.'

Cadmon understood that ideas were crystallising in Aelfred's mind. For his own part, he was very aware of the thrill he felt whenever Gwynedd was mentioned. 'I do see the way you're thinking, Al,' he said. 'But remember it's not my song. I've learned all about the Anglian gods and rituals. But I don't feel the same way as you do about them.'

'I suppose you don't,' Aelfred replied, a little vaguely because he was engrossed in his own reflections. 'I sometimes forget you weren't born one of us.'

Chapter 17

634–635 AD

Aelfred reflects as he comes of age

'So, Aelfred, you see the sign carved on this tree – the circle with the stripe through it? This is where you turn off the main path and follow for some distance the other trees which have the same mark,' Father said.

It was my eighteenth birthday, in June 635. As promised, Father and Uncle Alwyn were showing me where the royal treasure was buried.

The three of us walked on for several hundred yards through the trees which grew together thickly. 'Here we are,' Uncle Alwyn said as we reached a very slight gap in the trees. 'Now, could you tell the most extraordinary collection of treasure is buried beneath these twigs and leaves?'

I shook my head, wonderingly.

'Good,' Father said. He then continued, 'There are two very heavy sacks buried deep in the ground. We're not going to dig them up just now. We come and check every so often they haven't been disturbed. We could tell immediately if anyone had got in. You can probably see among the twigs a few stones. They form a circle with a stripe through it. If that isn't more or less as we left it, we would dig down to check. We haven't actually needed to look at the treasure since we buried it nearly four years ago.'

As Father tidied up some of the stones which were slightly out of line I asked, 'D'you think King Oswald will come to retrieve it soon?'

'I doubt it,' Uncle Alwyn replied. 'We've told his courtiers about it, but they're more than happy for it to stay secure here for the time being.'

* * * * * * *

It was an exciting moment: I had often wondered where the treasure was hidden, and now I knew. It was a weighty secret, and I had promised Father and Uncle Alwyn – several times – that I would not tell anyone else about the treasure, let alone where it was hidden.

This was, though, the high point of a very low key eighteenth birthday. I had told Mother and Father that I didn't want any sort of celebration. They were not surprised even though eighteen is the next most important milestone on the journey to manhood after thirteen. They are well aware how much I have struggled since Hatfield, and so didn't push me to change my mind.

Matters have improved for Woden's Ford in many ways since Grimbald's death in February 634 even though I still feel extremely low.

Shortly after the funeral Father refused a request from King Osric's people to supply men for a campaign against the Gwynedd occupiers. A few weeks later we heard that King Osric had been killed when he launched an ill-fated attack on their position.

Deira was thus without a king.

It still seems remarkable to me that Woden's Ford survived the Gwynedd occupation unscathed even though we heard that other parts of Deira had been occupied and even laid waste. I have often thought about the exchanges at the clan council when Father suggested negotiation with Cadwallon's troops. In the following weeks he did go away on a couple of mysterious trips. He wouldn't be drawn on where he went, but I do wonder whether he reached some sort of agreement whereby supplies would be passed to the Welsh and he would refrain from supplying men to Osric – all in return for protection for Woden's Ford.

If so, it was pretty cunning given that at the same time Uncle Alwyn was secretly part of the Deiran campaign to support Prince Oswald's return.

Anyway, almost immediately after news of King Osric's death came through Father and Uncle Alwyn and a contingent of men from Woden's Ford headed in great secrecy towards Bernicia with other Deirans who were sympathetic to Oswald. They didn't know when and where he would strike, but they were certain by now that Prince Oswald would return from exile to try to claim the kingship of the whole of Northumbria.

Father told me that the Deiran contingent knew that Oswald would have to defeat King Cadwallon, who was also moving north, and so wanted to be on hand to offer support. Father said that the 200 or so Deiran men, moving as carefully as they could away from settlements and split into small groups to avoid attracting attention, headed towards

Bamburgh on the assumption that would be Oswald's ultimate destination.

It was an extremely anxious few weeks at Woden's Ford. Memories of the Hatfield disaster were still raw.

This time there was a very different ending.

Father and Uncle Alwyn returned triumphant with all the men they had taken with them. In the event they had not met up with Oswald prior to the battle, but it hadn't mattered. A combined force of Dalriadans and the Northumbrians who had been with Oswald in exile surprised Cadwallon at Heavenfield in Bernicia. The prince had apparently looked inspired. His soldiers had fought like men possessed. King Cadwallon was killed, the Welsh were routed, and very few of them got away.

King Oswald, as he now was, soon sat unchallenged in Bamburgh on the throne of a reunited Northumbria. He met the Deiran contingent and thanked them for their support. Father and Uncle Alwyn reckoned they had earned the favour of the new regime. This seemed to be confirmed when they were invited to meet the king when he visited York a few weeks later.

As we had all thought, the new king had become a committed Christian under the influence of the monks of Iona during his exile in Dalriada. He now expected the whole of Northumbria to follow his lead. Uncle Alwyn said the brand of Christianity Oswald had brought with him was very different from the Roman, Augustinian version Queen Aethelburg and Paulinus had brought from Kent. He thought it was humbler, less ostentatious, less hierarchical.

I wasn't entirely sure what Uncle Alwyn meant, but not

long before my birthday we heard a bit more about King Oswald's approach to Christianity. He has founded a new monastery on the island of Lindisfarne, just off the coast near Bamburgh. It will be led by Brother Aidan who has followed the king from Iona. For the monks Lindisfarne will apparently be just a starting point for their ministry. Uncle Alwyn expects they will soon be tramping the paths of Northumbria, spreading their gospel of love and humility and a classless society, and setting up sub-monasteries far and wide.

* * * * * * *

Oswald's victory enabled a sad departure from Woden's Ford.

Uncle Alwyn and Aunt Brigit had done their best to look after Aunt Alice and restore her to health, but after several months they decided that she was beyond recovery. She appeared to neither have any idea who or where she was, nor to be able to recognise anyone, even Wulfhere. On the rare occasions when she spoke she made no sense, and she barely had enough strength to leave the house. She looked incomparably different: aged, diminished, ravaged.

Once peace returned to Northumbria it was agreed that she should be taken back to her family home in northern Deira, and that Alwyn and Brigit should adopt Wulfhere. Mother accompanied her cousin on the journey so that she could explain the tragic circumstances of the last few months to their family.

When Mother returned to Woden's Ford she said that the family were contemplating sending Aunt Alice to a nunnery up in the far north run by the King's sister. This seemed cruel to me – effectively putting her out of sight and mind. But Mother explained that most nunneries have developed serious expertise in herbal remedies for all sorts of conditions, and that they could also provide security and an atmosphere of tranquillity: in both respects Aunt Alice could be cared for much better in a nunnery than at either Woden's Ford or at her family home.

The demise of Aunt Alice and Grimbald seems somehow to symbolise all that's gone wrong since Hatfield. They had stood out for me as larger than life characters in the impressionable years between boyhood and full manhood.

Aunt Alice had appeared to my eager eyes almost impossibly beautiful. My feelings towards her had been a tangle of new-found physical attraction, embarrassment, awe, and affection. She seemed to understand my confusion intuitively and was always kind to me – but I often found myself tongue-tied when she did speak to me!

My feelings towards Grimbald were even more complicated. He was a man of few words, but he had always taken an interest in me. I was a little afraid of his temper, but had admired his power, strength and good looks, his unashamed paganism, and his unorthodoxy. I had been secretly thrilled by the scandal which had gripped Woden's Ford when Alice moved in with him, but I had also been ferociously jealous of Grimbald.

In different ways I miss both Aunt Alice and Grimbald terribly.

Aunt Alice's departure was in some ways balanced a few weeks before my birthday by the return of Aunt Bertha and her two sons from Bernicia. Her daughter, the oldest of the three children, had married in Bernicia, but Bertha wanted her sons – who are a little younger than me – to grow up in their father's clan.

Aunt Bertha tends to lift spirits wherever she is. She is still, of course, coming to terms with Uncle Wilfred's death at Hatfield, but she has energy and spirit, and I know that both Mother and Aunt Brigit are really pleased to see her back.

An unexpected benefit of Aunt Bertha's return has been the bond which has developed between her and little Wulfhere. He had said little and hardly smiled for well over a year after Grimbald's death and Aunt Alice's collapse, but Aunt Bertha has already managed to draw him out of his darkness. He lives with Uncle Alwyn and Aunt Brigit, but spends as much time as he can following Aunt Bertha around: the sound of his giggling laughter is one of the signs of hope which has sprung up in recent months.

* * * * * * *

Most of the remaining adults at Woden's Ford feel much more settled and hopeful than they did eighteen months or so ago. The shadow of the loss of so many men at Hatfield still lingers, and Father and Uncle Alwyn are reluctant to talk about Hatfield at all – but Northumbria once again seems to be stable, progressive and outward-looking.

For the most part the arguments about Christianity seem to be over as well now that Oswald's victory has removed any uncertainty about the Royal position. With Great Uncle

Edgar and Grimbald dead no one at Woden's Ford is really opposed, although I think Father is more ambivalent than the other adults.

Uncle Alwyn is even planning to build a church in the main village at Woden's Ford. He's asked one of the Deiran priests – a man who worked closely with Bishop Paulinus, but then had to go in to hiding for a while after the Queen and Paulinus fled back to Kent – to come and be the priest in charge.

I'm much less settled and hopeful about the future: in fact, quite the reverse.

I was devastated by what happened at Hatfield and its aftermath. Life changed so fundamentally. I keep thinking back to how confident and happy I felt on my thirteenth birthday. It's as if I was a completely different person five years ago.

I know I can't have been easy to live with. I feel particularly bad for Cadmon who spends so much time with me, and so has borne the brunt of my negative feelings and bitterness. He's getting fed up with my assertion that the conversion to Christianity is to blame for all that's happened because he's heard it so often.

I've been anxious, irritable and have found it difficult to sleep. When I have slept, I've often had a recurring dream in which I return to the spot where we found Grimbald's body, but it comes back to life and starts to attack me.

As a result, it's been difficult to concentrate on my work with Father and Uncle Alwyn, and I've even started to doubt my worthiness to become chief.

I want to do something to make Grandfather proud, to try

to push back the Christian tide – but I've had real problems with motivation, and consequently feel guilty.

For the most part I've kept these feelings bottled up. I can put on a good act. I can play effectively the various parts expected of me, whether high-spirited young noble, the diplomat, the heir apparent. I know Father is pleased that I've learned all the skills required for a warrior and hunter, grasped the essentials of land management, and can hold my own socially in the company of noble visitors and on our occasional visits to court.

The conflict between my inner feelings and external expectations is a real strain in our culture where everyone is expected to be boisterous. I feel I must be careful about who sees the effects of the strain.

I know my relationship with Mother and Father has suffered over the last year or so, and that Father, in particular, is frustrated.

Father is now over forty. He's a respected noble and warrior and held in high esteem at court. Yet the eleven years since Grandfather's death have taken their toll in many ways. As an adult myself now I can see that the conflicts and dilemmas surrounding conversion, the pain and grief of Hatfield, and the tension and uncertainty of the years of occupation and partition must have presented countless challenges.

Father still works very hard, but he's definitely slower and greyer, and he looks tired much of the time. He doesn't like talking about it, but I know he's wrestling in very similar ways with inner tension: between the pull of the pagan lore and values of our ancestors, and the teaching of Christianity and the expectations of tribal loyalty to Oswald.

But whatever he thinks privately, Father believes there's no point in wasting energy trying to change things unless there's a good chance of success – and he thinks Christianity is the future, whether we like it or not. I'm looking for black and white and very reluctant to accept shades of grey. We've argued a few times about his expectation that for pragmatic, political reasons I present publicly as a Christian and suppress my pagan instincts.

Mother is also aging, although she still looks younger than she is. She's quiet by temperament, but the disappointment at only having one child has had a lasting effect. I think she's much more committed to Christianity than Father is, and so feels less inner tension about her beliefs, but she never seems particularly happy. We've talked occasionally about deeper things, but I suspect she's reluctant to try to influence me too much one way or another.

Chapter 18

635–637AD

An arranged marriage

'I think this is a great opportunity, Alwyn: we can sort the succession, help Aelfred to settle down and focus on the practicalities of life, and boost the standing of Woden's Ford all at the same time. It's perfect.'

Rinc was talking to Alwyn as they walked across the home meadows in September 635. The two brothers were assessing flood damage along the river caused by an autumn storm.

'Tell me again about the opportunity,' Alwyn said as he examined the riverbank carefully.

'Well,' Rinc replied, 'as you know, since Oswald came to the throne we've been rebuilding relationships with the south and Europe. Northumbria's a power once again, and the East Anglians are looking for allies against Penda. A few days ago, a noble from the East Anglian court called on his way to Bamburgh. It turns out he's a pretty big fish. He'd been sent with messages from his king to Oswald. He has a seventeen-year-old daughter – called Edith, I think – and he knew that we have an unmarried son. There's already a vague family connection – possibly one of the daughters from here in the generation before Eadwell was sent down there to marry.'

'The bottom line is he's floated the idea of marriage,' Rinc concluded. 'On the face of it he outranks us, but it's important for him to develop ties with Northumbria.'

'And what will Aelfred think?' Alwyn queried.

'I haven't spoken to him yet, but I wanted to see what you thought. He's such a moody boy. He thinks far too much. And I know how badly Hatfield affected him. I really hope responsibility and fatherhood will force him out of the clouds. I want him to lighten up, Alwyn. And you know I'm keen to settle the succession. I always worry that if anything happens to Aelfred the next generation will be the first since Eadrich in which the direct line of succession would be broken. I'm not, of course, blaming Hilda, but having only one son leaves us very exposed.'

'I know what you mean,' Alwyn said. 'And I do agree. Would you like my help in any way?'

'I'm glad you asked, Al,' Rinc smiled as he replied. 'I told our East Anglian friend we'd think about his offer and give him an answer when he returns on his way back from Bamburgh. I'd like you to go with Aelfred down to East Anglia, look the girl over – discreetly of course – and negotiate the dowry terms and the date of the marriage, but only if you think it's a runner. As usual, I want to make sure we don't take on a dud girl!'

Alwyn agreed readily. The brothers had a close and respectful relationship and had taken their responsibilities to the clan as Eadwell's only surviving sons very seriously since Hatfield.

Aelfred agreed, too. He was not enthusiastic about getting married to a girl he had never seen, probably from a Christian family, but he knew very well that this was the approach to marriage which had been handed down by his ancestors, and so he respected it as such.

* * * * * * *

'I can't say I was optimistic about the prospects for the marriage as we travelled down to East Anglia. You know very well what Aelfred's been like ever since Hatfield. Well, it was more of the same: why should I marry a Christian girl? What if Edith doesn't like me? Can't Father find a girl from Deira? And so on, and so on.'

Alwyn had arrived back from East Anglia the previous day and was telling Rinc about how they had got on.

'Anyway, he behaved well when we got there: polite, courteous, even charming from time to time. I think it helped that Edith's a good-looking girl. You've seen her now, and so you know what I mean: tall, willowy, handsome. I certainly had no doubts. You can never tell, of course, what'll happen in terms of children, but I didn't get any impression of poor health or other issues. I didn't warm to Edith, to be honest. She seems quite haughty. But I wasn't too worried about her personality. I'm sure they'll work things out between them.'

'So, we sorted out the dowry and the plans for the wedding quite quickly,' Alwyn continued. 'The return journey was more complicated, of course. Edith, her mother, and the two maids Edith decided to bring along were all with us. To be fair, Edith's family sorted out accommodation for us; but it was rather like them and us. Edith spent much more time talking to her mother and her maids than to me and Aelfred.

I suspect she's a bit nervous about moving away from home. It's understandable, I suppose.'

'Well, many thanks once again, Alwyn. You've done a great job,' Rinc said, smiling. 'I can't imagine Aelfred being enthusiastic about anything at the moment, but at least he's not objecting! I know he's not looking forward to being the centre of attention at the wedding – he's never been keen on all that – but he'll do his duty. He'll even grit his teeth and accept a Christian ceremony. We've fixed a date the week after next. We've invited everyone we think should be there. I'll be glad when it's over, too!'

* * * * * * *

'It's like everything imploded and my memory has become jumbled. I can remember the wedding, which I hated, but I can only remember bits and pieces after that. I know you and Mother and Father have tried to fill in the blanks – but please remind me again what happened – I still haven't quite grasped it all.'

It was spring 637, sixteen months after the wedding. Aelfred was talking quietly as he and Cadmon fished on the river near Woden's Ford on a sunlit afternoon. It was Aelfred's first outing since being able to leave his bed a couple of weeks previously.

'I can see you're struggling to take it in,' Cadmon said. 'It must be so strange to have big gaps in your memory. I just can't imagine what it's like. It really is a tragic tale, I'm afraid. I suppose that's why your memory has shut it out. So, here goes.'

'Things settled down for a while after the wedding,' Cadmon began. 'In fact, New Year 636 was pretty good. I hadn't seen you in such good form since Hatfield. You seemed to be enjoying married life. I'll be honest, I can't say I really liked Edith much. She was a bit too full of herself – as were her two maids. I think they all felt they'd taken a step down in coming to Woden's Ford. But I wasn't married to Edith, and I was pleased you seemed to be getting on fine.'

Cadmon hesitated, as if gathering himself for the next part of the tale, and then carried on, 'Then, of course, Edith got pregnant, and the problems began. She was very sick almost immediately, and it went on for months. I felt sorry for her at first. I began to lose sympathy as she complained every day about how much colder and damper it was in Woden's Ford than in East Anglia. It was homesickness, no doubt, but I think everyone got fed up with her moaning. Your mother was certainly impatient from time to time – which is very unlike her. I imagine she was nervous. I'm sure Edith's pregnancy brought back all sorts of memories of her own trauma with childbirth.'

Cadmon paused again, glanced at Aelfred who was listening intently, and then continued, 'Anyway, Edith's sickness stopped eventually, and we all relaxed; but then the little boy was born several weeks before full term. I don't think anyone expected him to survive, and sadly he died three days later. Edith was fighting a losing battle with heavy blood loss and shock, and she died the next day, too. Your father lost control altogether. His anger was genuinely shocking. It felt like the loss of his grandchild set off an outpouring of accumulated grief and frustration. It had probably built up with your mother's failed pregnancies.'

Cadmon told Aelfred that he had remained dignified and composed until Edith's funeral, but when he returned to Woden's Ford afterwards he collapsed on the floor and remained in bed raving and feverish for weeks.

'Man, you were right out of it – saying all sorts of crazy things, trying to talk to Woden, your grandfather, Jesus. It was pretty scary, I can tell you!' Cadmon concluded.

Aelfred nodded vaguely from time to time, a faraway look in his eyes. There was silence for a few minutes after Cadmon stopped speaking, and then Aelfred exploded.

'It's absolutely not fair – not fair at all!' he bellowed. 'All Mother's babies die, then grandfather dies, then everyone dies at Hatfield, Grimbald gets eaten by a wolf, then my wife and baby die!'

'Cool it, Alf, you'll scare away the fish,' Cadmon laughed, trying hard to lighten the mood.

'I don't care, f... the fish!' Aelfred screamed. 'It's all the fault of Christianity. We've angered Woden, we've angered Eadrich and all our ancestors. They've punished us for turning from the old ways, the old rituals. It's only going to get worse. Perhaps I should die, too.'

Cadmon had become used to the twists and turns of Aelfred's moods since Hatfield, but this outburst plumbed new depths. He tried again to soothe Aelfred, the fishing now completely abandoned even though the two young men still sat by the river. 'How can you blame Christianity, Al? Old men die, plenty of babies and women die in childbirth, and men often die in battle and are killed by wild beasts. That's just reality. Look, I know it's been tough. But your mother and father will find another nice Anglian girl. One day you'll become chief. Life's too short to spend all your time thinking about things you can't control and bemoaning the past.'

It cut no ice with Aelfred. 'You're so superficial, Cad. Life's so much more than sleep, work, eat, repeat. We're not animals. We've each got a destiny to fulfil. If we fail, we betray our ancestors. We have to find that destiny.'

* * * * * * *

There were variations on this conversation over the following weeks, but although Aelfred and Cadmon remained on good terms there was no meeting of minds. Gradually the conversations about what had happened and why became less frequent and then petered out altogether.

Cadmon hoped that this was a positive sign, that perhaps Aelfred was moving on. Deep inside Aelfred, though, the knot which twisted together resentment about everything that had happened to him since Hatfield, the anger he felt towards Christianity, and loyalty to his grandfather was transmuting into the kernel of an idea.

At last, he felt the spark of motivation. The shock of the death of Edith and his baby had threatened to plunge him even further in to despair; instead, it had, eventually, galvanised him into action.

As the kernel of the idea grew and took the embryonic shape of a plan Aelfred knew there would be risks. He knew he would be accused of betrayal and treachery. But he persuaded himself that what he was planning to do was in the best interests of Clan Eadrich. He shut his ears to the inner warnings.

Aelfred's resolve hardened when he found, shoved carelessly in a storage area, a tiny silver pendant figure of Woden. He knew it had belonged to his grandfather. He suspected that his parents had not wanted it on display any longer because it didn't fit with the prevailing Christian culture.

Aelfred put the pendant round his neck, careful to make sure it was always hidden. He felt closer to his grandfather and, through him, to his ancestors. He persuaded himself that it was a sign that what he was planning was in some way approved, even authorised, by his ancestors.

For the first time since Hatfield Aelfred felt as if he was emerging from the black clouds which had engulfed him.

Chapter 19

spring 637 AD

Cadmon intervenes

I'm worried about Aelfred.

I've known him virtually all my life. I'm his slave, but he's as close as any brother could ever be. It's saddened me to see him deteriorate in so many ways since Hatfield.

He was never an outgoing child, and always quite serious, but until Hatfield he had been generally happy. Since Hatfield, his eyes seem to have lost their sparkle. To be honest, he's looked miserable most of the time.

I want to do whatever I can to help him, but I don't know how much I can reasonably do as a slave.

That's the conundrum I've always faced.

I've grown up effectively as an Anglian, as part of a noble family, drenched in their ancient culture.

I'm part of the family; yet I'm not one of them.

I am a Wealas – Welsh, or a foreigner in Anglian parlance – as well as a slave; and for the Anglians, Wealas and slave are interchangeable terms.

Until Gwynedd's victory at Hatfield I had taken little interest in my roots, or indeed in anything beyond daily life. As I've grown into adulthood though – I'm now nineteen – the ambiguity of my position has become clearer, as has awareness of my 'otherness'.

Even so I can't get too excited about religion, kings, ancestry and all the other issues which Aelfred frets about so much. My work in helping to keep Woden's Ford running is demanding and absorbs a great deal of energy. I reckon it would do so whether the chief of the clan was Christian, pagan or any other religion.

I'm generally satisfied with my lot. I get on well with Aelfred, and with Rinc and Hilda, even though I'm enslaved to them. I've enjoyed sharing Aelfred's noble education, and as a result I'm now a skilled hunter and fighter.

Aelfred told me once Hilda has had a soft spot for me ever since she found my mother lying dead with me crying beside her. Hilda told Aelfred the shock had triggered instant remorse for the way in which she had treated my mother – even though she continued to blame Rinc for bringing my mother to Woden's Ford in the first place – and so she had persuaded Rinc to keep me in the main house.

I've always sensed that Rinc was a bit sceptical about the way Hilda treated me as more or less Aelfred's brother, but I guess he's never felt strongly enough to argue the point. He's certainly treated me well enough over the years.

I don't think often about the future. I assume one day Aelfred will become chief and I will continue to serve him, but that's as far as my speculation goes. Each day is full enough without expending excess energy thinking about 'what ifs'.

I recognise I'll probably not be able to marry for many years. There's a continual shortage of young women within the peasant communities around Woden's Ford because so many die in and around childbirth. Everyone accepts that older men – often widowed – are given first pick.

I do wish I had a more straightforward identity. I am tolerated by the Anglians but certainly not one of them: I would not, for example, be allowed to marry an Anglian woman. On the other hand, I don't fit easily into the peasant, servant and slave communities. Although I'm from native British stock I am, unfairly because I have had no choice, seen as trying to get above myself. I feel a bit resentful occasionally, but on the whole I get on well with plenty of individuals in all the communities in and around Woden's Ford.

I'm relieved that Aelfred has recovered slowly from Edith's death and the serious illness which followed. It was shocking to see him lose his memory, but it returned gradually.

I've been somewhat reassured by Aelfred's calmer demeanour recently, but I feel I must take the highly unusual step of talking confidentially to Hilda about my concerns. I know she likes me and so I'm confident she will listen; but, nevertheless, I'm always mindful of my status as a slave.

* * * * * * *

'Of course, Cad,' Hilda said when I asked if I could talk to her. 'What would you like to talk about?'

'Aelfred,' I replied.

'I thought he was on the mend,' Hilda said in surprise.

'He is, I think, but I'm worried he's becoming obsessed – about his destiny, about Christianity, about his grandfather. To be honest, he often seems a bit weird. It may just be a passing phase, but …' I tailed off.

'Umm, I do know what you mean, Cad,' Hilda said pensively. 'It is, I suppose, only four months since Edith died, and so it's perhaps not surprising he's still pretty upset. I'll have a word with him and try to find out if there's anything to it.'

'Thank you, Cadmon,' Hilda continued warmly. 'I know you care for Aelfred. You're very good for him. I'm glad you've shared your concerns. But, don't worry, I won't tell him you did so.'

I'm pleased that I took this step, and very grateful to Hilda for respecting my concerns.

Chapter 20

summer 637–spring 638 AD

Aelfred's plan develops

A few days later Hilda had the perfect opportunity to raise Cadmon's concerns in an entirely natural way. Aelfred was on his own, concentrating on sharpening his dagger, while she was doing needlework. 'How're you feeling now, Aelfred? I know it's been a tough few months. Is there anything in particular you're planning to do during the rest of the summer?'

'Not much,' Aelfred replied briefly. 'Mainly working with Father and Uncle Alwyn, I guess.'

There was silence. Hilda debated furiously with herself whether to leave matters, or to risk annoying Aelfred by probing a bit harder. She thought back to what Cadmon had said and decided to take the risk.

'And how about a bit longer term, son: you're twenty now, you must have some ideas?'

Aelfred didn't respond for a moment, but Hilda could see his shoulders tense as he continued to work on his dagger. Then he stopped, turned to face her, and said, 'Is this some sort of inquisition, Mother? Have Father and Uncle Alwyn put you up to 'having a talk' with me?'

'Of course not, Aelfred: I'm your mother, I'm hurting for you, and I'm interested in what you think,' Hilda said, glad to have provoked a reaction but working hard to channel it.

Aelfred's expression softened. He had never felt very close to his mother, but he appreciated the way in which she tried to arbitrate at times between him and Rinc. He decided to take the plunge. 'I'll tell you what I'm thinking about just now. "The fear of every human being is of our own meaninglessness and nothingness". It's something Uncle Alwyn heard from someone. It's really struck home. You know how badly Hatfield hit me. I still miss everyone. I felt doubly cursed when we lost Edith and the baby. I felt like giving up – just going into the hills like Grimbald did and letting a wolf kill me. I really did feel as if there was no point in going on. I was genuinely afraid that I'd descended into utter nothingness.'

Aelfred paused, then looked straight at Hilda, and said, 'But I don't want my life to be meaningless. I've a duty to our ancestors to make something of it. I want to make Grandfather proud. I know Father wants me to settle down, to learn all the ropes of being the chief, and to have some Anglian babies. I do get that. But there must be more to life. I'm trying to work out a purpose, but it's not easy.'

Aelfred stopped well short of revealing his determination to push back the tide of Christianity. He knew Hilda would be concerned, would probably tell Rinc, and that things could then get complicated. But he was glad that he had been able to express to his mother some of what he was feeling.

Hilda was touched – and grateful yet again to Alwyn for the efforts he had made over the last decade to support and guide her son. 'That's really profound, Aelfred,' she said. 'I do kind of know what you mean. I don't find it easy to choose between my heart, my duty, and respect for our ancestors –

or even to know which is which most of the time!'

'I wonder whether it'd help to go and talk to some other folk about these thoughts and the way you feel?' Hilda continued after a brief pause.

As she waited for Aelfred to reply an idea popped into Hilda's head. 'What about visiting the monks of Lindisfarne?' she asked. 'I've heard they're very fair and ready to listen. Going to see them wouldn't commit you to believing what they do – I know you're not keen on Christianity; but it might help you to test out some of your thoughts, just to get a different perspective.'

'Aren't the Lindisfarne monks a bit odd?' Aelfred asked. 'I admit I haven't met any of them, but even Uncle Alwyn says they're … let's say unusual.'

The Anglian nobles were intrigued and puzzled by the strange men who had come from the far west, and whose values, lifestyle, clothing and aspirations were so entirely opposite to their own.

Hilda laughed. 'Well, you can't necessarily judge people by how they look and what they wear. They're meant to be very spiritual people. King Oswald himself must rate them very highly since he brought them to Northumbria.'

'I know, that is puzzling,' Aelfred said. 'I'm worried they'll undermine everything we've stood for throughout so many generations. What will happen if we turn our backs on our heritage? I can't work out why our king wants to take that risk.'

They chatted for a while amicably enough and Aelfred promised he would consider his mother's suggestion – but it was not a promise he intended to keep.

* * * * * * *

'So, Father, do you think King Oswald will try to get revenge for Hatfield any time soon? Surely we're more powerful than Mercia and Gwynedd now and could give them a good beating?'

Alwyn's son, Raedwald, who was seventeen, had asked the question. It was October 637, exactly four years after the Battle of Hatfield. Raedwald and Alwyn, together with Rinc, Aelfred, and Wilfred's two sons, Hilderic and Eadmund, were standing together beside a large stone cairn in a field at Woden's Ford along with families from right across the clan territory.

Rinc had established the collective memorial to the men of Woden's Ford who had perished at Hatfield soon after the battle since none of the bodies had been recovered. He had also instituted the annual ceremony of remembrance on the anniversary of the battle.

'I suspect war with Mercia is in Oswald's plans at some point, Raedwald,' Alwyn replied, 'but it's probably not imminent. You're right – Northumbria under Oswald has regained much of its strength. Alliances are being built with other kingdoms. Probably the most important is with the kingdom of Wessex to the south of Mercia. If Northumbria were to co-ordinate an attack with Wessex, then Mercia would be caught in the middle.'

'Do you think he *should* seek revenge, Uncle Alwyn?' Aelfred asked. 'Surely as a committed Christian he should forgive his enemies, not seek revenge?'

'It isn't an easy issue, Aelfred, I accept that,' Alwyn said thoughtfully. 'You're right about the expectation of forgiveness; but there's also an acceptance in Christianity that we live in a flawed world where people are less than perfect. I think war can be justified where the benefits might be expected to outweigh the bad consequences. And, trust me, war is brutal, and so many of its consequences are very bad indeed.'

Alwyn paused, as if considering his next words even more carefully, and then said, 'I believe the removal of King Penda in particular, who is a violent pagan, and the conversion of Mercia to Christianity would be worthwhile causes for war. Personally, I'm not sure revenge on its own would be a sufficient motive.'

'But surely we have the right to take revenge,' Hilderic said: he was the older of Wilfred's sons, also seventeen. 'All these men we've remembered today, including my father, were killed at Hatfield by Penda and Cadwallon. I know King Cadwallon got his comeuppance at Heavenfield; why shouldn't Penda suffer, too?'

There was a brief silence, as if no one wanted to attempt an answer. It was broken by Rinc. 'I'd have agreed with you when I was your age, Hilderic, I really would,' he said reflectively. 'It's perfectly natural in many ways to want to avenge your father's death. But now I can see we should think hard before getting into a cycle of tit for tat. I know our ancestors glorified war as an end in itself; but, as Uncle Alwyn says, war is so brutal and incredibly disruptive. The last four years would probably have been so much better for all of us if Hatfield hadn't happened. Why should we risk a repeat – or inflict the same sort of suffering on the ordinary people of Mercia – unless there was a very good reason?'

Rinc paused, looked to the heavens as if seeking inspiration, and then concluded, 'Having said all of that, I do agree with Uncle Alwyn. I think there's a good case for war with Mercia. And I suspect, sooner or later, our king will launch an attack on King Penda.'

There was silence for a couple of minutes, and then Eadmund – the youngest in the group, at fifteen – asked, a little timidly, 'Can you tell us what it was like at Hatfield, Uncle Alwyn and Uncle Rinc?'

Alwyn and Rinc looked at each other: Alwyn took a deep breath; Rinc shook his head.

'That's very difficult, Eadmund,' Alwyn replied, speaking slowly. 'It's almost impossible for those of us who've been involved in a major battle to convey what it's really like to those of you who haven't. I think Uncle Rinc would agree, much of Hatfield was so awful that it's as if our memories are closed off. I certainly can't remember much at all about the day.'

All four of the younger men looked sombre; Aelfred sensed that his three cousins were itching to ask more, but Alwyn's tone and the look on his face deterred them. There was a haunted look in his eyes which Aelfred had not seen before.

Aelfred, although only twenty, felt that his cousins by comparison were immature, and that this was reflected in their simplistic urge towards revenge. Wilfred's sons, in particular, had been through the trauma of losing their father, yet Aelfred believed that his own experiences, taken together, had been more difficult and had brought an unusual level of maturity.

Aelfred was unhappy. He knew that alone among the Anglo-Saxon kingdoms Mercia was holding fast to its pagan legacy. Based on what he had heard he admired Penda: to Aelfred there was simple logic and collective strength in the old pagan ways of ancestor worship, the quest for wealth and power, and trust in arms.

Aelfred did not want the Northumbrians to be defeated, but neither did he want to see Penda toppled and Mercia forced to become Christian. He kept these doubts to himself; but they provided further nourishment for his developing, still secret, plan.

* * * * * * *

For the next few months Aelfred got on with his duties in and around Woden's Ford. He supported his father and uncle as they managed the clan lands, ensured tributes were paid, and oversaw the peasants and slaves.

He went away for a few weeks in early 638 on his first military mission in King Oswald's army: a raid against the Picts beyond the far north of Northumbrian territory. He enjoyed it, but was glad to get back. 'It was so cold. I think I was more at risk from the ice and frost than from the enemy!' he told Cadmon.

Aelfred was reserved, but he had always been, and so no one suspected anything was amiss – or, if they did, they attributed it to lingering grief. He did not speak anymore, not even to Cadmon, about the continuing pain and resentment he felt.

Hilda watched closely. She, too, felt that Aelfred was settling down even though he did not seem to be planning to follow up her suggestion to go to Lindisfarne.

Yet deep within, nourished by the pain and resentment, Aelfred's secret plan continued to grow.

* * * * * * *

'Let's do that again, Aunt Bertha!' Wulfhere shouted excitedly.

'Right you are, young man, you're driving me hard, but it's fun – I think!' Bertha laughed breathlessly.

The eight-year-old boy and forty-year-old woman whirled back among the whooping and cheering dancers as the flames from the bonfire leaped into the night sky.

Watching on, Bertha's two sons rolled their eyes in embarrassment. 'What is she like?' Eadmund groaned, but he was grinning, too. Bertha's love of life and sheer enthusiasm were infectious.

It was Easter 638. The Christian priest whom Alwyn had installed in Woden's Ford had led a sunrise vigil and an Easter service. Eggs had been boiled, painted and rolled. Now, in the spring evening, there was a bonfire, music and dancing.

'It doesn't feel all that different to the old celebrations of spring,' Bertha mused, still breathing hard, as she came up to Hilda and Brigit. Wulfhere had gone off to find other amusement. 'The Christian service has been added on, but everything else is more or less the same. I don't really mind so long as we can enjoy life and celebrate.'

'I agree!' Hilda said fervently. 'By the way, Bertha, it's so good to see the way you go on with Wulfhere! He's so much happier now than in those early months after Alice became ill. You've really made such a difference by spending time with him.'

'I often wonder how Alice is getting on in that nunnery in Coldingham way up in the north of Northumbria,' Hilda continued. 'I guess it's a couple of years now since my uncle took her up there. It must be a pretty good nunnery if the king's sister's in charge. But I can't imagine she'll ever come out. It just seems such a waste of a life.'

None of the women said anything for a few moments, each lost in their own thoughts. Bertha then suddenly broke down in a paroxysm of sobs. Hilda and Brigit looked at each other in consternation and then, without saying a word, both put their arms around their sister-in-law. Bertha couldn't say anything as the sobs shook her body. After a few minutes the other two women led her away to her own home.

Bertha calmed down gradually, and said, 'Thank you both so much. I feel so pathetic. It's just with all the talk about resurrection and new life it quite suddenly struck me how much I still miss Wilfred. The mention of Alice somehow reminded me what we all lost at Hatfield. You'd have thought after four and a half years I'd be used to widowhood. For the most part I am; but occasionally I feel the loss and the loneliness so much.'

Bertha glanced at the two other women, as if to check they were still listening. They both nodded, and she continued, 'When I came back to Woden's Ford in 635 I was determined, for the boys' sake, to put the past behind us and look to the future. That's why I've never really talked about what happened after Hatfield. It was so terrifying and so bewildering. To lose your husband and your children's father is bad enough: to have to leave your home at short notice and travel ninety miles with the constant fear that marauding enemy soldiers might attack made matters even worse.'

Bertha paused, closed her eyes briefly as if to review the memories in her mind, and then carried on, 'The children were, of course, very unsettled. They were essentially Deiran but were plunged suddenly into a Bernician culture. Some kids teased them about their accents. Adults questioned them – and me – about where our loyalty lay. It felt really ironic. As you well know, Grimbald and others had kept on about me being a Bernician 'outsider' here for years; now some Bernicians wondered whether I had become a Deiran!'

Hilda and Brigit let Bertha talk, sensing her need to unburden. Eventually she paused, and then said, 'I'm sorry for rambling on like that, you've listened very patiently. I know I wasn't the only one to suffer as a result of Hatfield. I'm so grateful to you all for welcoming me back. It's great the boys now feel they have a home and a secure identity. But I'm worried by the way they're getting caught up in all the talk of revenge. It's not surprising in some ways they want to avenge Wilfred. But I fear we may be heading for another Hatfield. It was bad enough to lose my husband – I really don't want to lose my sons.'

There were tears in the eyes of all three women. Instinctively they clasped each other in a wordless hug which seemed to go on forever.

* * * * * * *

As spring advanced Aelfred suspected that Rinc and Hilda were hatching a new plan for his future. His suspicion materialised one day as he rode with Rinc.

'Look Aelfred, I know how awful Edith's death was for you,' Rinc said. 'All credit to you for getting on with life over the last year. But we've been thinking about a new wife for you. A family in Bernicia has made contact because they have a daughter of eighteen. They're relatives of Aunt Bertha. They're very well thought of by King Oswald, and they've got lots of land and wealth. I'd like us to go there to meet the girl. It'd be a great connection for Woden's Ford.'

For Aelfred, this was the spur for him to take his secret plan to the next stage and prepare to implement it.

'Of course, Father,' he replied quickly. 'I can see the sense in that. But there are some things I'd like to do over the summer, so perhaps we could put off the trip until about September?'

Rinc was surprised, he had expected some resistance – so equally quickly he said, 'That's fine, son; I'll be interested to hear about your plans.'

'Yes, I'll talk to you and Mother soon about what I want to do; there are a few things I'm thinking about,' Aelfred said.

Chapter 21

spring/summer 638 AD

Aelfred implements his plan

My mind raced over the next few days as I refined my plan and went over it again and again.

Cadmon and I had talked often about emulating the trip around the Deiran borders which Grandfather and Great Uncle Edgar had made as young men.

So, I planned: to tell Cadmon that we would make the trip in the summer – I knew he would be delighted; then tell my parents that we would start the expedition in mid-July and that it would take a few weeks; but as soon as we left Woden's Ford, ostensibly to start the trip, I planned to tell Cadmon that we were going to do something completely different.

I knew the royal treasure was still buried in the woods near Woden's Ford. When we left Woden's Ford I planned to dig it up and move it a few miles to a new location in the hills. We would then make our way south, disguised as itinerant metalworkers, travelling by night for the most part off the old Roman roads, to the court of King Penda of Mercia around 150 miles away.

I aimed to buy my way into Mercian service by telling them about the treasure hoard, take Mercian representatives back to collect it, and then act as an intermediary between

Mercia and Northumbria. I wanted to avoid war; but, above all, if there were war, I wanted my clan to return to the old ways – of Grandfather, of Eadrich, of Woden – and to be on the Mercian side.

I planned to remove a precious item from the hoard before I reburied it so that when I got to Penda's court I could use it to convince them of my integrity. I would also tell Cadmon that on reaching Mercia he would be a free man although I hoped he would choose to remain in my service.

I was convinced my plan would work; yet my conscience was deeply unsettled. I lay awake regularly at night arguing with the inner voices which accused me of planning to betray my kin and my king. They asked what would happen if the Mercians didn't believe my story, and also asked how my family would react if the Mercians did believe me, and I then returned as a thief and an emissary of an enemy kingdom.

The voices in my head became louder as the days went by precisely because I couldn't talk to anyone about my internal conflict; but I felt I had answered the questions and so blocked out the voices.

By early July, our overt preparations for the Deiran border expedition were well in hand: Cadmon was excited; and Mother and Father were pleased that I was acting so positively and fitting in with their plan for what they regarded as an excellent marriage.

Simultaneously I prepared to implement my real plan. I found an ideal spot to re-bury the treasure. I then traced a route from the current hiding place to the new location a few miles away in the hills which would be very difficult to track even with dogs once the loss of the treasure was discovered.

I had also mapped out in my head a possible route towards Tamworth, the capital of Mercia. This was based on conversations with traders from Mercia over the last couple of years, and with one of King Oswald's spies who had explored routes to the south extensively and who I had met on a visit to court.

Finally, on a sunlit July afternoon we set off: the good wishes of my family rang in my ears; pangs of conscience twisted uneasily in my stomach.

Within an hour I had told Cadmon that there was a change of plan, that he was to follow my instructions exactly, and that I would explain everything to him the next morning.

Chapter 22

Cadmon's Questions

'So, you're going to free me? But first we're going to walk to Mercia, persuade some of King Penda's folk to come back with us to retrieve the treasure, and then convince your family to join the Mercians?'

Aelfred nodded in reply to Cadmon's questions. 'That's the plan,' he said.

Aelfred and Cadmon had taken it in turn to sleep, keep watch and eat throughout the day after their night of digging up and re-hiding the treasure; now, in mid-evening, they were preparing to set off.

'Are you sure we're not in a dream, Al?'

'Nope, this is it, Cad: we're really going to make a difference. We're going to make Grandfather and Uncle Edgar proud,' Aelfred said heartily.

The weather had turned from sunny and warm to misty and chilly. Aelfred, for all his cheeriness, felt as though some of the mist had seeped into his soul. He expected to feel excited, enervated: instead, he felt isolated.

Anglians were brought up to think collectively: they were members of the tribe first, individuals second. This was an unnerving situation for Aelfred. The thought crossed his mind that it was not too late to turn back, rebury the treasure in its original place, embark on the Deiran border trip, and then return dutifully to Woden's Ford – but he quickly pushed it aside, as he had all his doubts over the last few weeks and months.

'Right, let's go: Mercia, here we come!' Aelfred said determinedly as they shouldered their packs. There were two or three hours of daylight left, but the woods afforded plenty of shelter from any curious eyes. The two men were expert in woodcraft, and so, even when darkness fell, they were able to make steady if slow progress.

Aelfred had given as full an explanation of his plans as he possibly could, but Cadmon had plenty of questions as they walked: about the treasure, about the route, about the risks, about how they would contact Penda's men.

Most of all Cadmon probed repeatedly Aelfred's motives. 'Why, Al, why? You have it all: heir to a great clan, prospect of a good marriage, already well known at court, a huge and loyal extended family. You're giving it all up, betraying your family – for what? I really, really don't get it.' Even in the twilight Cadmon's bafflement was evident.

'I can see from the way you're looking at me you don't get it,' Aelfred said. 'I'm sorry, I realise it's been a huge surprise. You've only had a few hours to get used to it. I've been thinking about it for months. I guess the idea's been growing inside me ever since Grandfather's funeral, fourteen years ago. I know I was only seven, but I made a vow of loyalty then to honour him and our ancestors. I genuinely do not believe Father and the rest are doing the same.'

Aelfred stopped walking, turned to face Cadmon, and said slowly, his tone of voice as serious as the expression in his eyes, 'I think it's my destiny to protect Woden's Ford from

Christianity, just as King Penda is protecting Mercia. That's far more important to me than wealth and power. I really believe, however bad it looks, I'm doing the best for Woden's Ford.'

'Can you not see that, Cad?' Aelfred asked, almost pleadingly, as he finished speaking.

'Not at the moment, I'm really struggling to make sense of it all,' Cadmon replied thoughtfully as they began walking again.

They fell silent as darkness gathered; with no moonlight their going slowed as they tried to keep a south-westerly line through the woods.

Cadmon did not stop puzzling though. He was shocked. He had trusted Aelfred throughout their lives. He had known that his moods were erratic, that he could be very intense, and that he had strong views; but he had never thought to question his loyalty to his clan and his king and the openness between them that had existed since their cradles.

Cadmon had been looking forward to the boundary expedition. He loved the outdoors, hunting and living in the wild. Initially the excitement of seeing the treasure and the novelty and mystery of what they had done overnight had blotted out his disappointment at the sudden change of plan; but once the adrenalin had ebbed away, disappointment and incomprehension had overwhelmed him.

Cadmon was hurt by Aelfred's secretive behaviour. He was also wondering whether Aelfred's grievances had clouded his judgement. The plan seemed to Cadmon outlandish, bizarre and fraught with risk. He liked the idea of becoming a free man, but he wasn't sure he could trust Aelfred to deliver. He wondered whether all the serious setbacks Aelfred had suffered over the last five years had undermined his ability to think rationally.

For the first time in his life Cadmon began, very tentatively, to contemplate the possibility of life away from Aelfred.

Chapter 23

Camp Woden

For the next four days and nights the two men made steady but slow progress. They concentrated on navigation, gathering and preparing food, walking by night, and alternately sleeping and watching by day.

They talked relatively little, and then mainly about practicalities and the route. They managed to keep to old, little-used paths and tracks and camped by day in secluded spots. They saw no one.

They knew they had probably crossed from Deira into the kingdom of Elmet, although there was no indication of any border crossing or other change in the landscape. Elmet had been essentially a Northumbrian tributary kingdom since its defeat by King Edwin almost twenty years previously. Aelfred and Cadmon reminisced about the stories Great Uncle Edgar had told of the campaign in Elmet – one he said that he had especially enjoyed because it had been a relatively easy victory for the Northumbrians.

By the early morning of day five, as they settled down after their night-march, they calculated that they had covered around fifty miles – still well under half of their journey. After they had eaten and talked briefly about the plan for the next night Cadmon fell asleep.

Aelfred was on first watch. It was a pleasant morning. The

gentle sun threatened to lull him to sleep as he sat against a tree. To keep his mind active he went over, once more, what he would say when he gained access to Penda's court.

Suddenly, inexplicably, every cell in his body seemed to tingle. Consciously he had heard and seen nothing, but he sensed a presence. He was alert to danger. Without making any overt movement Aelfred's hand closed on the hilt of his dagger and he tried to scan his surroundings.

He still saw nothing – until three men stepped out from the trees with arrows trained on him.

The middle of the trio was obviously the leader. He was of medium height and build, quite a few years older than Aelfred, and had close-shaved, reddish hair and grey-blue eyes. What struck Aelfred most forcibly was the authority which oozed intangibly from every pore.

Aelfred locked eyes with the leader for a short period which, to Aelfred, seemed very long.

Aelfred broke the silence, 'Who are you?' he asked.

'You need to give answers, not me,' snapped back the leader. Aelfred understood the words, but the accent and dialect were strikingly different from what he was used to in Deira. He guessed that the man was from Mercia having heard Mercian guests and traders at Woden's Ford and elsewhere.

'We're metal workers, travelling from Deira and looking for work in nobles' halls; we're between jobs at the moment,' Aelfred replied.

'So, why are you travelling at night through the woods rather than by day on main routes?' the leader barked. It quickly became clear that these men had been following their

200

movements closely for some time, and so it would be point-less to try to bluff.

Cadmon stirred from his sleep and looked up blearily. The leader shifted his gaze towards Cadmon. 'I think you're fleeing justice for some reason. You will come with us.' This wasn't an invitation. Aelfred and Cadmon were frog-marched away, bound and blind-folded so that they could not remember the route.

They walked for an hour or so through the forest, their captors entirely silent. 'Here we are,' announced the leader eventually, removing the blindfolds. 'Camp Woden.'

Thirty or forty shelters were spread amongst the trees and men and women were going busily about what appeared to be a variety of daily chores. To Aelfred and Cadmon it looked ordered, calm and reasonably well-established. They were motioned to a tent which was larger than most and obviously belonged to the leader.

'So,' he said, 'let me tell you about ourselves, and then we can get back to your story.' The leader – he never told them his name – explained that he and most of his companions were Mercian and that some were from Northumbria. They were all young men of Anglo-Saxon origin who wanted to preserve their heritage and build on it. They wanted to create a new kingdom of warriors completely loyal to Woden.

They had left their clans because they were fed up with the compromises and alliances with native kings and Christian-ity. The leader had left Mercia because he disagreed funda-mentally with Penda's alliance with the Christian Welsh against fellow Anglo-Saxon kingdoms. He said he'd heard that Penda was himself actually half-Welsh.

He said that Camp Woden was a model of the new way, and also a foundation for growth in population and territory. 'We're looking all the time for other men who want and will fight for change,' the leader explained. 'We want folk who're prepared to leave behind the existing kingdoms, who are utterly loyal to Woden, and who want to be part of a new kingdom.'

The leader's eyes shone. He spoke passionately. He had turned from captor to salesman. 'So, what d'you think? Will you join us? If you do, we'll not tell anyone about your escape from justice.'

Aelfred was both interested and repelled.

He disliked the man's arrogant, self-centred style; but what he had said had struck some chords. After all, Woden's Ford had developed over the last 300 years through an explicit aim to ensure that control of the clan's lands lay with men and women of Anglian stock. Aelfred himself wanted to see the Anglo-Saxon kingdoms unite on the basis of a commitment to ancient pagan values and the worship of Woden himself.

Yet there was something in the leader's attitude which did not sit right. There was a hint of, at best, suspicion of native people. Aelfred had heard rumours of organised persecution of native people elsewhere, but as far as he knew there had never been any violence or repression of natives in or around Woden's Ford purely because they were natives.

Aelfred was tempted, fleetingly, to join the band and contribute the buried treasure to the cause; but the unease he had experienced as he had listened to the leader far outweighed his tentative interest. He concluded that the man's ambition had blinded him to practicality: there was no way that Camp

Woden was the basis for turning any dream into reality.

'Thanks for the invitation, but we have work to do, and we want to get on with it,' Aelfred said as politely as he could manage.

The Leader switched instantly from salesman back to captor. 'As I said, I think you're escaping justice and the metalworker disguise is a cover story. Why else would you be travelling through the forest at night?'

Aelfred sensed the unpredictability of the man, his carelessness of others' lives; but after a tense exchange of denials by Aelfred and threats by the leader the latter suddenly seemed to lose interest. 'Go on your way then; whoever you are, you're obviously not our type. We want people who'll be committed to the cause. I'll get a couple of the men to blindfold you and take you back to where we found you.'

Chapter 24

A delay

Cadmon had been badly shaken by the encounter with the band of outlaws. He was well aware that the Eadrich clan had an explicit Anglian – or at least Anglo-Saxon – marriage policy: but oddly this had never seemed threatening either to him as a native, or, as far as he could tell, to those who worked on the land across the clan territory, most of whom were originally British.

But Cadmon wondered whether this could change. He knew that Anglo-Saxons held sway – in Northumbria and in many other areas – and that for the most part the native population were subordinate. Could subordination turn to something more sinister?

Cadmon was relieved that Aelfred had not wanted to throw in his lot with the outlaws – but he had sensed his hesitation. Could there be darker depths in the man he had known for twenty years? He was beginning to wonder how events might unfold if they ever did get to Mercia.

The pair didn't get much sleep after the outlaws had left them, not least because a large part of the day had passed by then. They set off on the next stage of the journey at around twilight as usual. They spoke a little about their experience at the hands of the outlaws, but Cadmon kept most of his thoughts to himself. He was growing more and more wary of

Aelfred. In any case they needed to concentrate hard on the route and on what was around them as darkness fell on the forest.

Aelfred had complained about tiredness when they had set off, but by the early hours he was obviously labouring. 'I feel awful, Cad,' he said. 'I'm exhausted and a bit shivery; we might need to stop sooner than we planned.'

'We can stop whenever you like,' Cadmon replied wearily, stifling a yawn. 'I could certainly do with more sleep, too.'

They went on for another half hour or so, at which point Aelfred slumped to the ground. 'I'm going to have to stop here,' he moaned. 'I need to sleep.'

Cadmon was alarmed, especially as Aelfred was asleep within two or three minutes. He covered him with his cloak and considered next steps – which weren't at all obvious. Dawn was, however, just beginning to break and so he was able to investigate the surroundings relatively easily. They were close to a junction of forest tracks, and one of them looked like a route to a settlement. Cadmon suspected it wasn't far away.

Cadmon decided that he must risk leaving Aelfred, try to find help, and hope that it wouldn't take long. He tucked him up as best as he could, and then ran down the track. Fortunately, a village was just twenty minutes away and there were early morning signs of life: a couple of dogs were barking, a cockerel was trumpeting, and two men were collecting water from a well.

Cadmon shouted as he approached – to signal he was coming peacefully and thus avoid having hounds set on him. The men looked round. They seemed surprised, but not particularly perturbed, which Cadmon took as a good sign. One of the men spoke, but in the native language. Ironically Cadmon had never needed to learn any language other than Anglian: the natives around Woden's Ford had long since adopted it as their first and for the most part only tongue.

Cadmon motioned his incomprehension and the man switched – albeit not fluently – to a Germanic language which he could understand. Cadmon explained that he was a travelling metalworker and that his companion had fallen sick in the forest. The men could easily have been suspicious, but they accepted Cadmon's story and offered help immediately. They got hold of a bedroll and stretcher, and the three men then hurried back along the track.

Aelfred had just woken up when they got back and was looking round groggily. Cadmon explained where he had been and introduced the two villagers. They said that they would take Aelfred back to the village and that he and Cadmon could both stay while he got well. Aelfred was in no position to argue: he conceded readily that he could not go on at the moment. He was sweating visibly and looked pale.

Once in the village Aelfred was taken into the wooden home that one of the men shared with his wife and two young children. He talked to his wife while she nodded and looked from Aelfred to Cadmon. They quickly found a space where Aelfred could lie comfortably.

The other man, whose name was Ceretic, said that Cadmon could stay in his home and led him there. His wife spoke virtually no Anglian, but she smiled broadly and repeatedly to assure Cadmon of her welcome.

Ceretic told Cadmon that they were in the village of Helme in Elmet. He offered to show Cadmon round and introduce him to the other villagers after he had eaten. A young woman, perhaps two years younger than Cadmon, came in at that point and Ceretic introduced her as his daughter, Dora.

Dora spoke to her father and he nodded. Ceretic translated, 'Dora would like to accompany us if that's all the same with you'.

'That's absolutely fine by me,' Cadmon replied

Dora smiled, and then said in the same Germanic dialect her father had used, but a little more haltingly, 'I would really appreciate it if you could also help me with your language. It would be good to have some conversation with a fluent speaker.'

'Of course,' Cadmon said, 'although you seem to speak the language fairly well already.' She laughed self-deprecatingly.

Ceretic and Dora were ideal guides. They loved Helme, were eager to tell Cadmon everything about it, and were popular throughout the village.

Ceretic was dark-haired, bearded and taller than average for a native British man. He was in his late thirties and seemed to have abundant energy and an inexhaustible sense of humour.

Dora was short and sturdy; her hair was neither fair nor dark but had a hint of red; she had a round face and green/brown eyes which seemed to dance and sparkle. She had an infectious sense of humour, was curious about Deira, and wanted to know all about Cadmon.

By the end of the introductory tour Cadmon felt he knew

everyone in the village, and that Ceretic and Dora knew a great deal about him.

Helme was a compact settlement which, Ceretic said, was home to about 100 people, all of them related in one way or another. He didn't have any idea how long Helme had existed, but he said that memories of life in the settlement had been handed down from many previous generations.

'Has there been much change since Elmet became part of the kingdom of Northumbria?' Cadmon asked.

'Not much in our daily routines, to be honest,' Ceretic said. 'We realised there was some fighting, but none of us was involved. We don't travel far on the whole, and we don't get many visitors. Life has just rolled on! The biggest change has been Anglo-Saxon settlements springing up in the area in the last decade or so. I guess some of the settlers came from Northumbria. It's worked out quite well so far. They seem fairly decent neighbours. Most of us have learned their language, and there's plenty of coming and going. As far as I know, there haven't been any major difficulties.'

'I'm not sure I entirely agree, Father,' Dora said, firmly but not argumentatively. 'There's nothing particularly wrong, but they do seem quite harsh people. You know, a bit selfish. They never try to learn any of our language, for example. And they can be very cruel, even to their own people who they think are abnormal in some way or have broken quite minor rules. But I know more of them will probably come. That's why I want to get better at their language. We need to build bridges.'

'Have you come across a band of Anglian outlaws?' Cadmon asked, describing the men they had met in the forest.

Dora half-closed her eyes as she thought, and then said, 'I think there've been one or two encounters when our men have been out hunting. There've also been rumours that a girl from another village may have been kidnapped by them. That's definitely worried some people although no one seems to be very sure what happened. She just disappeared.'

'A few of our folk worry that the Anglo-Saxons may try to take our land and turn us all into slaves; but most of us are not that concerned,' Dora concluded.

Ceretic glanced quickly at Cadmon and then nodded, 'I do know what you mean, Dora. They're not the easiest neighbours, but they're not too bad.'

The villagers were Christian and worshipped at a small chapel just outside Helme, but from what Cadmon could gather they appeared to combine their Christianity with rites and rituals handed down from pre-Christian times – and even seemed to have borrowed some aspects of their neighbours' old pagan practices.

* * * * * * *

The next day Aelfred was no better – if anything he was worse. He appeared to have contracted a particularly virulent fever. Aelfred's hosts and Ceretic and his family were adamant that Aelfred and Cadmon should stay until Aelfred was well enough to resume the journey. They appeared to have no qualms about hosting indefinitely two young men who on the face of it were Anglo-Saxon and who didn't speak their language.

In return Cadmon offered to help with tasks around the village. Life revolved around farming and hunting and the daily round of household and communal chores. Cadmon got the impression of a way of life which had continued relatively undisturbed for centuries. Cadmon's offer was taken up readily: he was detailed to fetch and chop wood from the forest to help to build up the winter store.

Dora was eager to spend as much time as she could with Cadmon over the next few days – and he was more than happy to oblige.

'I really like her, Al,' Cadmon said as he and Aelfred walked together one afternoon. Aelfred was trying to rebuild his strength before they resumed their journey to Tamworth. 'I've never felt this way about a girl before: we seem to think in the same way, and get on so well. She's good fun and really thoughtful; and she's curious to learn more about the wider world. I'll be sad to say goodbye.'

'You want to be careful, Cad; she'll be lined up to be married to another bloke, perhaps in another village. They won't want her messing around with someone they think's an Anglian,' Aelfred warned.

'I haven't noticed any suspicion; in fact, the whole village seems incredibly relaxed and kind. I almost wish we could stay!' Cadmon replied.

* * * * * * *

In the end Aelfred and Cadmon had to stay in Helme for almost two weeks. Aelfred hardly stirred for several days; it took him several more to regain sufficient strength to carry on the journey.

They were both deeply impressed by the villagers' easy hospitality and their willingness to welcome them into their lives, however temporarily. Both Cadmon and – once he began to recover – Aelfred particularly enjoyed the informal gatherings after the evening meal.

The weather was good and the evenings still long. Groups of neighbours would get together, begin by talking about the events of the day, and then often reminisce about the past. Some evenings games were played, other times there was singing. Every evening there was mead, ale and lively humour.

It dawned on Aelfred that the villagers' reminiscences were almost all parochial and domestic: they did not seem to have been involved in many events beyond the village and its locality, or at least the memories of any such events were relatively unimportant to them.

Aelfred reflected that in his clan the vast majority of tales revolved around battles, feuds and raids. He found himself quite liking the peaceful rhythm and narrative in Helme in spite of the villagers' Christian allegiance; but he wasn't yet ready to say this out loud.

'It's such an ordinary life here, just the same day after day. It must get pretty tedious,' Aelfred said to Cadmon one day as they talked about how they were finding life in Helme.

'Isn't that the same for most folk most of the time?' Cadmon asked in reply. 'Surely it was much the same at Woden's Ford. At least here they don't seem to talk endlessly about fighting. That must surely be a good thing.'

'But what's the purpose? That's what we all need – an opportunity to make a difference, change things,' Aelfred mused.

'What, like those outlaws in the forest? I think I prefer a peaceful life of honest toil than one dominated by hatred and planning for war.' Cadmon couldn't keep an edge out of his voice. He had heard Aelfred often enough talk about 'purpose', but he still felt raw from their recent encounter at Camp Woden.

The two men pulled back from what was threatening to become an irritable argument; the conversation diverted to plans for the next stages of their journey.

There was an unease now in the relationship between the two men which had not been there before they had left Woden's Ford.

Chapter 25

Visitors from the North

A couple of days later Cadmon and Dora were meandering back from the forest, both carrying loads of firewood. 'Please tell me more about the great halls of Deira,' Dora asked.

Cadmon laughed, and said, 'I'm not sure there's much more I can tell you. They're not really that exciting! Why are you so interested?'

'I'm really curious.' Dora said. 'I've never been more than a few miles away from the village, and nor have most of my folk. I think one of my great uncles did travel a bit, but the rest of us have lived and worked in this place for ever. I love it, and I love my family. But I can't help wondering what else is out there. And you seem so well-travelled and interesting!'

Dora finished on a wheedling note, and Cadmon laughed again. He paused, and then said, 'Do you mind if I tell you a really important secret, Dora?'

'Of course not,' Dora replied, surprised but clearly gratified.

'You'll promise not to tell?'

'Of course,' she said solemnly.

'Well, I'm not an Anglian, and we're not travelling metal workers. I'm Welsh, from Gwynedd, and Aelfred's slave. We've run away from Deira. Aelfred's planning to free me

213

soon. I can't tell you anymore, but I want you to know I'm a native of these lands.'

It was clear from her expression that Dora didn't know quite how to react. She had never heard of Gwynedd, but she appreciated this was a significant moment.

She looked at Cadmon, and then asked very simply, 'Will you come back for me when you reach wherever you're going and become a free man?'

It was Cadmon's turn to be surprised, but he had no chance to reply. They were within sight of the village, but now saw three men approaching on a different path which would soon converge with theirs. It was clear, even from a distance of a few hundred yards, that these men were unfamiliar. They were dressed in long dark travelling cloaks even though it was a mild summer afternoon, their heads were shaven, and they carried simple packs on their backs and poles in their hands.

'I've never seen them,' Dora said as Cadmon looked at her questioningly. 'They must be travellers. We never see travellers normally, then suddenly five arrive all at once!'

They were by now within earshot. Two of the men were of medium height and young, perhaps slightly taller and a little older than Cadmon. The third was quite a bit taller and older, and it was he who spoke first as they all halted.

'Good day to you,' he said quite formally, but politely and heartily, in Anglian. 'We have travelled far and are pleased to have found your village. Is there anywhere that three tired and hungry men could rest?' Cadmon could understand him easily, but it was obvious that it was not the man's native tongue.

'I'm also a traveller, and I've found the villagers to be very hospitable,' Cadmon said. 'Dora here could perhaps direct you to her family. I'm sure they'll find a place for you to stay if you come in peace. Where have you travelled from, if you don't mind me asking?'

'We've travelled from the far north, from the monastery on the isle of Lindisfarne. My name is Brother Felgild. I can assure you we come in peace, and we bring peace,' the big man said.

Of course, thought Cadmon to himself: they had not seen any of the monks around Woden's Ford, but Aelfred's Uncle Alwyn had been to Lindisfarne and had described their unusual appearance.

Cadmon explained that he was from Deira and had grown up near York.

'Ah, I know York well,' the big man replied warmly, his dark blue eyes lighting up in a broad smile.

Dora had followed most of the conversation. She was intrigued. Here was another window opening on to the wider world. 'I'll take you to my father: you're very welcome,' she said warmly.

A few of the village children had come to find out more about the strangely dressed men. They accompanied the five adults for the last few hundred yards, firing questions at Dora as they went.

* * * * * * *

As Cadmon expected, the three monks were welcomed graciously, and accommodation was found in different homes. The code of hospitality seemed to override all other considerations.

That evening most of the adults gathered to hear more from the monks. Brother Felgild told the villagers about the monastery at Lindisfarne and said he was one of the founding monks.

'I was born in Dalriada far to the west, started training to become a monk on the island of Iona when I was only eight years old, and then travelled to Northumbria with Brother Aidan just three years ago. My two companions – who are natural brothers as well as monks – have only arrived recently.'

Felgild said the mission of Lindisfarne was to build the community on the island, and also to take the Christian gospel out across the land. This was one of their most southerly missions so far. They were planning to travel on to a new sub-monastery on the East coast, and from there they would return to Lindisfarne by sea.

The villagers were excited by the talk of the lands in the far north and west, although they had only the vaguest concept of what Dalriada might be like. They couldn't envisage a landscape of islands, mountains and sea lanes, and peppered the monks with questions.

Brother Felgild was more than happy to talk about his homeland, but after a while moved the conversation on to matters of faith. He asked the villagers about their worship and their beliefs, and then started on what Aelfred and Cadmon assumed was a standard sermon to encourage those who were already Christian.

He talked about the love of God, about how God had

placed a conscience deep in every person so that they instinctively recognised what was right, but that the sinful human nature too often encouraged behaviour which was wrong. He talked about Jesus and the Holy Spirit who were living manifestations of God and who could help Christians to walk in God's way. He explained the Christian hope of Heaven, and how everything on earth would pass and that life everlasting with God would make human existence seem like a fleeting shadow.

The villagers were receptive and eager. They said that priests visited only occasionally, and so they had to practise their Christian faith themselves.

Ceretic then raised an issue which, judging from the nods and supportive murmurs, Aelfred and Cadmon realised was a topic of much debate in the village – just as it had been at Woden's Ford for the last few years.

'I wonder, Brother, whether you'd give us your views on burial arrangements,' Ceretic said. 'It's a very sensitive matter, of course, but there've been all sorts of practice over the last few years. I know the old pagan way, certainly among the Anglians, has been cremation and the burial of grave goods – as many as possible of the latter. We've heard the proper Christian way is entirely opposite – bury the body whole and put in no grave goods at all.'

'We're really confused, to be honest,' he continued. 'In fact, just a few days ago a man in one of the nearby Anglian settlements – which are all Christian – was buried rather than cremated, but his family included some of his most valued possessions as grave goods.'

Brother Felgild was non-committal in reply, sensing that

this was a hornets' nest and that he could easily get stung, 'Look, I completely understand folk feel really strongly about this, for obvious reasons. But the style of burial is far less important than the faith of the individual in life; it's the soul of the Christian that'll live forever, not the physical body. The objects we treasure on earth, however valuable and loved, will remain on earth.'

* * * * * * *

Aelfred lay awake later that night. The words of Brother Felgild whirled in his mind. An unexpected dialogue was going on inside his head: between his commitment on the one hand to the ancient Anglian, pagan ways and the private vow he had made to his grandfather and through him to all his ancestors, and on the other hand an unbidden sense that there was a better way.

Brother Felgild's sermon was reminiscent of arguments for Christianity he had heard from his Uncle Alwyn and others; but what had struck Aelfred powerfully was his simple, utterly confident, gentle manner. Felgild spoke with the conviction and assurance of someone who knew he was right and wanted to communicate this most important message to others – not for his own benefit but for theirs.

There did not appear to be a shred of pride or vanity or ambition in the man: he was prepared to walk hundreds of miles to talk about his faith because he loved his god and wanted to share him with others.

And yet, and yet: it was a religion of milksops, not even fit for Anglian women and children; it would weaken the Anglian race; it was a gospel of defeat. The words of his beloved pagan grandfather and great uncle echoed down the years.

Aelfred slept fitfully. In the morning he sought out Brother Felgild. It was to be Aelfred's and Cadmon's last day in Helme before they resumed their journey, but Aelfred wanted to talk to the monk.

He found all three monks playing games energetically with the village children – to their mutual delight and the amusement of the village adults. The monks were clearly as much at ease having boisterous fun as they were preaching the Christian gospel.

Aelfred watched enviously. He had never been able to relax with others: children and adults alike seemed to sense his reserve. Once the game was over Aelfred caught Felgild's attention and introduced himself: there had been no opportunity to do so in the excitement of the monks' arrival the previous day.

'I was really interested in what you had to say last night,' he said. 'Would it be alright to ask you a few questions?'

'Of course,' Felgild responded enthusiastically. 'I always love to talk about God: I wouldn't be a monk if I didn't! I'm planning to walk over to visit the family of the Anglian man who died recently. Would you like to come with me?'

Aelfred agreed and let Cadmon know. Cadmon was more than happy to stay in Helme and spend as much time with Dora as he could on their final day together.

'I'm guessing your family's accepted Christianity because King Oswald and before him King Edwin did so, but you've never been quite sure,' Felgild said as they set off.

Aelfred was startled, but reacted cautiously, 'What makes you think that? Has Cadmon been talking to you?'

'Not at all,' Felgild replied, smiling. 'I can see in your eyes, and I saw in your body language as I spoke last night, that there's a struggle going on inside.'

Aelfred was silent for a few moments. He was not used to being probed about his feelings – especially those he wasn't even aware of himself; and yet, although he had only just met Felgild, he felt remarkably comfortable with him.

'Right, here goes: I want to know how you can be so certain that the Christian God exists? How's that for starters?' Aelfred asked, probably a bit more belligerently than he intended because he was a little nervous.

Felgild was unflustered by what came across as a challenge. 'That's a completely understandable question,' he said calmly, 'and not at all easy to answer – simply because there are so many aspects to it. I can't give you absolutely solid evidence. I can, for example, point at that rock and tell you it exists. I suspect you'll believe me because the evidence is there in front of your eyes.' Felgild motioned towards a boulder lying near the path as he spoke.

'It's a bit more difficult to point to the wind and ask you to believe in it; but although you can't see the wind, you can see how it's affecting the trees today as they rustle. You can see the effects even more clearly when it's much stronger. I guess God's a bit like that. I've never seen Him, but I've felt His presence in my life and seen His impact all around me. That's why I have absolute faith He exists.'

'I experience every day an amazing creation. Its beauty and

complexity tell me about the existence of a loving creator,' Felgild continued, his arm sweeping in a wide arc to encompass all they could see. 'I've read the scriptures. I've heard others talk about the evidence of God's work through history and through the birth, death and resurrection of Jesus. I've seen God change lives of those around me, and answer prayers in my own life.'

The monk hesitated, as if to allow Aelfred to respond, but when he didn't Felgild carried on, 'Our God's a living God, but not a tame God. I've seen the wild geese fly in the skies above Iona and Lindisfarne where the land, the sea and the air meet. In so many ways they symbolise God: elemental, powerful, wild. Even the way they fly illustrates the loving heart of God. Each goose takes its turn at the front to bear the brunt of the wind and shield the rest. It's a perfect template for life.'

Felgild paused again, and then concluded, 'I guess I would sum up by saying we know God 'is', but it's a mistake to try to define Him, especially in our own image. Christianity's about encountering the divine presence, not just learning about it.'

Aelfred had listened carefully, but he was determined to be sceptical and so said, 'All this love stuff sounds great, but surely totally impractical. Christianity's like a death knell for communities: if they turn the other cheek, they'll be wiped out.'

Felgild remained calm as he replied, 'Of course all human societies are founded on power and wealth; but the great challenge of the gospel is to look at life through a different set of eyes. The material world is wonderful, and I adore it. You can't live on Iona and Lindisfarne and not cherish creation in all its wonder; but it's transient, as are we – like mist in the morning. Yet God promises eternal life to those who believe. It must surely be better to invest in eternity, rather than worry too much about our goods and chattels and status here on earth, don't you think?'

'The first commandment of Christianity is to love the Lord your God, and to love your neighbour as yourself,' Felgild continued. 'I agree it's revolutionary; but can you imagine what life would be like if we were all less precious about our wealth and status, and more prepared to forgive? We'd have a virtuous circle of civilised, neighbourly behaviour, rather than a vicious cycle of war and revenge.'

'Jesus said the birds and flowers don't have to worry about what they wear and what they eat because God provides,' Felgild concluded. 'I'm not suggesting for a moment we should all become careless and live lives of total abstinence; but it's a question of priorities and focus.'

The conversation went back and forth as the two men walked. Aelfred found he was enjoying the debate even as he became irritated that Felgild appeared to have a reasonable answer to every question. They talked about the differences between paganism and Christianity, and about how Christians just as much as pagans respected kinship and the heritage passed down from ancestors.

Aelfred was interested to learn that the monks of Lindisfarne were making contacts in the other Anglo-Saxon kingdoms as well as across Northumbria. Felgild said that even in pagan Mercia there appeared to be willingness in some quarters to at least listen to what they had to say. Aelfred didn't tell

Felgild that he was planning to travel to Mercia. He wondered which quarters in Penda's pagan kingdom were listening to the monks' gospel.

After an hour and a half they were drawing near the Anglian settlement which was Felgild's destination. Aelfred said he felt uneasy about accompanying Felgild on effectively a pastoral visit, and Felgild agreed that he should turn back.

* * * * * * *

Aelfred's mind churned as he retraced his steps towards Helme. He had never heard such a passionate and yet reasoned statement of the Christian faith. He had talked on and off to his Uncle Alwyn when he was younger and so heard his take, but in recent years he had avoided the subject, and Alwyn had respected Aelfred's obvious unease.

Aelfred told himself that Felgild would say all that, wouldn't he: that's his job, and he's been brain-washed since he was a child. He reminded himself that this new-fangled religion didn't even begin to measure up to the tried and tested lore handed down from Woden and the gods through generations of his ancestors.

Aelfred recalled the passionate belief of his grandfather and great uncle in the old gods, in the right to defend and gain power and wealth for their kin, and the promise of glory in the afterlife that awaited great Anglian warriors.

Yet Aelfred couldn't get out of his mind the simple reasonableness of what Felgild had said and the way he had said it. There was something profoundly different about the monk which both attracted and unsettled Aelfred. He had utter faith, not in human might but in something invisible and immeasurable – and he was prepared to sacrifice everything to spread that message. He exuded powerful humility.

Aelfred reflected, too, on the irony of his determination not to follow his mother's advice to go and talk to the monks of Lindisfarne, and the fact that they had now followed him! How she would smile, he thought.

Aelfred physically shook himself as he walked, as if he could force his jumbled thoughts and feelings back into order. 'Let's get to Mercia,' he told himself sternly. 'Then we'll experience a fully and unashamedly pagan kingdom, and Christianity won't seem so clever. I can't believe the monks have made much impact down there, whatever Felgild says.'

Aelfred convinced himself that he had pushed the conversation with Felgild out of his mind as he turned to plans for resuming the journey to Mercia the next day.

The next few hours were a blur of farewells and thanks to the villagers who had been so hospitable and welcoming. Aelfred felt a little guilty that they had been there under false pretences – they had used assumed names and stuck to their cover story throughout; but he reminded himself – as he had done continually since leaving Woden's Ford – that the journey to Mercia was for the greater good of the whole of Northumbria, including Elmet, and that deceit and subterfuge were thus justified.

The morning of their departure was cool and breezy. Aelfred and Cadmon had agreed that they were now sufficiently far from Woden's Ford that they could afford to travel by daylight and more openly without fear of recognition or pursuit. So, for the second time in just a few short weeks, they set off with good wishes ringing in their ears towards a destination which was very different to where the well-wishers thought they were going.

Chapter 26

Next Steps

Throughout their lives Cadmon had always been the more talkative and extrovert, Aelfred the quieter and more introspective. The roles were reversed as they set off south through the hills on the next leg of their journey.

Aelfred fulminated about the naivety of Brother Felgild, the flaws in Christianity, and its total impracticality for people building for the future. Cadmon sensed that Aelfred was almost protesting too much: Felgild had obviously got under his skin.

Cadmon wasn't in the mood to listen to Aelfred's monologue and, rather irritably, asked him to give it a break. He wanted some time to reflect on all that he had seen, heard and felt over the last couple of weeks.

The last day in Helme had been frustrating. Dora's mother had been ill, and so Dora had had to spend more time than usual on household chores. They had, however, managed to catch a few minutes alone. Cadmon had committed to come back to her once he was a free man, and Dora had committed to wait.

Cadmon's feelings were mixed: on the one hand he was elated that he had, he believed, found his life partner; but he was impatient to be able to return, and apprehensive in case circumstances prevented him.

Mingled with his feelings for Dora was a profound sense of liberation. Cadmon felt that a burden of inferiority had lifted from his shoulders. He had grown up knowing that he was a native, but almost ashamed – subconsciously acknowledging the Anglian narrative that the native people of Britain were a subject race. King Cadwallon's victory at Hatfield had given him a glimpse of a different reality, but life had reverted to normal under King Oswald.

Yet in the last two weeks he had seen and experienced native British people living free – and it felt good. The experience had helped him to see slavery as entirely unnatural and unjust, and also to realise how ludicrous it was to brand all natives as wealas – foreigners – when they had been on the island for generations before the Anglians arrived.

Cadmon was not averse to Christianity; but he reflected on the irony that the monks talked about finding freedom in their god when so many folk were enslaved by the Anglo-Saxon powers whom they served.

Cadmon had never spent much time trying to either analyse his inner feelings or to address big philosophical issues. Now he felt that his mind was bubbling and spitting in all directions, like a pot of broth boiling on a fire. The turbulence was showing in his expression. Throughout his life a smile had always seemed to be hovering on the edges of his dark eyes, a reflection of his cheerful, unfussy temperament. He now looked pensive and preoccupied much of the time, his brow slightly furrowed.

'Look, Al,' Cadmon said after they had walked on in silence for a while, 'I get that you don't like Christianity. I can see Felgild riled you. It'll certainly be interesting to hear what the Mercians think about it when we get there. But how do you feel about native British people being left to get on with their lives, whatever their religion?'

Cadmon could see that Aelfred was surprised by the question, and that the thought had not really occurred to him – even though they had lived in a native village for a couple of weeks with no signs of any Anglian overlords.

'Well, I don't know, Cad. They were great people, no question. I've got nothing at all against British folk. But what are you suggesting?' Aelfred asked thoughtfully.

'For one thing, it was really nice to be in a place where you weren't referred to as a foreigner, and where British people weren't just servants and peasants,' Cadmon said.

Aelfred was evidently puzzled. He pointed out that he planned to give Cadmon his freedom. He asked again what he was suggesting.

Cadmon's frustration pulsed in his voice as he said, 'I was captured as a baby by your father after your uncle killed my father, brought to a foreign kingdom, orphaned when I was nine months old, and enslaved. That's simply not right. We've always got on well; but I could see when we met those outlaws in the forest you had some sympathy with them. You've taken a risk by leaving Woden's Ford – but it's only because you want to strengthen the old pagan order. It's that order which has kept me and my people under a yoke.'

'I'm not a foreigner, a Wealas,' Cadmon concluded firmly. 'I'm certain my ancestors have been in these lands far longer than yours. We should be treated fairly, not as inferior. Native British lives matter just as much as Anglian lives.'

Aelfred was getting frustrated, too, and even angry. 'I don't agree with everything my family's done, Cad, but we've invested hundreds of years of blood and sweat in making Woden's Ford successful. We've given livelihoods to countless people, native and Anglo-Saxon. I didn't like the folk at Camp Woden any more than you did; but I can't blame them for wanting to preserve our culture and heritage. I don't see what's so bad about that.'

They argued on for a while, and became increasingly annoyed with each other, but eventually both lapsed into sullen silence. Cadmon sensed that Aelfred's deep mindset was unmoved: the Anglians and other Germanic folk were in charge, natives were to be treated with respect if they deserved it, but they were 'other'.

Cadmon could no longer imagine living in any place where he was treated as subservient purely because of his ancestry. He had decided that he would serve Aelfred loyally until he freed him, but he wanted then to find genuine freedom.

Something had shifted deep within Cadmon. As they walked he tried to express to himself what he now felt.

'I feel alive!' he said to himself suddenly. He was startled by his insight, but it felt right.

* * * * * * *

As they continued to head south over the next few days neither man referred again to the relationship between Anglo-Saxons and native British; but it felt to both of them that the frustrated words they had exchanged lay only half-submerged, forming an awkward barrier. They spoke little, and then mainly about practicalities.

The tension and the divergence in their views which had arisen on several occasions since they had left Woden's Ford was impeding the easy flow of their relationship which had been maintained for twenty years.

The hurt which Cadmon had experienced when Aelfred, as he saw it, had duped him was still very raw indeed. Each new argument rubbed salt in the wound.

Aelfred felt disappointment and irritation that Cadmon seemed unable to grasp what he was trying to achieve. Characteristically, though, he withdrew more and more into himself. He gnawed inwardly at the irritation, but he did not express it directly to Cadmon.

The two men were able to make relatively quick progress after leaving Helme, walking by day on open roads and tracks. The landscape was a mix of rugged, rolling hills clothed in foliage of every conceivable shade of green, brown and faun; narrow, wriggling valleys through which rivers flowed and tumbled; great cliffs of solid rock; farmland where the arable crops were reaching their golden fullness and the cattle grazed peacefully; and thick woodland.

Aelfred and Cadmon were not particularly concerned about avoiding people as they walked, but they slept in the open for the most part, as far away as they could from any probing questions.

As they got closer to Tamworth Aelfred felt both more excited and more nervous. He went over repeatedly with Cadmon the kinds of things he would say once they got there, but also kept fretting about all sorts of scenarios from the possible to the catastrophic.

After four days of hard walking, they reached a hostelry one evening near a crossing of the River Trent where roads from the north and west met. The owner told them they were only about ten miles from Tamworth. He offered accommodation and a meal, and readily accepted both their tried and tested cover story that they were itinerant metal workers from Northumbria looking for work in and around the Mercian court, and the Northumbrian coins with which Aelfred paid.

It was a welcome relief for both men to be able to wash thoroughly after a few days of sleeping in the wild and so feel prepared for the final leg of the journey to Tamworth. They were ready for a hearty meal when they went through to the dining area of the hostelry. They sat down on wooden benches, their legs stretched out to ease the stiffness.

As they waited three men sat down at a table close by. They spoke to each other in British, but switched to fluent Anglian when their food was brought to them. They talked amiably to the hostelry owner about their plans to travel to Tamworth the next day and the weather prospects. The men had an air of easy authority.

As the owner walked away Cadmon caught the eye of one of the men, and said, 'I couldn't help hearing you're heading to Tamworth tomorrow; so are we. Would you mind me asking what business you have there: you've obviously travelled quite some distance.'

If the man was surprised by the direct approach he didn't show it. 'Not at all,' he said. 'We're heading to the court of King Penda. We're agents of Mercia's ally, the king of Gwynedd. We're bringing messages from him. We've come on foot rather than on horseback because we didn't want to attract attention in the wild lands north and west of here. There's constant fighting between the Mercian nobles and the warlords there. We didn't want to get caught up in it. Now we're in Mercia we actually feel on much safer ground.'

'I'm Morvyn, by the way, and my companions are Caradoc and Einion,' he said as he finished.

Cadmon's heart beat wildly: for the first time he was talking to men who came from the land of his birth, who spoke the language his parents would have spoken, who may have trodden the same ground as them – and who may even have been involved in the victory over Northumbria at Hatfield.

Aelfred reacted differently. Even though he had temporarily turned his back on Northumbria his instincts were Northumbrian, and Gwynedd had long been an enemy kingdom; yet he was also intrigued that the men were heading for the court of the pagan king whose reputation had drawn him to this very point.

Aelfred told the Welshmen that he and Cadmon were metalworkers who had become disillusioned in Northumbria and were heading to Tamworth to try to find work in or around Penda's court. The Welshmen seemed unconcerned even though Northumbria was the rival of both Mercia and Gwynedd. The five men were soon swapping information about their respective journeys.

Cadmon was eager to find out as much as he possibly could about Gwynedd and the men were more than happy to satisfy his curiosity.

Aelfred asked about the nature of the relationship between the kings and peoples of Gwynedd and Mercia. 'It's an alliance of convenience, mainly against your folk – but I don't think we're particularly liked in Mercia: tolerated at best,' Caradoc said. 'And the feeling's mutual, to be honest. With all due respect, the Anglo-Saxon people haven't endeared themselves to the natives of this island.'

By this stage, the mead and ale were beginning to have an effect, and there were no other guests in the dining area. Morvyn was particularly voluble. 'That's right,' he said hotly. 'We want back our lost lands, the lands the Saxons have overrun. One day the kings of Gwynedd will rule the whole island. That's what the old prophesy says – 'The Conversation of Merlin with his sister'. I, for one, believe it absolutely.'

'Come now, Morvyn,' Caradoc said. 'Remember where you are and who you're with. That's the ale talking.'

Morvyn was incensed. 'I tell you, we've a right to every particle of this island. It's been stolen from us.'

'I know that's what the prophesy says,' Caradoc said, 'but I'd be happy if, in return for supporting Penda, the Welsh kings could get back control in the border lands. I think Penda has his eye on them: it would be really bad news if they were swallowed up in Mercia.'

Aelfred and Cadmon were intrigued for different reasons. Cadmon's Welsh consciousness was growing. The notion that all the land controlled by Anglo-Saxons by rights belonged to the Welsh was further grist to the mill for him. He had felt hairs on the back of his neck rising as Morvyn had talked about the old prophesy.

Aelfred was interested in Penda's alleged expansionist plans. He asked how the people of Gwynedd, as Christians, felt about allying with a pagan, Anglo-Saxon king against other

Christian kingdoms. 'Well, yes, we're Christians – but I guess most of us are men of Gwynedd first and foremost, and Welsh second,' Einion said. 'We want what's best for Gwynedd, and also for the rest of the Welsh kingdoms. If a tactical alliance with a pagan can keep our influence in the border lands, that's fine by us.'

Completely unbidden, the words of Brother Felgild about the vicious cycle of attack and revenge popped in to Aelfred's mind. He pushed away the naive concept of a world in which all neighbours could live together in harmony. He told himself he was entering the real world of power and might. He fingered the figure of Woden hanging around his neck.

It was getting late, but as they retired for the night the five men agreed to travel on to Tamworth together in the morning. Aelfred felt a tremor of excitement: after all the planning he was almost there! He couldn't hide from himself though a degree of trepidation: the next day he would be entering the lair of a very powerful wolf.

* * * * * * *

As the men set off the next morning Cadmon made sure to fall in with Morvyn. Even without the influence of ale the Welshman talked a great deal. He was very well-versed in the history and mythology of Gwynedd and clearly a proud patriot.

There was a charisma about Morvyn which Cadmon was trying to understand. In many respects he did not stand out: he was of medium height and build, his brown hair was thinning and receding, and his straggly beard and moustache were speckled with grey. His hazel eyes, though, were intense and restless, a window in to what Cadmon suspected was a powerful and creative mind. His voice, too, was at odds with his appearance: deep, resonant, and inexplicably attractive.

Morvyn told Cadmon about the majestic mountains and valleys of Gwynedd, the culture of bards and poetry, and the ancient history. He also talked about more recent history. He had fought for the Mercia-Gwynedd alliance at the battle of Hatfield, and had then stayed in King Cadwallon's army of occupation until they were beaten by the returning Oswald at Heavenfield. Morvyn recalled the fluctuating feelings of the Gwynedd warriors during that period, and the dejection among the few survivors as they had escaped over the northern hills after Heavenfield.

Aelfred pumped Caradoc and Einion for information about Penda's court. It turned out that they had both visited Tamworth a couple of times before and met many of the men of influence.

After they had been walking for an hour or so they became aware of a party of horsemen approaching in the opposite direction. There were about thirty, all heavily armed. The leader, a big man in his late forties, halted the party as they drew level. 'Who are you and where are you heading?' he asked, calmly but in a tone which did not encourage equivocation.

'We're going to your master's court, my Lord Harald, on the business of our king of Gwynedd. We're carrying important messages,' Morvyn responded confidently.

The leading horseman looked surprised, but recognition came almost immediately. 'Of course,' he said coolly. 'I do recall your last visit. The king's elsewhere just now, but I'm sure you'll be well received. Why are you walking, though – you must have travelled a long way?'

'We wanted to travel as unobtrusively as we could through the lands of the border war bands. We thought it'd be safer on foot, my Lord,' Morvyn said. He was clearly the most senior of the three agents and the spokesman.

Harald nodded, not unsympathetically. 'Yes, they're definitely a wild lot. As it happens, we're on our way to join up with some other Mercians, and then we're going to give them a kicking. We know who the worst of them are, and we're going to find them. We'll maybe see you back in Tamworth.'

With that the party cantered off, many of the horsemen looking curiously at the group of pedestrians who were known to their leader.

Aelfred and Cadmon were full of questions about the encounter having deduced that the leader was an important noble at Penda's court. 'How do you know one of the leading courtiers of the King of the Mercians?' Aelfred asked.

'I told you, we've been to Tamworth before and met plenty of Penda's men. The second time the king was giving a great feast for some Francian traders, and we were invited. Let's just say there was plenty of mead, Harald imbibed heavily, and he spent quite a bit of time talking to us about all sorts of things! I'm surprised he does remember us given the state we were all in, but we did spend a few hours together.' Caradoc laughed as he recounted the experience.

'So, what was Harald like?' Cadmon asked.

'Very drunk!' said Einion. 'Other than that, it was difficult to tell. But he certainly has a reputation for being ruthless.

Like you saw just there, he's quite a warrior, and Penda trusts him to lead big raids.'

Aelfred was impressed. The Welshmen were obviously not bluffing. They were familiar enough in Tamworth to be recognised by one of Penda's main men.

A thought which had been at the back of Aelfred's mind in very vague form now moved front and centre. His plan on reaching Tamworth had been simply to go to court and then try to gain an audience with someone senior enough by explaining that he was bringing important and secret information from Northumbria.

He could now see an opportunity to expedite matters. He was naturally cautious; but having taken a huge risk already he judged that he might as well be hanged for a sheep as a lamb if it did all go wrong.

'I need to tell you something,' he said as they all walked on together. The Welshmen sensed the change in Aelfred's tone and signalled that they were listening carefully. 'Cadmon and I haven't been entirely straight with you, but for good reasons. We are from Northumbria, and we're unhappy with many things up there; but we're not metalworkers. We've actually got some really sensitive information which we want to make sure gets to the highest authority in Mercia.'

'Hmm, I'm not particularly surprised. I could sense you were on some sort of mission. Well, you've met up with the right folk. Do you want us to help you to get an introduction?' Morvyn asked.

Aelfred tried to hide his delight: that is exactly what he'd been hoping. 'If it's no trouble, that'd be great,' he said eagerly.

'Not at all. It'll help our cause if we can bring something new to Penda's folk,' Morvyn said. 'The rivalry with Northumbria isn't going away any time soon, and so anything that gives Mercia an edge will be welcome to Penda.'

Chapter 27

In the Wolf's lair

The party arrived in Tamworth in mid-afternoon. To an objective eye there was little about the settlement that was exceptional. Wooden buildings of various shapes and sizes were scattered on either side of the River Tame, intersected by paths and tracks which were mostly dirt although some were roughly cobbled. People and livestock were going about their daily business.

Yet to Aelfred the very ordinary settlement seemed almost ethereal, otherworldly. He had thought so much about this moment for the last year. He had wondered continually what it would be like to arrive in Tamworth and what he would do when he got there. He felt as if he were in a dream and could see beyond the prosaic physical reality: this was his promised land.

The three Welshmen led them through the settlement to the area where Penda, his family and some of his personal war band and most powerful nobles and courtiers lived. The buildings were larger, more substantial, obviously more prestigious.

The men already knew that King Penda was holding court in another part of Mercia, but there was plenty of activity nevertheless. One of the servants recognised the Welshmen, and the party was soon ushered into a room occupied by a small, rather portly, balding man.

'Aha, it's the three wise men of Gwynedd,' he exclaimed. 'You've come back to do some more wheeling and dealing, I take it. I hope your king's sent you with a sensible offer. I really don't want you to have wasted such a long journey.'

The Mercian then looked curiously at Aelfred and Cadmon. 'And who are these – ummm – individuals you've brought with you?' he asked. His tone was sneering, to the point of rudeness, as he looked Aelfred and Cadmon up and down.

Aelfred was well aware that he and Cadmon were a little unkempt after their adventures of the last month or so, but he took an immediate, instinctive dislike to the Mercian noble.

Morvyn, though, was unflustered. Gone was the bluster of last night, the wild words; the royal envoy was on show, refusing to respond in kind. Aelfred was impressed as Morvyn said, 'Thank you for seeing us, my Lord Brice. It's a pleasure to be back in Tamworth. We actually met Lord Harald on the road just a few miles away, and he assured us we'd be welcome. We were also very fortunate to meet these two fugitives from Northumbria. They have some valuable information to share with you.'

Lord Brice maintained his slightly bored expression, but Aelfred noticed a flicker of shrewd interest in his eyes as he said, 'Northumbrians, eh: not spies, I trust? We've caught a few spies from Deira and Bernicia in the last few years. I won't say just now what happened to them, but believe me, young men, you'd do well to avoid their fate.'

'We're definitely not spies,' Aelfred said, perhaps too quickly as he noticed Brice narrow his eyes a little. 'We're fed up with what King Oswald's doing. We want to do what we can to help King Penda. We've got something really important to offer.'

'Well, I do very much hope so,' Brice said briskly. 'Now, I have other things I must see to, but I'll meet you both later. And, of course, I look forward to hearing what the king of Gwynedd is offering, too. So many offers, we in Mercia are very grateful.'

'Now, please take our friends away and find them lodgings,' Brice said to a waiting servant as he finished.

The five men were led to a group of guest houses a few hundred yards away alongside the River Tame. The water was ruffled by a breeze and the clouds scudded across the sky: it was a cool, overcast evening.

The others talked as they ate in a nearby hostelry a little while later. They were joined by two traders who had travelled from East Anglia. They bemoaned the continual fighting and tension between kingdoms which was hampering trade.

Aelfred was silent. He was not in the mood for small talk and couldn't concentrate. He was so close to the point where his gamble would either pay off or fail badly. He was trying to process his reaction to Lord Brice, and also pondering how best to approach the next and crucial conversation with him.

It was almost dark by the time a messenger arrived to summon Aelfred and Cadmon – but not the Welsh agents. They jumped up eagerly and followed the messenger back to the room in which they had met Lord Brice earlier. It was lit now by flaming torches; a fire burned to ward off the evening chill.

'So,' Lord Brice said, without any attempt at pleasantries and with the same sardonic smile they had witnessed earlier playing across his face. 'Convince me you're not Oswald's spies, and that I shouldn't execute you immediately.'

Aelfred had half-expected some sort of challenge, an attempt to shock – and he had an idea about how to get on the front foot. 'My Lord,' he said, pulling from his pack the solid gold sword pommel he had extracted from the hoard and handing it to Brice, 'this is why you should spare our lives and give us the chance to help Mercia. Let's call it a deposit, a sign of our integrity.'

Brice's eyes widened as he examined the pommel and registered the obvious value and quality of the object. His usual tone was firmly in place, though, as he asked, 'It's a lovely little trinket, but how's it going to help King Penda win his next war?'

Aelfred knew that he had the Mercian's attention and so launched into his story, speaking quickly, 'This is just one item from a major hoard of Northumbrian royal treasure hidden in a secret place in Deira. I'm the son of a Northumbrian noble. Seven years ago King Edwin asked my father to store a portion of the royal treasury. I knew where it was hidden, and I've now moved it to a new location. I want to offer the treasure to Mercia because I believe Northumbria has gone down a wrong path. I want the Anglian people to be united in the old ways, the ways of our ancestors. I believe Mercia can spearhead that drive for unity. Cadmon and I are the only people who know where the treasure is hidden. He's been my slave since birth, but is now a free man. We're prepared to lead you to the treasure. I hope afterwards that I can persuade my family to join the Mercian cause by showing them how strongly I feel.'

There was silence once Aelfred finished speaking, as if Cadmon and Brice were momentarily overwhelmed by the volume and intensity of Aelfred's words. Cadmon told Aelfred later that his passion seemed to fill the room.

Brice spoke eventually, but appeared to go off at a tangent, 'King Oswald,' he said slowly. 'We really don't know what to make of him. Now King Edwin we understood. He clearly became a Christian for cynical, political reasons. He wanted the friendship of Kent and Francia to help him become the most powerful king on the island. He saw Christianity as a means to a very earthly end; but it didn't help him avoid a very nasty end at Hatfield.'

'We're really not sure whether Oswald is cleverer than Edwin, or simply a fool,' Brice continued. 'It could be he sees Christianity as a very neat way to keep his subjects quiet. Behave in this life and obey the king, he and his Irish monks tell the people, and you'll have a good afterlife. It's a very convenient message for a king – and so different from our old belief that the way to eternal glory is through fighting and killing. Yet his Christianity doesn't stop Oswald from plotting to overpower his enemies.'

Brice paused, and then went on, 'Oswald might, too, see Christianity as a way of showing to the European powers that Northumbria is a modern, outward-looking kingdom. We in Mercia certainly don't think that's necessary. We're making plenty of contacts with the Francians and others without becoming Christians, and trade's picking up nicely.'

'Or perhaps Oswald really does believe the Christian

gospel and his western monks?' Brice posited. 'If so, he's stupid. Christianity will weaken the drive and energy which have gained our people so much power and land over the last few hundred years. Look at Mercia: we would never have built this mighty kingdom in the last forty years if we'd kept turning the other cheek as their Jesus tells them to do.'

Brice paused again, looked at Aelfred and Cadmon in turn, and then said, 'But whether he's a fool or a genius, Oswald's a threat to us. He's signed up Wessex as an ally for one reason and one reason only – because he wants to smash Mercia. I'm glad you're seeing sense, my boys, and abandoning your king. But how can I be sure you're telling the truth and not leading us into a trap?'

'You'll have to trust us,' Aelfred said as insistently as he could. 'Why would we make this journey and go to all this trouble just to lure a handful of Mercians into an ambush? There's a great deal more treasure like this pommel buried just 150 miles away. It will certainly help your King with the costs of war against Northumbria if it comes to that.'

Brice probed for more detail, but although Aelfred was prepared to talk about the contents of the treasure sacks, he refused to give any specific information about the location of the hiding place.

After a few minutes of cross-questioning it was clear that Brice had reached a conclusion. 'I am prepared to trust you,' he said, 'but woe-betide if you double-cross us. If we retrieve the treasure, and it's as valuable as you say it is, then you'll be rewarded. We'll find you a high-born Mercian wife – I've just the girl in mind actually. And we'll give you some land. You'll become one of us. And your friend can become a free man in

Mercia.' Brice nodded towards Cadmon as he finished.

Aelfred was delighted. He had hoped to be able to persuade the Mercians, but he had feared that – at the very least – it would take some time. Lord Brice's offer, coming so suddenly, sounded almost too good to be to true. Aelfred felt giddy with relief and excitement. It seemed momentarily as if all the air had been sucked out of his lungs.

Aelfred took a deep breath, smiled, and said earnestly, 'Thank you, sir, I really am very grateful. I will not let you down.'

Brice smiled, too, but thinly: there was no warmth in his expression. 'We should move quickly now to retrieve the treasure,' he said decisively. 'We'll sort out a plan to accompany you to the hiding place, and then let's get on with it. In the meantime, for your own protection, we should put you in separate houses and give you some guards. I just wouldn't want anyone in Tamworth to get any funny ideas about a couple of young Northumbrian bloods staying so near the royal court.'

With that Brice rose, picked up the gold pommel, and left the room. A few minutes later guards appeared to lead Aelfred and Cadmon away to their accommodation.

As he prepared to go to bed a little later Aelfred mulled over the events of a long and momentous day. The euphoria he had felt when Brice had made his offer had ebbed away; instead, he felt strangely hollow.

'I've thought for so long about how to get 'there', to fulfil my goal,' he said to himself reflectively. 'Now I appear to have arrived, but 'there' seems somehow so empty and lifeless.'

Unbidden, Aelfred's mind seemed to present a contrast

between Brother Felgild and Lord Brice: to his surprise he found himself missing the former and recalling his selfless reasonableness.

'I'm tired,' Aelfred told himself. 'I'm still suffering the after-effects of the fever after several days of hard walking. The excitement will come once I've rested.'

Aelfred had told Cadmon and the Mercian who had led them to their lodgings that he would take the next couple of days to regather his strength before the return trip to Deira to fetch the treasure.

* * * * * * *

Cadmon had never at any stage in his life had trouble sleeping. He had often told Aelfred, who was a notoriously light sleeper, that it was because he had nothing to worry about.

Tonight, though, he could not sleep. His mind was racing.

The first twenty years of his life had been very ordinary; the last month had been extraordinary.

He was a fugitive, a traitor and a thief – but also now a free man in an enemy kingdom, and in love with a girl to whom he had committed to return.

As he tossed and turned, he clarified what he wanted: to marry Dora, and to play a part, however small, in fulfilling the prophesy that the Welsh would regain their lost lands.

Cadmon was also clear about what he didn't want: to live in or support Mercia in any way, other than as part of the tactical alliance which Gwynedd appeared to have with Penda.

He felt sad that he would have to part company with Aelfred, something he could not have even imagined several weeks ago. Yet this was easier because of the events of the last month and the changes he had witnessed in Aelfred.

Cadmon knew that the Welsh agents were the key. He made up his mind what he would do over the next couple of days while Aelfred was resting. He then promptly fell asleep.

* * * * * * *

The next day Cadmon was up early. From what he could gather from the young Mercian outside his room, he and Aelfred were to be guarded and discouraged from leaving their rooms overnight, but during the day were free to move about as they pleased.

Cadmon went in search of the Welsh agents. He found them about to meet with leaders of Penda's war band for a day of talks about possible collaboration. Cadmon told them he had something he wanted to discuss, and they agreed to meet in the early evening.

It was Cadmon's turn to spend time fretting about what he would say. The day dragged.

Finally, Cadmon was seated with the Welshmen in a quiet corner of the hostelry they had visited the previous evening. 'Look,' he said after a few minutes of listening to the Welshmen complain about how badly they felt they had been treated by Penda's warriors. 'I want to come completely clean with you about why Aelfred and I are here in Tamworth; but what I'm about to tell you is extremely sensitive. I'm sorry, but I must ask you to swear to secrecy.'

The Welshmen sensed the urgency and solemnity in Cadmon's voice. They agreed readily to his terms.

Cadmon continued, 'Aelfred told you we weren't metalworkers, and that we'd fled from Northumbria with information which we felt would be of interest to Penda's men. That's true; but it's not the whole truth. First, I want to tell you I am – was – Aelfred's slave, and I'm not an Anglian. I was born in Gwynedd of ancient Welsh stock. I was captured with my mother as a baby and have lived in Deira ever since. I'm as Welsh as you are!'

Morvyn let out a low whistle, and then said, 'I did sense your great interest in everything to do with Gwynedd. I could put it down to my skill as a storyteller, but I wondered whether there was something else going on!'

His two companions laughed. Caradoc said, 'You just like hearing your own voice, Morvyn. Let's be honest: you'd talk about Gwynedd in an empty room!'

Cadmon went on once the initial surprise had sunk in, 'The second thing I want to say is I would like to join you. I feel my eyes have been opened in the last few weeks. I'm Welsh, and I want to re-join my people. Aelfred has given me my freedom, but I don't feel I owe the Anglians any loyalty. What's more, I could bring with me an introductory gift which will be of real value to you and your king as you try to recover the lost lands.'

The Welshmen were now listening intently, the jovial banter of a few minutes ago set aside. Cadmon told them about the treasure hoard, said that he could lead them to it, but explained that they would need to move quickly if they were to get there before Aelfred and the Mercians. He also told them about Dora and his plan to marry her and live in Gwynedd.

'You're absolutely sure you want to go through with this? I know this sounds harsh, but you'd be a double traitor.' Caradoc's voice was deadly serious as he looked Cadmon in the eye.

'I've thought about that,' Cadmon said, equally gravely. 'But I reckon I've effectively been held a prisoner for over twenty years. I'm now negotiating my path to freedom. My life wasn't at all bad by the standards of many slaves. But I surely have a right to be free in my own country. I see the treasure as reparation for what's been done to me, my mother and my father.'

'Fair enough,' Morvyn said, 'I can certainly see your point. And we would definitely like the treasure. I'm sure you and your girl will be rewarded richly and be given a nice home in Gwynedd. So, what's the plan?'

They agreed that Cadmon would slip away from Tamworth the next afternoon and travel as surreptitiously as he could back towards the hostelry by the River Trent where they had met two days previously, and then wait under cover. The Welshmen said that they would be able to leave Tamworth perfectly openly and to no one's surprise the day after Cadmon left. They could all meet near the hostelry, and the Welshmen would then try to obtain horses so that they could travel quickly north to Deira.

Cadmon could hardly believe what he had done, but he was utterly confident in the rightness of his action. At the same time, he felt sorry that his lifelong association with

Aelfred should be coming to an end in such an underhand manner. He could not tell Aelfred what he was planning, and he knew that Aelfred would be genuinely puzzled once he had disappeared.

* * * * * * *

At the same time that Cadmon and the Welshmen were finalising their plan, Lord Brice was toying with his food in his home a few hundred yards away. He was oblivious to the dinner table chatter of his wife, Wynflaed, and his two sons and a daughter.

'What's on your mind, Brice?' Wynflaed asked once the children had left.

'Nothing in particular, why do you ask?' Brice replied distractedly.

'Because your mind isn't here,' Wynflaed said, succinctly, and slightly impatiently. 'I don't think you've heard a single word any of us has said. It doesn't look like you've eaten much, either. Something must be worrying you.'

Brice was, in truth, still preoccupied by his encounter with Aelfred and Cadmon the previous evening. The Mercian earl could not still nagging doubts in the corner of his mind about their story and the decision he had taken. He had not been able to concentrate fully on anything all day, although he had nevertheless been pleased with the discussions with the Gwynedd men.

Brice looked at his wife appraisingly. He didn't normally discuss what he regarded as work matters with her; but whenever he had done, she had been able to offer helpful insights. He had a great deal of respect for Wynflaed's mental and intuitive powers. He was always mindful, too, that as a niece of King Penda she was extremely well connected. He felt fortunate to have married such a high-born woman, but he was realistic enough to know that she could make life difficult for him if she felt unhappy.

'Right, I'll tell you – but, as usual, please keep this to yourself,' Brice said.

'Of course,' Wynflaed said, a hint of impatience still in her voice, as if she were offended that he could consider a niece of the king to be anything but completely trustworthy.

Brice recounted Aelfred's tale and explained what he had decided and why. 'I'm still fairly sure I've made the right decision,' he concluded. 'I think it'll be good for me, and for us, if we can secure the treasure. I'm sure the king'll be pleased. But there's something about the whole story that doesn't smell quite right. I'm a bit worried it might be some sort of trap, and that I'll end up looking a fool.'

Wynflaed had listened intently. She now raised her eyebrows as she nodded her head several times. 'That's remarkably interesting,' she said. 'For what it's worth, I think you've done the right thing. It doesn't sound to me like the boys are lying. I also think it's a good idea to offer Lord Harald's second daughter as a bride. Sigeberg's quite a charmer. I'm sure the Northumbrian boy will feel even more positive towards Mercia once he meets her.'

She looked thoughtful, and then went on, 'The Northumbrian connection is interesting. I don't think I told you, but last week I met a Christian monk from Lindisfarne, an island way up off the Northumbrian coast. He'd contacted my mother somehow, and she arranged for him to talk to a few of us. What he said didn't make much sense to me, but it was fascinating to hear what's going on elsewhere.'

It was Brice's turn to be surprised. 'I thought the king wasn't at all keen on Christianity. So why did he allow a monk from an enemy kingdom to spread his strange ideas?'

'The king's certainly not planning to become a Christian, you're absolutely right,' Wynflaed replied, smiling. 'But he hasn't banned Christians from Mercia altogether. I don't think he sees any harm in folk listening to them. After all, he allies with Christian Welsh kings in war, so I don't think he can be too choosy.'

'I suppose so,' Brice replied, 'but I'm still surprised. You'll let me know if you plan to become a Christian, won't you!'

'Of course!' Wynflaed said, laughing.

'Thank you for listening, anyway,' Brice said. 'I'm glad you think I've made the right decision about the Northumbrians. I'll have a chat with Harald once he gets back from this latest raid. I don't think he'll be too long. At the very least I should tell him I've got an idea for a son in law!'

* * * * * * *

Cadmon was awake early the next morning. The sun was already streaming in through the window. For a few moments he couldn't work out where he was.

As he tried desperately to orient his mind memories of the previous evening suddenly flooded back: the decision to throw in his lot with the men from Gwynedd stood in stark relief.

Cadmon breathed in deeply and closed his eyes. Had he really taken such an irreversible step, he asked himself? Was he making a huge mistake?

He reminded himself once again of all the reasons why he had decided to leave Tamworth and Aelfred to join up with Morvyn and the others. As he did so he calmed down: he still felt certain that he was doing the right thing.

Cadmon was planning to leave Tamworth in the late afternoon. He decided to spend a little time with Aelfred before then, although he knew that would not be easy. He prepared as much as he could for his departure, and then went to Aelfred's lodging around midday.

Aelfred was pleased to see Cadmon. He said he was already feeling the benefit of a rest and expected them to be on their way north within a couple of days. Cadmon didn't want to start talking about the next steps Aelfred had planned in case he gave himself away, and so diverted the conversation quickly.

Cadmon asked Aelfred what he would do once he was settled with a Mercian wife. He was surprised by his flat, evasive reply. It seemed quite a contrast to the last time he had seen him. Aelfred had spoken with such passion when making his case to Lord Brice just a couple of days previously. He had appeared so delighted that he had both made it to the heart of the Mercian court and effectively been offered everything he wanted – perhaps more than he had expected. Cadmon could see now, from Aelfred's eyes and his body language, that he was feeling deflated, but he put it down to a combination of anti-climax and tiredness after his illness and the journey from Helme to Tamworth.

Aelfred asked Cadmon about his longer-term plans now that he was free. Cadmon talked very generally about his longing to marry Dora, but he was careful not to give any hint about where they might live. Aelfred asked directly whether he would settle in Mercia. Cadmon gave a non-committal reply about needing to talk to Dora and her family. If he noticed any equivocation Aelfred didn't mention it: he seemed genuinely interested in how Cadmon envisaged marriage, how he would get on with Dora's parents and other relatives, what Dora would feel about possibly leaving Helme.

Aelfred gradually brightened up. It was a relaxed and comfortable chat. Some of the tension of the previous month seemed to melt away.

Cadmon felt wistful as they parted as well as pangs of guilt, especially as Aelfred said, 'See you tomorrow.' It was clear that Aelfred had no inkling of the ruse Cadmon was planning.

Within a couple of hours Cadmon was heading out of Tamworth by the most circuitous and covert route possible. Another episode in his extraordinary personal saga was beginning.

Chapter 28

Questions and decisions

L ord Brice was told early the next day that Cadmon had disappeared. He also learned that Lord Harald had returned from his raid the previous evening.

Brice had been planning to see Harald once he returned anyway, but the news about Cadmon prompted him to seek out his fellow earl immediately. The nagging doubts in his mind about the two Northumbrians were now more insistent than ever.

Brice reflected on his relationship with Harald. As two of King Penda's senior courtiers they worked together closely, and they had done so for many years. Brice respected Harald and valued his opinions, but he didn't trust him. He was also jealous of him. Brice had long acknowledged to himself that Harald was taller, stronger, better-looking and a smoother talker: he worried continually that as a result Harald had a better reputation at court.

Brice was in a quandary. He was always on the lookout for ways of enhancing his own reputation. He believed that delivering a fabulous treasure hoard to the king would do just that. He didn't want to share any of the glory, least of all with Harald. On the other hand, he was worried that something could go horribly wrong. If it did, he wanted to be able to spread any blame. On balance he had decided that he would need to share at least some of the glory in order to provide a degree of protection in a worst-case scenario.

'So, my good Lord Harald, did you manage to sort out the Cornovii boys and mete out some justice?' Brice asked cheerfully once he had tracked him down.

'We certainly did, Brice,' Harald replied. 'It was a very successful raid indeed. We burned a few Cornovii villages, hanged a few chaps, and generally spread some fear and misery. Rough justice, I would say! Even if the men we executed weren't the ones who've been causing the most trouble, I suspect the warlords will think twice before they plan any more mischief.'

'That sounds great, Harald,' Lord Brice enthused. 'Those native tribes to the west are such a menace. In the end I'm sure we'll have to move west and either conquer them or push them back in to Gwynedd and the other Welsh kingdoms. For one thing, it's a pain in the neck having to deal with their raids; but there's a lot of really good land out there as well – and I'd rather we had it than the Cornovii.'

'I agree entirely,' Harald said. 'It's the obvious next step for Mercia; but I guess the king's wary about upsetting the Welsh kingdoms. They might react badly if he moves too openly to absorb the land between us and them. He still sees them as crucial allies against Northumbria.'

'I know,' Brice replied. 'It puzzles me that the king's so intent on enmity with Northumbria. I guess he wants Mercia to become the most powerful Saxon kingdom; but to my mind it'd make more sense to sort things out in the west first and put the Welsh in their place. Anyway, that brings me neatly to what I want to talk to you about just now. I gather you met the envoys from Gwynedd as you went out on your raid?'

'Yes,' Harald confirmed. 'Seeing them brought back mixed memories of the last time they were in Tamworth actually!'

'Well, they arrived here and, for once, we had some useful discussions with them. They actually just left this morning to head back to Gwynedd,' Brice continued. 'The main purpose of their visit obviously was to talk about military collaboration. But they also had a couple of rather strange Northumbrian lads in tow. And I'm really not sure what to make of them.'

'I did see two other men with the Welsh,' Harald said, 'but they weren't introduced. Tell me more, I'm intrigued!'

Brice filled Harald in on Aelfred and Cadmon and their story and explained his decision to send men with them to Deira to recover the hoard. He also showed him the gold sword pommel. Earl Harald was as impressed with the pommel as Brice had been, and equally as fascinated by the prospect of the hoard.

'If Aelfred is genuine and he guides us to the treasure, I've promised him a quality Mercian bride as part of his reward,' Brice concluded. 'He claims to be the son of a Northumbrian noble, I assume he's not married already, and he's a handsome chap – so I think he'd be a good match. In fact, I was wondering whether he might be suitable for your second daughter?'

'That's a great idea, Brice,' Earl Harald said enthusiastically. 'We've been thinking about a husband for Sigeberg, and so thank you for bearing her in mind. But I think I'll wait and see what this chap delivers before mooting the idea with her or my wife, if that's alright!'

'So, when does the party leave to get the treasure?' Harald then asked.

'The day after tomorrow, at least that's the plan,' Brice replied. 'I've assigned four of our toughest and most resourceful men to accompany the Northumbrians. They know the terrain further north really well. But to be absolutely honest, Harald, I've got doubts about the whole thing. I can't make up my mind whether Aelfred is genuine – or if he's a spy, or a fantasist, or just a plain liar.'

'To complicate matters even further the second man, Cadmon, who's Aelfred's ex-slave, has now disappeared – seemingly into thin air,' Brice continued. 'They're not prisoners, and so Cadmon may just have decided to claim his freedom while he could; and, of course, he may yet return. But his disappearance has raised loads more questions for me about what the pair are up to.'

'What do you think, Harald?' Brice asked, tilting his head to one side, his expression a puzzled frown.

Harald laughed as he said, 'It's certainly quite a mystery. I can well see why you're undecided. What's my instinctive reaction? There's a ring of truth to Aelfred's story. I can see why some people in Northumbria are disenchanted with the conversion to Christianity. I also get why they may look towards us. Mercia is the coming power – and, of course, we're the last pagans standing.'

Harald looked thoughtful, and then carried on, 'The plan sounds over-elaborate if his aim is simply to lure a few of our men into an ambush. Personally, I would go with your original decision. We don't have much to lose if things go awry except a bit of embarrassment. And there's potentially quite a lot to gain. This pommel is certainly exceptionally good quality. If there's more stuff like it buried in Deira we might as well try to get our hands on it. If the slave gets there first, double-crosses his ex-master, and scoops up the treasure it'll be annoying; but nothing ventured nothing gained is normally my motto.'

'But they're all top of the head thoughts,' Harald concluded. 'You've met the chaps, and so it's your call, Brice.'

Brice was reassured to some extent: if it did go wrong Harald would now share some of the blame. Yet the discussion had not assuaged his doubts.

'Thanks, Harald, that's immensely helpful,' Brice said. 'But I have to say I'm still in two minds. Something in my waters is telling me there's a great deal more to this than meets the eye. I think I'll still ask our chaps to prepare to accompany the Northumbrians the day after tomorrow; but if Cadmon's not back by first thing tomorrow I'm going to call if off.'

'In that case I'll also have Aelfred executed as a spy. I'm half-certain already that's what he is,' Brice continued. 'I take your point there might not be much to lose; but there's a risk the Northumbrians will capture and use our men as hostages. I doubt whether our chaps would give much away even if tortured. And I'm sure we wouldn't pay any sort of ransom. But it wouldn't be a good look for us.'

'I do get that, Brice,' Harald said thoughtfully. 'I hadn't thought of our men being taken hostage. I agree it'd be better to be rid of Aelfred if you've any doubts rather than to let him go back to York. Better to be safe than sorry is another of my mottos. I accept it contradicts my other motto, but I think you can 'venture safely', so to speak!'

* * * * * * *

As Brice and Harald discussed their next steps, Aelfred was contemplating the way ahead after two days of almost total rest. The sun had already been high in the sky when he had awoken. He knew immediately that he felt better for the rest. He was not back to maximum energy levels, but he wanted to get started on the journey back to Deira to retrieve the treasure as soon as possible.

He had enjoyed spending time with Cadmon the previous day: that had helped to take the edge off the distaste he had felt for Lord Brice. He knew, though, that he was forcing himself to feel positive.

Aelfred was still trying to understand the reception he had received in Tamworth. The stationing of a guard outside his lodging had puzzled him. He had felt offended initially. Why do they not trust me, he had wondered? On reflection, though, as he had rested and recovered, he was inclined to be more understanding. Cadmon and he were the only people who knew the whereabouts of the treasure, and so the Mercians wanted to make absolutely sure that the knowledge was protected. Keeping them in separate rooms provided extra insurance, Aelfred suspected.

The guard was sitting outside, looking very bored. Aelfred asked him to pass on the message that he was now ready to begin the journey north.

The Mercians were obviously itching to get moving, too, because within a couple of hours four very capable-looking warriors turned up to discuss plans for the journey. Aelfred explained to them the general area in which the treasure was buried and roughly how much there was. They said that they would prepare horses and supplies for the journey, and that they would set off as early as possible on the next day but one.

The Mercians judged it would take about five days to get to the hiding place, travelling openly on horseback while in Mercian territory and covertly on foot once in Northumbria. They said that they would leave the horses at the home of a Mercian noble near the border with Northumbria.

Once they had gone, Aelfred asked the guard to send a message to Cadmon asking him to come so that he could tell him about the plans. Aelfred was surprised when the guard returned a little later to say that he couldn't find Cadmon, his room was empty, and no one else seemed to have any idea of his whereabouts.

Aelfred decided to find the Welsh agents in case Cadmon was with them. He learned that they had set off back to Gwynedd earlier that morning having completed their discussions with Penda's men.

As the hours passed, Aelfred became worried as well as irritated by Cadmon's absence. He decided to see Lord Brice: he had by now convinced himself that the Mercians were holding Cadmon as a hostage pending the safe retrieval of the treasure.

Brice denied this flatly. He said that Cadmon had disappeared into thin air. Aelfred pressed him hard: he said that he had seen Cadmon the previous day and that he had not mentioned even the possibility of leaving. But he got nowhere, and Lord Brice threatened to become extremely angry.

Aelfred was still convinced that the Mercians were holding Cadmon, but he could not prove it and so had to accept that he would have to wait, and ultimately may even need to travel without him.

Chapter 29

Races against time

At about the time Aelfred was confronting Brice – in the early evening – Cadmon was meeting in a secluded spot near the River Trent with the three Welsh agents. He had arrived safely and unseen from Tamworth the previous evening, slept in the woods, and whiled away time during the day.

The four men decided quickly to separate the next morning. Morvyn would attempt to buy horses on which Cadmon and he could travel to Deira to retrieve the treasure. Caradoc and Einion, meanwhile, would return to Gwynedd on foot to report to the king on the discussions with the Mercians and on the possibility of finding Northumbrian treasure.

Cadmon thought that this was sensible because two travellers in Deira would be less noticeable than four. He agreed with Morvyn that if anything happened to Morvyn, or they were captured, he would try to push on alone or escape so that he could retrieve the treasure and make his way to Gwynedd.

The Welshmen left Cadmon to sleep rough for a second night and went on to the hostelry. Morvyn started to ask around about the possibility of buying two horses. He said that his two colleagues would be riding back to Gwynedd while he had to return to Tamworth. He had enough royal gold available to silence any questions and soon had a deal.

The next morning Caradoc and Einion set off on the newly acquired horses, ostensibly towards Gwynedd. Morvyn made a show of starting to walk back towards Tamworth, but then went to meet Cadmon at the agreed rendezvous, away from inquisitive eyes. Once the four men were together again, Morvyn and Cadmon took the horses and set off at top speed for Deira, while the other two men began to walk towards Gwynedd.

By nightfall Morvyn and Cadmon had ridden forty miles over difficult terrain. Cadmon was an expert rider, but he had experienced few rides like this. Morvyn seemed relaxed, but the horses definitely needed a rest.

* * * * * * *

As Cadmon was beginning his whirlwind ride north Lord Brice was preparing to leave his home for the day. He was wondering whether Cadmon had returned and contemplating the steps he would have to take if he hadn't.

Brice had no compunction about potentially having to order Aelfred's execution. There was a good chance that he was a spy, but if he weren't no one in Mercia would shed any tears about the death of a young Northumbrian noble. Yet Brice admitted to himself that he would be disappointed if the chance to deliver a major treasure hoard to King Penda were to evaporate with Aelfred's life.

Brice was startled when Wynflaed interrupted his train of

thought by asking, 'How're you getting on with those Northumbrians you were telling me about, dear? I had a strange dream about them last night. I really don't know what to make of it, but it reminded me to ask you.'

Brice glanced at her sharply, and then replied, 'It's crunch time today actually. One of the lads, Cadmon, has vanished into thin air. The other one, Aelfred, then had the cheek to confront me last evening and accuse us of holding Cadmon hostage pending collection of the treasure. I was furious. I told you I wasn't sure about those two. I'm even more convinced now they're up to no good – although I'm not quite sure what. So, I've agreed with Harald that if Cadmon doesn't return today we'll execute Aelfred. I simply can't take the risk of letting a possible Northumbrian spy just wander away; and I'm certainly not keen on ...'

Brice didn't finish his sentence because of the look of utter horror on his wife's face.

'What is it, dear? You look as if you've seen a ghost or something,' Brice continued, full of concern.

'You cannot execute that boy, Brice!' Wynflaed managed to say, but it was an effort. She was trembling visibly.

'What? Why not?' Brice asked, his face screwed up in consternation now as well as concern. He was genuinely bemused.

Wynflaed took a few moments to compose herself, although her voice was still shaky when she said, 'I told you I had a dream. Well, like most dreams it was all mixed up and strange, but the monk from Lindisfarne I was telling you about was definitely involved. He was trying to protect a young man. I'm not quite sure why – obviously, I haven't actually seen either of them in the flesh – but I was sure in the dream it was one of your Northumbrians. The young man seemed to be in danger. It felt important he should be protected. It also felt in the dream as if I were meant to do something.'

Wynflaed was struggling to express herself, but managed to continue eventually, 'I woke up in quite a state, I can tell you. But when I thought about it, I felt better because I knew you'd decided to believe the Northumbrians' story and to have them escorted north to collect the treasure. Then you suddenly tell me one of the men has disappeared mysteriously, and you might have the other executed today!'

Brice was not often lost for words, but he was utterly flummoxed on this occasion. Finally, he said, 'I can see why you're upset, dear, that sounds very distressing. But it was only a dream. And, as you say, a fairly mixed up one at that. But I'm not quite sure why you're expecting me to change a decision because of a dream. We can't run a kingdom that way.'

'Come on, Brice,' Wynflaed cried, 'that's not fair. I agree there are all sorts of dreams. But it is one of the ways in which the gods communicate with us. Our people have always tried to understand and interpret dreams. Yes, my dream was strange, but the message was clear. I'm telling you right now, I'll be very unhappy if either of those men were executed. We run a real risk of upsetting the gods. I don't want to suffer the consequences.'

Brice looked aghast, and, again, did not know what to say. He knew that once Wynflaed was convinced about something she would not be moved easily – and that she would do whatever she could to get her way.

They looked at each other for a few moments. Wynflaed broke the silence eventually, now speaking more gently, 'I know it's not an easy decision for you, Brice. It's a very odd situation indeed, I get that. I also realise there could be risks in sending four of our men north with these chaps. I've never interfered with your work; but I cannot overstate how strong a premonition I have following my dream. I really do believe something awful could happen to us if you were to put either or both of those men to death.'

She paused, and then said, 'I promise to have a word with the king on your behalf if things do go wrong and it turns out the Northumbrians have tricked us. The king is very committed to his family as you know. I can't promise he would listen to me, but it might help.'

Brice sighed, looked away, and then turned back to face his wife. 'Right you are, dear,' he said heavily. 'I have heard you. I promise not to have either of them executed.'

'Thank you, Brice, that really does mean a great deal,' Wynflaed said simply.

A few minutes later Brice found out that Cadmon had not returned.

Brice quickly sought out Lord Harald and brought him up to date. It was a warm, humid morning: the combination of the stressful conversation with Wynflaed, the temperature, and his hurry had made Brice sweat profusely. 'So,' Brice concluded, wiping his brow with his hand, 'I don't think I really have much choice. I don't think a chap should always change his mind just because his wife's had a dream. But it's a bit different when the chap's wife is the king's niece! Against my better judgement frankly I'm going to give the go ahead for our four men to accompany Aelfred tomorrow even if Cadmon doesn't return. Then let's see what happens.'

His fellow noble nodded his head, smiled sympathetically, and said, 'Well, hopefully you'll see the benefits of being married to the king's niece if it does go wrong. I'm sure Wynflaed'll keep her promise and put in a word for you! It's a pity the king's still away actually. This is a decision we might have put to him if he were in Tamworth. But I understand speed is of the essence. Anyway, I'm still perfectly prepared to support the decision.'

Brice smiled gratefully. 'Thanks, Harald, I appreciate that,' he said, and then continued, 'By the way, have you heard anything about a monk from Northumbria visiting and talking to some of our people? Wynflaed told me she went to a gathering in the last week or so. That seems to have prompted her dream.'

'I did hear something about that, yes,' Harald replied vaguely. 'I can't say I was too interested. With Mercia's reputation growing far and wide, we seem to be attracting all sorts of weird and wonderful folk to court. They want to buy and sell goods, and also ideas. Personally, I treat them all with a pinch of salt.'

'I don't know, Harald,' Brice replied ominously. 'I don't like the idea of these Christians spreading their ideas in Tamworth. It could be the thin end of the wedge. Look at what happened in Northumbria. Before we know it, the king will have converted, and then he'll be ordering everyone else to do the same.'

Harald laughed. 'Come on, Brice, lighten up. I really cannot see King Penda falling for that. He's having far too much fun!' he exclaimed.

* * * * * * *

A few hundred yards away, blithely unaware that his life had been in the balance, Aelfred began his last full day in Tamworth.

He spent some time with his four Mercian escorts as they prepared for the journey, chose a horse for him from the royal stables for the first leg, and talked about options for the walking stages.

It turned out that all four men knew Deira reasonably well: three of them had fought at the battle of Hatfield, and all of them had been in and out of Northumbria since on various spying missions. They wouldn't talk much about either the battle or their undercover missions, but it was clear to Aelfred that these were warriors who were highly regarded and trusted by Penda and his hierarchy.

Aelfred felt absorbed and excited while immersed in the detail of preparation, but worried and sad whenever he thought about Cadmon. He still expected him to reappear and found it hard to imagine making the journey north without him; but as the hours passed, he became more pessimistic – and bitter towards the Mercians whom he still believed were holding Cadmon hostage.

He also sensed an indefinable atmosphere of mistrust. The four men were courteous but aloof. Lord Brice made a brief appearance to wish them well on their journey but barely acknowledged Aelfred. Aelfred assumed he was still irked by his accusation about Cadmon.

Aelfred told himself it wasn't surprising that the Mercians were cautious around him: he was an outsider from an enemy kingdom who had promised much but not yet delivered.

Try as he might, Aelfred could not shake off an underlying feeling of hollowness and loneliness. Yet again, unbidden, the contrast with the sincerity and warmth of Felgild occurred to him. He thought he had pushed the conversation with Felgild to the margins of his mind, but fragments kept popping into the forefront and distracting him.

* * * * * * *

After the first day of riding Cadmon slept soundly in a make-shift camp in thick woodland, his cloak pulled tightly around him. Morvyn had assured him that he was a light sleeper and would be awake instantly in the event of any unexpected approach by either a wild beast or another human. The horses, tethered to a tree, stirred occasionally but were as tired as the two men.

They were on their way again early the next morning. Morvyn was focused and determined, and he knew the terrain well because of his experience in the army of occupation between the battles of Hatfield and Heavenfield.

There was little opportunity to talk because of the speed at which they were riding, often in single file. Cadmon day-dreamed about the future: about the moment he would arrive back in Helme, the look in Dora's eyes, the excitement they would feel as they set off for a new life in Gwynedd.

He tried, too, to imagine what Gwynedd would be like, piecing together all that he had heard from Morvyn and his companions, and the little information that Rinc had given him about the circumstances of his and his mother's capture. He wondered whether he would be able to find the village where he was born and perhaps even track down some relatives.

By the time they had travelled fifty miles the horses were exhausted, and they found a suitable spot to camp. They were within thirty miles of the treasure and so should reach it the next day. They spent the evening planning the retrieval and the start of their journey to Gwynedd. They went over possible scenarios, including what they would do and say if captured. They had had no trouble so far, but they were approaching the heart of Deira and knew that they must be wary.

'I'm really nervous about tomorrow, Morvyn,' Cadmon said. 'I can feel butterflies in my stomach. Questions keep coming into my head: will we beat Aelfred to the treasure? Will I be able to find it? Will we be able to escape from Northumbria with the treasure?'

'It's not surprising you're nervous, lad,' laughed Morvyn, who was about twenty years older than Cadmon and a perpetual optimist. 'It's going to be a big day, but I'm sure we'll be fine. We've got this far without any difficulty, haven't we?'

'I really do hope you're right,' Cadmon said passionately. 'So much is riding on this for me. I was content with my lot until just a few weeks ago; but leaving Woden's Ford has stirred up masses of issues. I used to laugh at Aelfred when he talked about the importance of having a purpose in life. I just wanted to live a day at a time, not think too much about either the past or the future.'

Cadmon stopped, looked away, and then back at Morvyn

as he said, 'It sounds grand, but now I want justice. I really feel the pain of being an orphan, a slave, an inferior in my own land. The pain's been buried all these years, I guess. I felt inspired when you told me about the prophesy that the Welsh will drive out all the Anglo-Saxon folk. Maybe it'll never happen. But I now have a vision and a purpose. I want to marry Dora, and to then be part of a great movement out of Gwynedd. It would be so unfair if anything were to happen to me tomorrow. But if it does, please will you try to find Dora and tell her how much she meant to me, and that I was planning to get back to her.'

In spite of his best efforts Cadmon could not stifle a sob as he finished in a welter of words.

'Of course, Cadmon,' Morvyn said putting his arm round the younger man's shoulders. 'I'd make every effort to find her; but it won't come to that. You'll meet up with your girl, and you'll find glory in Gwynedd, you mark my words!'

Cadmon smiled gratefully through his tears.

'I know what you mean about purpose,' Morvyn continued. 'I've never married, never had children, because I wanted to devote myself to Gwynedd's cause. I've always just wanted to serve the king. At times I've struggled. But, on the whole, I've found our surface desires are often the noisiest and most demanding, but not necessarily the most satisfying.'

As Cadmon went to sleep he remembered the last time he had seen the treasure – when he and Aelfred had buried it. He reflected, yet again, with wonder, at all that had happened in the weeks since.

* * * * * * *

Aelfred's day had started early, too, riding out from Tamworth with the four Mercian warriors. As on the previous day, they were quiet, talking only when necessary about the practicalities of the journey. Aelfred wondered whether they were warders or escorts.

Try as he might Aelfred could not dispel the melancholy he had experienced in the last few days. His mood was not helped by the damp, overcast weather. He missed Cadmon more than he could have imagined. He could not help feeling disenchanted by his experience of Mercia – the people he had met had seemed cold, harsh and cynical.

They rode hard and had covered almost fifty miles by the time they arrived at their destination on the edge of Mercian territory. Aelfred paid little attention to the route or his surroundings. He felt curiously detached throughout the day, as if he were observing himself from afar.

He was not in the mood to engage with the noble and his family who hosted them; pleading tiredness he retired early to bed.

Some hours later Aelfred awoke with a start. He had been in the most vivid dream he could remember. It had felt remarkably life-like. He had been walking in the hills near Woden's Ford when a voice had told him that he could ask for anything he liked. Aelfred strained to remember to whom the voice belonged, but all he could recall were the deep timbre and the clarity of the words.

Aelfred's response in the dream had been to ask to know the truth.

He could remember nothing else, certainly not a response to his request: he assumed he had awoken at that point.

As he lay awake, he reflected how different the request he had made in his dream had been from the typical desire of his clan and his people for more wealth and power.

Suddenly, unbidden, two thoughts occurred to him. It was as if they had entered his mind fully formed. He was so surprised that he sat up in bed in a mixture of excitement and dismay.

The first thought was an insight into Cadmon's unexpected departure. Aelfred recalled Cadmon's feelings for Dora and his deep interest in everything that the Welshmen had had to say about Gwynedd. Aelfred knew, in a way he could not explain, that Cadmon was not being held by the Mercians, but had taken advantage of his free status to go back to find Dora and then attempt to return to the land of his birth.

Aelfred remembered the last moment he had seen Cadmon as he had left his lodging and the unfathomable look in Cadmon's eyes. Aelfred there and then forgave Cadmon for not telling him he was leaving. He knew he was trying to protect both Aelfred and himself as best he could: if Aelfred did not know, he would not be able to tell the Mercians.

The second thought was that he must abandon the journey to retrieve the treasure and head immediately to Lindisfarne to continue the discussion with Felgild!

Aelfred tried to push away this amazing, seemingly ridiculous notion. He told himself that it was a product of his negative feelings of the last few days, that he couldn't risk so much to give up on his mission at this last moment, that

Felgild's words about Lindisfarne must have contained some sort of charm.

Yet the idea would not budge. The more he examined it the more peaceful he felt.

His mother had suggested the previous year that he meet the monks of Lindisfarne. Felgild had invited him to visit the monastery whenever he wanted.

On both occasions it had felt like the last thing he wanted to do. Now, incredibly, going to Lindisfarne seemed like the right thing to do, and far more attractive than retrieving the treasure and spending more time in Mercia.

* * * * * * *

As Morvyn and Cadmon set out on what they expected to be the final leg of their quest they decided to take it much more slowly for the sake of the horses.

A combination of walking and trotting had taken them about ten miles by mid-morning, still about twenty miles away from the hiding place. As they trotted along a woodland path they could see coming towards them a party of six riders, all clearly well-armed. The other men deliberately barred their way, but unthreateningly at this stage.

'Good day, my friends,' the leading rider said in a level voice. 'May I ask where you're heading?'

'Certainly,' Cadmon said. He and Morvyn had agreed that, as he spoke with a Northumbrian dialect and accent, he should take the lead if they were stopped. 'We've travelled from Wessex. We're taking messages to King Oswald's court at Bamburgh.'

'That's a long and important journey for two men to make alone,' the horseman said, the note of scepticism evident in his voice, the question-mark implicit but undoubtedly hanging in the air.

'We wanted to be as unobtrusive as possible as we skirted Mercian territory. We thought two riders would attract less suspicion than a larger party,' Cadmon replied.

'I can tell you're Northumbrian,' the interlocutor said, 'but what about your friend?'

'I'm from Wessex,' Morvyn said. 'I'm pleased to be doing my bit to build the alliance between Northumbria and Wessex.'

The horseman narrowed his eyes, furrowed his brow, and tilted his head towards Morvyn. 'Have you always lived in Wessex, pal?' he asked.

'Yes, certainly,' Morvyn replied confidently.

'Ummm, there's something about your accent that's familiar. But you don't sound like Wessex men I've met before – although, to be fair, I haven't met many,' the Northumbrian said slowly, his face still screwed in concentration.

'Of course,' he said after a few moments, his face clearing, and then immediately darkening into a look of intense dislike.

'I could swear he sounds remarkably like the men of Gwynedd who occupied Northumbria after Hatfield,' the man said to his companions. 'Which of us will ever forget the indignity Cadwallon's army heaped on us during that year? I thought I'd heard the last of the cursed Gwynedd lilt after they were beaten at Heavenfield.'

The other horsemen said nothing, but their expressions were hostile.

'That's not true,' Morvyn said insistently. 'I'm a Wessex man, I give you my word.'

The situation, however, had shifted irrevocably.

'Well, you may be right,' the leader said, still evenly. 'But we're under orders to look out for spies from Mercia and Gwynedd. There've been plenty of sightings of spies over the last few years, and I can't yet be certain we're not looking at two more. I would like you both to dismount. We'll then take you to York for questioning.'

Morvyn realised that he had no alternative. He did as he was told, dismounting slowly as one of the riders jumped from his own horse and came to take him captive.

But, as Cadmon started to follow suit, Morvyn glanced at him and flicked his eyes towards the deep woods to his left.

Cadmon, who was fit and agile, took the hint, launched himself from his horse, and bounded towards the trees.

But the barely noticeable eye contact had been noticed by one of the riders. It gave him just enough time to ready the spear he was carrying, and then hurl it towards Cadmon's retreating back.

The throw was deadly accurate. Morvyn could only watch in horror as his young companion fell forwards and lay motionless.

None of the watchers doubted that Cadmon had died instantly. This was confirmed by the leading horseman who dismounted, walked over to Cadmon, pulled out the spear, and rolled the inert body. 'Well done, my man, that was some shot. Our friend will spy no more,' he said.

'Now,' he continued, turning to Morvyn, 'I suggest you tell us the truth, or you'll meet a similar fate.'

The Northumbrians bound Morvyn's hands and tied him to his horse's reins. Cadmon's body was secured on his own horse which was tied to Morvyn's. One of the Northumbrian riders then led the two horses by a rope, and the other five riders followed on behind as the convoy set off for York.

* * * * * * *

For the rest of the night after his dream Aelfred had wrestled with the sudden impulse to head to Lindisfarne. As he got ready for the day he felt as if he had not had enough sleep; but even so he was experiencing an inner calmness such as he could not remember.

The Mercians again focussed entirely on the journey and the task in hand as they left the horses behind at the home of the Mercian noble and began to walk; conversation was infrequent and perfunctory.

Aelfred didn't mind. He relished the time to process his feelings, and to question the insistent voice in his head telling him he must travel to Lindisfarne. The churning, negative mood of the previous day had gone. He now felt remorse for all that he had done over the last few weeks, but it was producing clarity about the way ahead rather than traumatising and disabling guilt.

Was he experiencing now what he had hoped for all those years ago in the River Swale? Aelfred wasn't sure. He couldn't believe so suddenly that Christianity was true and that his grandfather and great uncle and generations of ancestors had been wrong.

Yet he knew, with a conviction that he could not understand, that he must try to get to Lindisfarne and follow up the conversation with Felgild which he had started in Elmet: he must know the truth.

He decided that, as a first step, he must break away from the Mercians as soon as he possibly could. He had worked out roughly where he was. He believed that he could make his way to the sub-monastery on the east coast to which Felgild and his companions had been heading after their time in Elmet. He assumed that from there he might be able to get a boat ride to Lindisfarne.

The weather changed over the course of the day: from overcast to bright and increasingly warm. The Mercians said that they wouldn't need the tents they had brought that night and that they could sleep in the open. Aelfred sensed his opportunity.

As they settled later to sleep under the stars Aelfred manoeuvred himself to the outside of the circle. The Mercians were not at all suspicious; Aelfred realised now that they were primarily escorts rather than guards.

Aelfred lay still. He fought his tiredness as he tried to stay awake. Once he was certain that the others were deeply asleep, he began to shuffle carefully, silently and slowly away from the circle. Once he was a few yards away he eased himself upright, checked that none of the Mercians was stirring, and then stood up very cautiously.

He began to tiptoe away, taking extreme care to avoid stepping on anything which would emit any sound. He speeded up gradually. He began to run once he felt he was completely out of earshot.

He was carrying nothing but his cloak; he felt as light as a feather.

* * * * * * *

Once in York Morvyn was taken to what appeared to be a cellar. He was told it was an old Roman prison. Two different Northumbrian men came in and without any introduction began to question him aggressively. For a while he stuck to his story that he was from Wessex and was bringing messages to the royal court at Bamburgh.

His captors simply did not believe him. 'We've met men of Wessex before and they don't sound anything like you,' one of them said. 'Either you tell us the truth, in which case there's a chance we'll let you go, or you don't, and you'll die horribly.'

Morvyn didn't trust his captors, but he decided he had nothing to lose. Telling them most of the truth was unlikely to jeopardise Aelfred's mission: even if Aelfred had not already retrieved the treasure, Morvyn was not going to give his captors even the vaguest hint of its whereabouts. Yet telling them of the loss of the royal treasure would be demoralising for Northumbria, and that was not a bad thing to his mind.

He told them that Cadmon had escaped from Woden's Ford, reburied a royal treasure hoard in a secret location, then fled towards Gwynedd, and had met him on the way. Morvyn admitted to being from Gwynedd. He said Cadmon had offered to show him the treasure and then accompany him to Gwynedd where he wanted to settle. He didn't mention Aelfred or his two companions or the discussions in Tamworth. He maintained that only Cadmon had known where the treasure was hidden, and that he had been relying entirely on him to guide them to it.

Morvyn's captors looked at each other. It sounded a far-fetched tale, but it clearly had enough of a ring of truth. They asked some questions about how and when they had met and about their journey north, and then pressed Morvyn about the whereabouts of the treasure. 'How can you be so sure our late friend was telling the truth? Maybe it was a pack of lies?' they asked.

'Maybe, but I'm certain it was the truth,' Morvyn said. 'What did he have to gain by leading me along if there was no treasure? If he had wanted to rob me, he could have done so much further back.'

There was a short silence as the two men assessed what they had heard. 'I think our next step will be to contact Rinc, the thegn of Woden's Ford, bring him here to meet you, and see if he recognises the body of his ex-slave,' one of the captors said. 'We'll decide what to do with you after that. In the meantime, this is your home. Enjoy our hospitality!'

The men laughed as they walked out; Morvyn didn't.

* * * * * * *

Aelfred kept running. Fortunately, the moon was shining brightly. Aelfred was reminded of the night he and Cadmon had left Woden's Ford and reburied the treasure.

He knew the Mercians would expect him to head north towards the treasure, and so he headed due south for some time. When he came to a large stream he waded along it for a few hundred yards to cover his tracks, got out on the other side, and started heading north-east.

He slowed eventually to a walk. As dawn broke he noticed something in the sky ahead. An early kestrel was hovering, its wings beating furiously, its head perfectly still, its eyes trained on the ground for potential prey.

It seemed to Aelfred to be a sign. There would be turbulent times ahead, he would have to be very active – but he had been given an inner peace which would enable him to stay clear-headed.

He was very tired, very hungry, but felt calm.

He found a convenient spot, lay down under his cloak, and slept deeply.

Chapter 30

Conclusions

Rinc was in the fields at Woden's Ford chatting to some of the peasants about plans for the harvest when he saw two horsemen in the distance, clearly in a hurry and galloping towards them. As they drew near Rinc signalled to them. They slowed and halted as they recognised him.

Rinc knew the two men slightly. They were members of Oswald's war band who were stationed in what used to be the royal court of Deira in York, now the local headquarters of the Northumbrian king. He was surprised but not worried. Rinc was a thegn who was trusted by Oswald, and so it would not be unusual for a royal message or summons to be sent to Woden's Ford.

His surprise turned quickly to shock and incredulity as the men told Rinc their news. 'You cannot be serious!' he said. 'Aelfred and Cadmon left here around six weeks ago to travel round the borders of Deira. We expect them back any day. Aelfred'll then travel to Bernicia to meet his future bride.'

It was as if Rinc was challenging the men to change their story.

'I'm sorry,' the older of the two said, as sympathetically as he could. 'We were both there yesterday when the man who has been named as your slave was asked to stop. He was with a man who has confessed to being from Gwynedd, and who we believe is a spy. We saw the slave die. The other man is in the royal prison in York. He's adamant they came to Northumbria to collect some hidden treasure. It'd be really helpful if you could come back with us to identify the dead man – if, of course, that's who he is. And it would be good if you could question the Welshman yourself.'

'Don't worry, I'm coming,' Rinc said vehemently. 'But first I want to go and check something.'

Rinc felt as if a whirlwind had touched down, lifted him off the ground, and deposited him in a completely different place. Twenty minutes previously he had not had any significant cares in the world: his main preoccupation had been about how well the harvest was going.

He told the royal messengers to return to York, and to explain that he would follow on very quickly. He then asked one of the peasants to run to summon his brother, Alwyn, and another to saddle their two best horses.

Half an hour later Rinc and Alwyn were cantering through the woods towards the place where they had hidden the royal treasure seven years previously. Rinc had filled Alwyn in on the startling news. Once the forest got too thick they dismounted, tethered the horses, and ran on, following the secret marks on the trees.

Rinc was hoping against hope that the news was wrong – a deliberate hoax or a garbled misunderstanding. He and Alwyn checked the treasure every few months: they had last done so about three months previously, and it had been safe and sound.

Once they reached the hiding place, they started digging furiously with the spades they had brought. It was soon clear that the treasure had gone. The brothers looked at each other aghast. A welter of emotions was roiling within Rinc: anger, fear, consternation, shock.

'How? Why? Where?' he agonised aloud. He did not have the control to articulate anything more.

Alwyn, who had always been cooler and more rational in tense situations, was almost equally stunned. 'I don't know,' he said limply. 'But I think we should go to York immediately and talk to this Welshman.'

Rinc nodded. The brothers ran back to the horses, dropped off the spades at Woden's Ford, and galloped all the way to York. They were there within an hour. They had not spoken a word since they had left the empty hiding place where the hoard had lain for so many years.

Rinc and Alwyn were shown the body as soon as they arrived. 'It's Cadmon alright. I just can't believe it. Something's gone terribly wrong,' Rinc said.

One of the men who had interrogated Morvyn the previous day was with Rinc and Alwyn. He refrained from pointing out to Rinc that he had just stated the obvious; he merely nodded sympathetically to acknowledge the positive identification of the body.

'I'm sorry,' the man said. 'I know this must be difficult, but let's go and talk to our Welsh friend.'

'Yes, let's – and let's shake some sense out of him,' Rinc said, his voice crackling with anger and pain. Alwyn put his hand on his shoulder as they walked between rooms in the prison, but Rinc shrugged it off.

Morvyn was looking tired and dishevelled when the three men walked into his cell. He had obviously had a rough night. Rinc looked at him with cold fury, but Morvyn did not make eye contact.

'Right, you Welsh dog, let's hear the truth!' Rinc demanded, the cold fury spreading from his eyes to his voice.

Morvyn looked at Rinc for the first time and said evenly, 'I told the truth to your friends yesterday: I can't remake reality.'

Rinc smashed his boot on the stone floor and shouted, 'Don't be clever with me, Wealas! You lot are all instinctive liars. I want to know what happened – every last detail.'

Morvyn was unperturbed by the outburst. After a few moments he recounted his story exactly as he had told it the previous day. Rinc listened intently, and then said, 'But what's happened to my son? And where's the treasure buried? Don't tell me you don't know because I won't believe you.'

'I don't know,' Morvyn said simply.

The exchanges went on for a few minutes. Alwyn also quizzed Morvyn, less aggressively, but the Welshman was unshakeable.

Rinc rose with an air of finality. 'I simply don't believe him,' he said, now in a more controlled voice. 'What I do believe is that Aelfred foolishly broke his promise to keep the secret of the treasure and told Cadmon about it during their trip. Cadmon then murdered Aelfred, reburied the treasure, and somehow linked up with this thief.'

The brothers looked at each other in utter dismay, but they had no idea what else to ask Morvyn. Rinc then turned to the guard and said, 'Right, have him executed, and then throw both bodies to the dogs: that's the only way to deal with murderers, traitors and thieves.'

Morvyn shook his head as Rinc and Alwyn walked out,

leaving him with Oswald's man; but Morvyn knew it was over. In Welsh he said in a calm voice, 'Into your hands I commit my spirit,' and made the sign of the cross over his heart.

* * * * * * *

Back at Woden's Ford a couple of hours later Rinc and Alwyn sat with Hilda. They were all silent, each of them buried in their own thoughts. Hilda was looking baffled as much as shocked. Her husband and brother-in-law had just told her all they knew. She had initially refused to believe them.

'Are you sure it was Cadmon's body? And how can you be certain Aelfred was murdered?' she had asked.

The two men had assured her that there was absolutely no question both that Cadmon was dead and that the treasure had been taken from its hiding place. Rinc had repeated three times his theory about Aelfred's fate, but he admitted that it was only a theory for which he had no hard evidence.

Hilda broke the silence. 'I simply cannot accept Cadmon murdered Aelfred. I know those two boys better than anyone else. I brought them both up. I saw the depth of their love for one another. They may have fallen out from time to time, but they wouldn't hurt each other. I accept Cadmon's dead, and my heart weeps for him. But I will not believe Aelfred is dead until either I see the body, or I hear from someone I trust who's seen it. He's alive somewhere. I wish I knew where, but he will return.'

The woman who for so many years had often appeared to

be a sad, melancholy presence at Woden's Ford was transformed in to a she-wolf. Her dark eyes flashed, her voice was strong and insistent, every fibre in her body seemed to throb with passion.

'I may have only given birth to one healthy child, but I will not give up on him lightly.' With these words Hilda rose and left the two men staring at each other.

'I take her point that there isn't any evidence, but I can't see how Aelfred is still alive,' Alwyn said after a few moments. 'Surely if he were alive he would come back here. I know he could be difficult at times, but he wasn't a traitor. D'you think it would be worth getting our best hunting dogs down to where the treasure was hidden and see if they can pick up any trace? It's probably a long shot, but it wouldn't do any harm.'

'Yes, let's do that,' Rinc replied in a flat monotone. His body language matched the tone of his voice: it was as if the earlier fury had blown through him and now left him sagging emotionally, drained of his life-force.

Alwyn looked at him, was on the verge of saying something, but then thought better of it. He went alone to fetch the dogs. As he had suspected, it was a fruitless exercise. He put down some clothes which Aelfred and Cadmon had worn just before they went away for the dogs to smell, but the dogs could not pick up any matching scent.

He returned three hours later. It looked as if Rinc had not moved. He sat in the same slumped position. 'Come on, Rinc,' Alwyn said as gently as he could manage. 'I know it's tough, but life must go on.'

Alwyn half-expected – and perhaps hoped for – an indignant

response. Instead Rinc said resignedly, 'I know, it just seems so utterly unbelievable, so wrong, so completely crazy.'

The brothers agreed that all they could do for the next few days was to send out men to look for clues in the widest area possible, but neither of them held out much hope that they would find anything.

Hilda returned at this point. Her eyes were red, but she carried herself proudly. 'I'm sorry,' she said. 'I didn't mean to suggest earlier you were lying. I know each of us has to handle this in our own way. I'll just wait patiently for Aelfred to make contact. He's out there somewhere.'

* * * * * * *

'I'm absolutely certain he's still alive. I don't know where Aelfred is, or when I'll see him, but he's not dead.'

Hilda was talking to Bertha and Brigit the next day. Her eyes were still red-rimmed, and there were dark shadows under them, but she looked calm.

'Poor, poor you,' Bertha said sympathetically. 'I can see you didn't sleep very well last night. It's not surprising. It feels a bit like Hatfield all over again. But as well as the uncertainty there's mystery, too. Even though we weren't sure whether they would come back after Hatfield, at least we knew roughly where the men had gone, and why.'

'Yes, it's just so bewildering,' Brigit agreed, shaking her head slowly. 'Let me make sure I understand what we know, Hilda. Aelfred and Cadmon went off on their trip a few weeks ago and were due back around now. You hadn't heard from them, but you weren't expecting to anyway. Now we hear that Cadmon returned to Deira, without Aelfred but with an unknown Welsh man, to recover some treasure which we didn't know about but which the boys had stolen, and was killed as a spy just a few miles away by our own king's men. In the meantime, Aelfred seems to have vanished into thin air.'

'That's about it,' Hilda replied sadly. 'It does sound incredible when you say it out loud. What hurts so much is Aelfred must have planned the deception extremely thoroughly. Rinc has told me the existence and whereabouts of the treasure were known only to those on the clan council and to Aelfred. It was a very closely guarded secret. I certainly had no idea about the treasure: I assume neither of you did, either?'

Bertha and Brigit shook their heads in answer to Hilda's question.

'I just can't stop wondering what they intended to do with the treasure,' Brigit said, bafflement etched on her face. 'Alwyn says it was hidden in the forest just a few miles away seven years ago, and never touched from that day on – until Aelfred and Cadmon removed it and apparently hid it somewhere else in Deira. They must have had some idea what they were going to do with it. Do you think this chap from Gwynedd had been in touch with them somehow? Perhaps they arranged to meet him, and then he and Cadmon tricked Aelfred? It seems preposterous, but why else was Cadmon coming back alone with the Welshman?'

'I guess that's possible,' Bertha said. 'It's hard to believe, though. Cadmon was always such a cheerful, respectful lad. I know he was a slave, but I often forgot he wasn't Aelfred's little brother. What could have possessed him to trick Aelfred, or even worse? It's so sad to think of Cadmon being killed effectively as an outlaw. But perhaps it served him right in the end.'

Bertha paused thoughtfully, and then went on, 'You just never know what's going on in other folks' heads, whatever things look like on the surface. Is it even possible that after all these years Cadmon wanted revenge for the way his father was killed and his mother enslaved?'

'No, no, no!' Hilda shouted. Her sisters in law looked at her in surprise: they had never heard an outburst like this from Hilda.

Hilda continued, her voice still quivering but quieter, 'It's a complete mystery, but I simply cannot accept Cadmon hurt Aelfred or was out for revenge. I even find it hard to believe he could trick Aelfred. As you say, Bertha, they were like brothers all their lives – and they got on so well.'

The three women were quiet for a few moments, and then Hilda said, 'I've wracked my brains for any sign whatsoever that might throw any light on where Aelfred is now. He's always thought a great deal – perhaps over-thought things. And we all know he's quiet and can be very secretive. I was very worried after Edith's death he would do something really extreme. Remember how ill he was, and how low his mood dropped? In fact, Cadmon was really concerned, too, and came to talk to me. But over the last year Aelfred had seemed to be getting on with things without any difficulty. I was quite pleased by the way he appeared to recover. I certainly didn't see any sign he was about to do anything so outrageous.'

Hilda's sisters in law both nodded, their brows furrowed, and then Brigit said, 'I do absolutely see what you mean, Hilda. I certainly didn't see anything which caused me alarm; and Alwyn didn't mention any concerns to me, either. Aelfred's always been very intense though. He was surprisingly anti-Christian from a very young age. He's never hidden his doubts about our change of religion. Do you think there's any chance he could have gone off to a pagan kingdom where he might feel more comfortable?'

'I do take the point, Brigit, and it's a reasonable thought,' Hilda replied. 'But I really can't see him doing that. He's very anti-Christian, but he's also very loyal to us. I can't imagine he'd even think about leaving his family behind. One of his main objectives in life was to make Eadwell proud: I don't think running away to Mercia, or anywhere else, would do that. Even the way he agreed, without any fuss, to marry this lass up in Bernicia who you identified for us, Bertha, suggests he's still very committed to the clan.'

There was another pause, and then Hilda said, 'I did suggest when he was so low last year that he go to Lindisfarne to talk to the monks up there – you know, just to get a different perspective. He said he would think about it. But I'm not sure he ever took the idea very seriously. I suppose it's just about conceivable he's decided to go there, but I think highly unlikely.'

'I cannot for one moment imagine Aelfred going anywhere near Lindisfarne,' Bertha said firmly. 'He was so anti-Christian.'

'It's such a strange situation,' she continued. 'I'm sure Rinc and Alwyn will carry on searching for Aelfred and the treasure. But I guess it's almost impossible to know where to look because there are no clues at all.'

'Yes, it's incredibly upsetting and frustrating,' Hilda said, sighing. 'I'm sure Aelfred's alive; but even so it's awfully hard when all you can do is wait and pray.'

Hilda then continued, in a rather peevish tone, 'What's made me feel even worse over the last day is that Rinc actually seems more anxious about recovering the wretched treasure hoard than with finding Aelfred. It's important because it's the king's treasure, and it'll be a very big deal if we've lost it. I understand completely that Rinc's angry with Aelfred for effectively stealing it. But Aelfred is his flesh and blood and heir. Surely not having any idea where he is should be the bigger worry.'

Bertha rolled her eyes and replied heavily, 'Men will be men!'

Chapter 31

Finale

The three days after he left the Mercians and struck out on his own towards the east coast monastery were the hardest of Aelfred's young life.

He carried no weapon, no money and no supplies.

His limbs ached from the exertions of the last few weeks.

His brain felt continuously foggy because of insufficient sleep.

He had a general idea of where he was heading, but he didn't know how to get there with any certainty or how long it would take.

The weather turned wet and cold as an early autumn storm hurled itself across the British Isles.

Aelfred was still trying to make sense of his sudden change of direction – and battling the doubts and questions which swirled in his mind, and, in particular, the feeling that he was betraying his grandfather and great uncle.

Depending on the circumstances, Aelfred pretended to be either a wandering, simple-minded beggar, or a pilgrim. He managed in this way to just about get enough to live on from people he met along the way, to find shelter of sorts, and to ensure that he kept heading in the right direction towards the coastal monastery.

He was soaked continually. He sensed the damp entering

every nook and cranny of his body. Even in the downpours, though, he was able to look beyond his immediate situation. As he crossed a stream which had become a raging, muddy torrent he saw symbolism. His own life had felt a bit like this at times, but all rivers reached a more tranquil stage as they reached flatter land and the sea; he hoped that he would soon enter a less turbulent period, too.

He arrived eventually at the monastery and knocked wearily on the wooden door. The monk who opened it took one look and exclaimed, 'Brother, come right in! You definitely look as if you could use some hospitality!'

The combination of shock, fatigue, uncertainty, tiredness, hunger and the wet weather had taken their toll. Aelfred had not recovered fully from his fever in Elmet, and he was now dog-tired.

The monks cared for him for the next week as he re-gathered his strength. They listened carefully to the parts of his story Aelfred felt he could share. He told them that he and a companion had travelled from Northumbria to Mercia but had become separated. He told them about his encounter with Felgild. Aelfred was interested to learn that the monks had already heard about him from Felgild when he had visited the monastery. Aelfred said that he wanted to visit Lindisfarne and talk at greater length with Felgild.

The monks didn't probe or press. They guessed that he was telling them a partial story, but they were content to give him time and space: they were monks after all, not detectives. They said there was regular interchange with their mother monastery at Lindisfarne, and that as soon as he was well enough one of them would ferry him up the coast.

* * * * * * *

The total rest in the monastery gave Aelfred plenty of time to reflect. Ever since he could remember he had felt conflicted and ill at ease for much of the time. For the last twelve months most of his waking moments had been devoted to thinking about and planning the journey to Mercia; the last few weeks had been consumed entirely in its execution.

Aelfred was now on the verge of a dramatic transition from one phase of his life to the next – in fact, from one life to another, he realised, given the probably irreversible step he was taking. He found it very difficult to imagine now that he could ever become the chief of Clan Eadrich.

As he lay in bed one night Aelfred cast his mind back over other transitions and seminal moments in his life: his grandfather's death; conversion and baptism; being mentored by Great Uncle Edgar and his thirteenth birthday; the fallout from the battle of Hatfield; finding Grimbald's body; being shown the hidden treasure on his eighteenth birthday; his ill-fated marriage and its traumatic end; the flight from Woden's Ford; the encounters with Felgild and Lord Brice; his remarkable dream and its consequences.

Aelfred wondered whether there was any pattern to it all. Was this next step he was about to take somehow preordained, inevitable? Was it the consequence of a series of random events and the way he had reacted to them? Had some external, supernatural force been leading him, shaping his will, controlling his actions?

He remembered how often throughout his life people had asked him which Aelfred had turned up today: a reflection of the many different selves he seemed able to take on and off, and his ability to hide his true feelings.

Aelfred reflected how his mother and Uncle Alwyn had talked often about how folk spend much of their time trying to satisfy others rather than following their hearts.

Had he at last found his heart, his true self, Aelfred asked himself? Had the unbidden thoughts which had kept entering his mind since that encounter with Felgild been those of his true self? Or was this yet another self, one he had adopted because he had been impressed, in spite of himself, by Felgild?

Aelfred decided that he didn't know and actually didn't really care. He did know that he had never felt more right, more relaxed, and more peaceful. He was not striving any more for anything.

He drifted gently into a deep sleep. For the first time he could remember he slept at length and dreamlessly. He woke eleven hours later.

* * * * * * *

By the end of a week of rest, healthy food, unquestioning care, and quiet reflection Aelfred felt ready for a sea journey.

The Irish monks were expert sailors and loved the sea, and so there were plenty of volunteers to make the journey north to Lindisfarne. Aelfred was a much less experienced sailor, and so very grateful to the two brothers who were in charge of the little boat as it plied up the Northumbrian coast for two days. The gales had abated, and it was a trouble-free voyage.

As they approached Lindisfarne on a clear, pleasantly warm evening a skein of geese flew low over them in the classic V formation. The noise as they called to each other carried in the still air.

Aelfred was transported back to his conversation with Felgild in Elmet, remembering his comparison of the Holy Spirit to wild geese. Aelfred's heart swelled. He was excited about what lay in store now he had reached his unexpected destination. He shook his head at the strange turns his life had taken over the last few weeks.

Aelfred and the two brothers were welcomed warmly, particularly by the two monks who had accompanied Felgild in Elmet. Aelfred explained that he had come to continue his conversation with Felgild. If they were surprised by this succinct explanation, they didn't show it. They certainly didn't question Aelfred. They told him that Felgild had been away on another mission but was due back the following day. Until then, they said, Aelfred must make himself completely at home on the island and do as he wished.

Aelfred awoke the next morning to the feeling that he had entered a giant cocoon. The mist which so often stole in from the sea up and down the east coast blanketed Lindisfarne. As he strolled around the island, he could see very little. The tide was in and so the causeway which linked it to the mainland was impassable by land.

The overall impression was of complete isolation. It felt as if Lindisfarne had retreated in to an abstract, unique and utterly peaceful dimension. Aelfred reflected that this matched his own interior feelings: since his dream he felt as if he had entered a different dimension in which the mores and values which had governed the first twenty-one years of his life no longer applied.

Felgild arrived later in the day, walking over the causeway once the tide had receded. He was thrilled to see Aelfred again, but he told him he wasn't particularly surprised.

'Why?' Aelfred asked. 'I certainly didn't expect to see you again at any time, never mind so soon.'

'It was very obvious to me you were searching for many things,' Felgild said, smiling. 'On the face of it, you were pushing against the message of Christianity. But I suspected you still had lots of unanswered questions. We monks do believe in the power of prayer, you know, and I've been praying for you ever since. I'm not saying you didn't come here of your own free will, but let's say I sense another force at work, too!'

Aelfred was intrigued, thinking back to the way the idea to travel to Lindisfarne had seemed to come from nowhere, and to Hilda's out of the blue suggestion the previous year.

'Thank you for praying for me, and for the welcome I've received,' Aelfred said. 'I'm still not sure I believe. But looking back, I can see I definitely left you in Elmet with many more questions than I'd had previously. I'd really like to spend some time with you now trying to understand Christianity.'

Felgild agreed readily, and so over the next few days the two men were closeted together for hour after hour. For Aelfred the sessions served as a confessional as well as a tutorial about Christianity. Felgild had told him gently but bluntly that he could only help him if he was completely transparent about his whole life and, in particular, what had prompted his flight from Woden's Ford.

Unlike the vast majority of Anglians the Irish monks were literate, and so Felgild also suggested that he might write down a summary of what Aelfred told him. Aelfred was keen to learn to read and write, and so thought this was an excellent idea as he would have a record on which he could build in later life.

After spending most of his life in an internal dialogue with himself about his feelings, fears and dilemmas it was something of a relief for Aelfred to be able to empty the whole jumbled collection into the lap of someone else – particularly as Felgild was a consummate listener and did not pass judgement at any point.

Aelfred included in his confession the precise details of his theft and relocation of the royal treasure. He wanted to omit nothing from his account. Felgild's eyebrows rose at this point, but he made no comment and kept writing diligently.

Felgild was extremely interested in Aelfred's dream and the feelings of peace and calm which had settled on him ever since. 'So, you asked to know the truth,' he said. 'Do you feel freer now than you did when you had the dream?'

Aelfred paused before he answered, 'It's been very strange. I had a definite feeling I should come here; but initially, and ever since, I've wrestled with the idea. It seemed so bizarre to give up everything I'd been planning and to turn my back on what I believed. Yet the more I wrestled, the calmer I felt. Does that make any sort of sense?'

Felgild replied, 'Jesus himself once said "You will know the truth and the truth will set you free." I'm not sure anyone, however wise and good, can know the full truth; but it does seem to me you're perhaps closer than you were. I guess that leads me to ask what you want to do next. You're certainly in a good place to seek truth, but it's obviously not for me to impose any plan on you.'

'I really don't know, Felgild,' Aelfred said reflectively. 'I know it's not the Anglian way, but I'd like to spend time here at least trying to understand Christianity and the work of the community.'

He continued after a few moments, 'I also know I must, somehow, make amends for the way I've treated my clan. I want to find a path towards reconciliation. But it's difficult to see what that looks like for a self-confessed traitor and thief!'

'Would a start be to get a message to your parents?' Felgild asked. 'You could let them know first and foremost you're alive, because they may be wondering; second, you could confess to what you've done; and third, you could offer to meet them if they feel they can forgive you.'

Aelfred was quiet for a few minutes as he pondered Felgild's question. Felgild simply sat back and watched and waited.

Aelfred said eventually, 'I've been wondering for a few days exactly how I might do all that, but I haven't got any answers yet.'

'How about something like this?' Felgild offered. 'A boat's going from here to York the day after tomorrow. It'll take four of our brothers down to start a mission in southern Deira. I could write out what you'd like to say to your parents. The brothers could go to Woden's Ford and read the message to your parents.'

Aelfred smiled. 'I like that!' he said. 'It gives them the information, but leaves them free, without any pressure, to decide what to do next. I'll have done what I can.'

They spent a little while agreeing the terms of the message which would be carried to Woden's Ford. Aelfred then said that he needed to rest. He told Felgild that his energy levels had dropped over the last couple of days and that he had an intermittent headache. They agreed that the intensity of the confessional sessions following on from the physical exertions of the last few weeks were probably having an effect, and that he should take a break for a few days.

* * * * * * *

Just over three weeks had passed at Woden's Ford since Cadmon's death. To say it had been a difficult and tense time was an understatement.

The patrols sent out to try to find any evidence of the missing treasure, or indeed Aelfred, had drawn a blank.

Rinc had had to confess to King Oswald, through his representatives in Deira, to the loss of the treasure. He had agreed to increase his tribute to the king in both produce and manpower unless and until the treasure was found.

Hilda had continued to believe stubbornly that Aelfred was still alive. She was on tenterhooks continuously. She genuinely expected him to walk back through the door at any moment.

It was into this uncomfortable atmosphere that the Lindisfarne monks walked. They told the servant who met them that they had news of Aelfred. It was as if they had unleashed a bolt of lightning. There was a flurry of activity as Rinc and Hilda were informed and rushed to meet the monks.

Once they were all gathered, Rinc and Hilda looking as if they were about to be sick with nervousness, Brother Comgall said, 'I'm sorry for descending on you in this way. The first thing I want to tell you is Aelfred's alive.'

Hilda, all pretence at primness abandoned, screamed with delight, 'I knew it! I knew it! Where is he? Is he on Lindisfarne?'

Comgall smiled and held up his hand. 'I know it must have been a stressful time for you, and so I'm really pleased I can give you good news. Yes, he's on Lindisfarne, and I have a message from him.'

Rinc was no less stunned by the news, but he was already wondering why Aelfred had not come in person. 'Why has he sent a message rather than come himself?' he asked.

'That's explained in the message which he dictated for you,' Comgall said, reaching into his pack for the scroll of vellum. 'Shall I read it out for you?'

Rinc and Hilda nodded, their feelings too intense to allow any words.

The message took a few minutes to read:

I am alive and living temporarily in the monastery in Lindisfarne. I am sorry that when I left Woden's Ford I misled you completely about my intentions. Cadmon and I stole the royal treasure from its hiding place and relocated it. I cannot tell you the precise location in this message in case it's intercepted en route. We travelled to Mercia with the intention of using the treasure to buy our way into their favour. I did this because I'd lost confidence in the direction Northumbria was taking under Oswald. I felt that to embrace Christianity was to betray our ancestors. I wanted to shock you all in to joining with Penda rather than fighting him. I now see that it was an entirely wrong and selfish thing to do. I am deeply sorry.

I freed Cadmon when we got to Tamworth. He left to go, I think, to meet up with a girl he fell in love with on our journey and then possibly on to Gwynedd – he was very taken with three men of Gwynedd we met in Tamworth. I decided to go to Lindisfarne instead of leading the Mercians to the treasure. I want to really understand Christianity. I think I may have misjudged and underestimated it.

I know how extremely disappointed you will be with my behaviour, completely understandably. I will not blame you if you never want to see me again, and indeed disown me. If, however, you feel you can forgive me I would very much like to meet at a place you choose to renew our relationship.

Rinc and Hilda listened in rapt silence. When Comgall finished, their demeanours were a study in contrast.

Hilda was weeping tears of joy and sorrow as she cried and smiled at the same time. She had not told anyone that she had prayed for the last year for Aelfred to find a way to Lindisfarne

Rinc looked thunderstruck.

They agreed quickly that they would travel to Lindisfarne as soon as they could to meet Aelfred. For Hilda forgiveness was a foregone conclusion. Comgall later told Felgild that he was not sure whether Rinc was prepared to forgive: he was at that moment more interested in finding out the whereabouts of the treasure.

It was settled that Aelfred's parents would travel to Lindisfarne overland, leaving two days later with an escort of five warriors. The journey would take longer than by boat, but Hilda had had some difficult experiences on sea voyages in the past and so preferred to travel by land.

* * * * * * *

Felgild and the other brothers meanwhile had become more and more worried about Aelfred. Rest didn't seem to help. He began to alternately vomit, shiver and sweat profusely. The monks had a great deal of accumulated knowledge of herbs and treatments that might alleviate a range of symptoms, but all their efforts were in vain.

Aelfred struggled to keep food down and became progressively weaker. One afternoon, when Aelfred appeared to have rallied a little, Felgild sat with him in his lodging. The sun streamed into the room. The sound of gulls and other seabirds drifted across the gentle sea breeze.

'I'm sorry, Aelfred,' the monk said, looking utterly dejected. 'I'm afraid we have to face facts. You're getting steadily weaker. There's nothing we seem able to do to help. It looks to me as if you didn't recover fully from the fever you caught in Elmet. The demands you've placed on yourself since then seem to have set off a much worse version.'

'Do you think I'll recover?' Aelfred asked baldly; the thought of death had occurred to him as his strength had seemed to seep away. He wanted to confront it head on.

'Well, we'll do everything we can to make sure you do,' Felgild said. 'But I'd be wrong to give a guarantee. You're far too young to die, but it's not looking good at the moment.'

The monk seemed more upset than Aelfred, tears welling in his eyes. Aelfred reached out his hand and placed it on his friend's arm, saying, 'Thank you for being so honest, Brother, I really appreciate it. I don't feel very hopeful myself. In fact, I know I'm losing ground.' As if to illustrate the point he broke off as a deep cough wracked his body.

Aelfred continued once he had recovered, 'But I'm really not afraid of death. That surprises me, to be honest. I don't know whether I've found truth, but I feel incredibly peaceful! I can see why you think I've encountered a profound and living presence – I guess what you call God. But I still don't understand Christianity fully. In fact, I'm not sure what to believe! I'm so grateful to you for explaining the gospel so clearly. But deep down I still feel the pull of the pagan gods, too. Perhaps it's in my blood.'

Aelfred was weighing his words carefully. Felgild sensed that he didn't need to reply. After a few minutes Aelfred resumed, 'I really don't feel as though I was misled by my father and grandfather and great uncle. Their pagan values were products of their times and of generations of belief and practice. They lived and breathed what they believed. They passed on their faith to me in complete sincerity. I can't blame them for being anti-Christian. They simply didn't have the chance to comprehend the full depth and breadth of the gospel. To them, Christianity must have appeared to be just another set of tribal symbols – and so a threat to their way of life.'

Aelfred paused, and then went on, 'So I'm grateful to my ancestors, and I'm genuinely proud of my heritage. Having said that, I know for sure now that the old ways are not the only ways – and not necessarily the best, either. I really, really do hope my people can find the will in future to break the cycles of violence and revenge.'

Aelfred stopped speaking again. He looked out of the window, and then fixed his gaze intently on the monk and said, 'That's why, if I do die, and my parents come to Lindisfarne, I don't want them to be told where the treasure is hidden. That particular hoard is a product of war. It would probably only fuel more violence if it were recovered.'

Aelfred hesitated, and then said decisively, 'I want it to stay hidden forever.'

Aelfred then concluded quietly, 'Please also try to find Cadmon. And please let him know that I was deeply sorry for misleading him and forcing him on such a merry dance. I really hope he has by now found his heart's desire.'

It had been a great effort for Aelfred to make this little speech. He lay back on his bed exhausted. Felgild wept openly. Once he could speak, he said, 'You're a brave man, Aelfred. You've not been afraid to hold to your beliefs, and then to change them even when there were great risks in doing so. I can't say all your actions have been a credit to you; but you've been prepared to go out on a limb when you believed that was the right thing to do. I'm so pleased you've found peace. Personally, whatever you think, I'm certain you've had an encounter with the Living God of the Christian faith.'

'Let's hope you recover and thrive,' the monk continued. 'But if you don't, I'll be proud to tell your parents you died nobly and bore no grudges. I certainly won't tell anyone about the location of the hoard. And we will, of course, try to track down Cadmon and pass on your message.'

Aelfred smiled and thanked Felgild, but the strength was now draining from him almost visibly.

Felgild hurried away. He returned to Aelfred's bedside a few minutes later with several other monks and a silver container of oil.

They committed the young Anglian to God and performed the last rites.

Almost as if he had been waiting for the end of the ceremony Aelfred closed his eyes and breathed his last.

Epilogue

Rinc and Hilda arrived on Lindisfarne three days after Aelfred's death. They were distraught but drew some comfort from the deathbed message Felgild was able to pass on. Rinc did ask whether Aelfred had confided the whereabouts of the treasure, but Felgild (having sought prior absolution from Brother Aidan, the leader of the community) told him that he did not have any information he could share on the subject.

Hilda was devastated because her hopes of reconciliation had been so high. She said that she could not contemplate returning to Woden's Ford. Rinc did not try to dissuade her.

The monks agreed to look after Hilda on Lindisfarne, and, once she was well enough, take her to the priory at Coldingham run by Ebba, King Oswald's sister, where her cousin, Alice, had been taken a few years previously. Hilda recovered, her Christian faith flourished, she became a valued member of the Coldingham community, and lived there until she died many years later.

Hilda overlapped with Alice by less than a year. Alice never emerged from the darkness which had engulfed her after Grimbald's death, but she died peacefully.

Rinc was saddened by his son's death, but he found it hard to come to terms with what Aelfred had done. He was frustrated that the treasure should be lying somewhere in Northumbria but could not be reclaimed. His stock at King Oswald's court fell slightly, but the larger tribute rendered annually by Woden's Ford helped to minimise the damage to his reputation.

Everyone across the Woden's Ford community experienced shock and grief for weeks as they tried to absorb the news of the tragedies which had, so suddenly and unexpectedly, befallen Hilda, Aelfred and Cadmon. The loss was felt keenly.

At the same time Woden's Ford was intrigued and gripped by the news of the secret treasure hoard. Rumours about the contents spiralled out of control. Theories about its where-abouts abounded – some of them far-fetched and bizarre.

Alwyn's and Wilfred's children, in particular, were tantal-ised by the thought of the wealth that must lie in the ground, perhaps within just a few miles of Woden's Ford. From time to time over the next few years one or more of them, lured by the prospect of discovering the hoard, would pepper Alwyn, Rinc and Aldrich with questions, and then launch a mission to try to find it. After several fruitless expeditions they accep-ted that it was a genuinely lost cause.

Eventually, as one by one Aldrich, Rinc and Alwyn died, leaving no one who had actually seen the treasure left alive, the tale of the hoard faded into the realms of family mytho-logy. After a few generations even the myth vanished from oral history.

With Hilda gone, Rinc married the young Bernician woman whom Aelfred had been due to wed even though she was more than twenty-five years his junior. She bore healthy twin sons within a year. Rinc, however, was killed in a major battle near Oswestry in 641 during which King Oswald was defeated – and also killed – by a combined Mercian and

Welsh force. Alwyn took over as chief of the clan since Rinc's sons were still babies.

Woden's Ford remained more or less intact under the leadership of Eadrich's successors for more than 200 years. From the second half of the ninth century onwards into the tenth century, however, the land was captured, parcelled up, and redistributed repeatedly as Danes, Vikings, and Anglo-Saxons fought for control across much of what was to become England. Eadrich's successors were absorbed into the wider population of what eventually became North Yorkshire. The oral history of Woden's Ford from the middle of the fourth century onwards, which had been maintained for so long, evaporated.

The four Mercian warriors who had been escorting Aelfred spent some time looking for him, but they gave up when they could find no sign. They decided not to return to Mercia empty-handed and to almost certain death, became outlaws, and eventually melted into the Anglo-Saxon warrior bands which inhabited the boundary lands between Mercia, Northumbria and East Anglia.

Lord Brice was livid when it became apparent, as he saw it, that he had been duped. He believed that Aelfred's tale of the hoard was a lie. Wynflaed did put in a good word for Brice with her uncle, King Penda. To his credit, Lord Harald supported him, too.

Brice suffered no repercussions at the Mercian court; but that did nothing to allay his anger. He assumed that Aelfred had led the four Mercian warriors into a trap simply to humiliate Mercia. The bad feeling Brice stoked in Tamworth over the next few years helped to fuel the Mercian assault on

Oswald's army at the battle near Oswestry in 641, and the savage treatment of the Northumbrian king's body after his death.

In 655 the Northumbrians finally gained revenge when Penda was killed in battle against them. Mercia was occupied and, at last, became a Christian kingdom. In an ironic twist, hundreds of years later a statue of Penda, the last pagan king in the British Isles, was included on the west wall of the great cathedral in Lichfield – in the Christian diocese which was established by St Chad, a few years after Penda's demise, in the heart of his old kingdom. It was doubly ironic that St Chad had arrived in Mercia as a missionary from Lindisfarne.

Caradoc and Einion made their way back to Gwynedd without mishap. They accepted eventually that things had not worked out for Morvyn and Cadmon. They tried to persuade others in Gwynedd to launch an expedition to find out what had happened, and, lured by the mystery, perhaps to try to recover the treasure, too; but there was little enthusiasm for what sounded like a risky and speculative venture. They got some monks to write down their account anyway and to file it safely.

The relationship between the Welsh and the Mercians continued to be uneasy. Wars and various alliances alternated over the decades. Eventually, in the eighth century, King Offa of Mercia built a giant dyke 149 miles long – presumably, although the reasons are unknown, to mark the border and try to keep the Welsh out.

Dora waited in vain for Cadmon to return to Helme. She resisted as long as she could Ceretic's encouragement to marry an older man in a neighbouring village, but she accepted eventually that Cadmon would not come back. She lived out her years within five miles of her birth.

Lindisfarne went through numerous vicissitudes, especially during the Viking era after their first attack in 793, but it has remained home to a living Christian community to the present day.

* * * * * * *

The Woden's Ford treasure hoard lay on undisturbed, eventually beyond any human consciousness, for decade after decade after decade in the place where Aelfred and Cadmon had buried it – until 2037, 1399 years after their deaths.

In that year a Welsh archivist, Tim Jones, who had become passionately interested in the story of the Staffordshire Anglo-Saxon Hoard (discovered near Lichfield in 2009), found the faintest whisper in some ancient Gwynedd records of another vast seventh century treasure hoard in Northumbria. It was a reference to the account by Caradoc and Einion on their return from Tamworth in 638 which had been filed away so carefully.

Tim travelled to north-east England. He was, he admitted to friends, lured by the prospect of discovering a remarkable hoard.

He scoured every record deposit he could find in Yorkshire, Durham and Northumberland. Eventually, to his astonishment, buried deep in a dusty file in an obscure archive in Northumberland, he found a collection of ancient parchments which had been transferred from Lindisfarne at some point. They had escaped the attention of the Viking raiders who had been looking for glitzier prizes.

One of the parchments was clearly dated 638 AD. With the help of linguistic experts Tim deciphered what turned out to be Felgild's record of Aelfred's confession – including his remarkably detailed description of the location of the royal treasure.

Tim was spellbound by Felgild's narrative. He searched doggedly through the other ancient Lindisfarne records for any trace of what had happened subsequently, but the trail went cold. Felgild's record contained a wealth of information, but also begged innumerable questions.

Tim wondered about Aelfred: what sort of man was he? What did he look like? Did he go back and retrieve the treasure? Or did his slave, Cadmon, who had apparently left him in Tamworth, double-cross Aelfred and take the treasure himself? Perhaps Aelfred renounced the world, became a monk, and left the treasure in the ground? Or maybe the monks themselves recovered the treasure and used it to fund the development of their community?

In high excitement Tim set about telling others and organising an expedition to track down the treasure. Lured, just as much as Tim had been, by the prospect of a remarkable and historic discovery, he attracted to his cause: archaeologists from a regional museum; a local business which was prepared to pay for sophisticated metal-detecting equipment; and a journalist and photographer from a Yorkshire newspaper who wanted to capture the moment of discovery for posterity.

Everyone in the team was in a state of high anticipation, but at the same time very edgy, as they finally set off towards the Yorkshire Wolds, a few miles away from York. Each person wondered the same things: were the directions in the ancient parchment accurate? would the treasure still be there?

With the help of the metal detectors, they did, after a thorough search, finally locate the exact spot. It was a wild and lonely corner, tucked in the hills. There was certainly no sign that anyone had stepped that way in the previous fourteen centuries.

With trembling hands, the archaeologists dug: carefully, but quickly.

Their ecstasy knew no bounds as they freed the ancient, mouldering sacks which Aelfred and Cadmon had buried nearly 1400 years earlier and set eyes on the wondrous hoard of treasure they contained!

Historical Timeline

Some Key Dates

597 AD: St Augustine lands in Kent at head of small mission from Rome with aim of converting the Anglo-Saxons

606 AD: King Aethelfrith of Bernicia annexes the neighbouring kingdom of Deira and becomes king of Northumbria

Prince Edwin of Deira goes into exile – probably to Gwynedd, then Mercia, and finally East Anglia

616 AD: King Aethelfrith defeats a coalition of Welsh forces at the Battle of Chester

616 AD: Edwin, with support of King Raedwald of East Anglia, defeats and kills Aethelfrith and becomes king of Northumbria

Aethelfrith's wife, Queen Acha – who was Edwin's sister – goes in to exile in Dalriada. She takes her children, including twelve-year-old Prince Oswald

Early 620s: Edwin conquers the small kingdom of Elmet, and it becomes part of the kingdom of Northumbria

626/27 AD:	King Edwin converts to Christianity, influenced by his Kentish wife and her ally Paulinus who became Bishop of York
	Mass baptism ceremonies follow across Northumbria, including at Catterick
633 AD:	Battle of Hatfield – Edwin defeated and killed by alliance of Penda of Mercia and Cadwallon of Gwynedd
633–34 AD:	Cadwallon's army stays in Northumbria
	Osric and Eanfrith become kings of Deira and Bernicia respectively, but are killed by Cadwallon's forces
	King Oswald returns from exile, defeats Cadwallon at Heavenfield (near Hexham in modern Northumberland) at head of combined Dalriadan/Northumbrian force, becomes king of reunited Northumbria
635 AD:	Oswald invites Aidan to come from Iona with monks from Dalriada to found monastery at Lindisfarne
641 AD:	Oswald defeated and killed by combined Mercian/Welsh forces near Oswestry (in modern Shropshire)
655 AD:	King Penda of Mercia defeated and killed by Northumbrian forces at Winwaed (probably near modern Leeds)
	Mercia becomes Christian

Alphabetical List of Named Fictional Characters

Abertha: mother of Cadmon (married to Gerant)

Aelfred: son of Rinc and Hilda

Aldrich: brother of Eadwell

Alice: wife of Godwyn and cousin of Hilda

Alwyn: third son of Eadwell, brother of Rinc

Bertha: wife of Wilfred, oldest son of Eadwell

Brice: Mercian noble

Brigit: wife of Alwyn

Cadmon: son of Abertha and Gerant; slave to Aelfred

Caradoc: agent of King of Gwynedd

Ceretic: man in Elmet

Comgall: monk of Lindisfarne

Dora: woman in Elmet

Eadrich: Founder of Eadrich clan in mid-4th century

Eadmund: younger son of Wilfred

Eadwell: 8th chief of Eadrich clan, direct descendant of Eadrich

Edgar: oldest brother of Eadwell

Edith: young woman from East Anglia

Einion: agent of King of Gwynedd

Felgild: monk of Lindisfarne

Gerant: father of Cadmon (married to Abertha)

Godwyn: fourth son of Eadwell, brother of Rinc

Grimbald: son of Edgar

Harald: Mercian noble

Hilda: wife of Rinc, Aelfred's mother

Hilderic: older son of Wilfred

Mildred: wife of Edgar

Modig: friend of Eadrich in 4th century

Morvyn: agent of King of Gwynedd

Raedwald: Alwyn's son

Rinc: oldest son of Eadwell, married to Hilda, father of Aelfred

Wilfred: second son of Eadwell, brother of Rinc

Wulfhere: Alice's son

Wynflaed: wife of Brice, a Mercian noble